Praise for
Good Riddance

A *New York Times* Editors' Choice
A LibraryReads Pick

"Effortlessly charming . . . The book inspires a very specific kind of modern joy." —*New York Times Book Review*

"A clever romantic comedy from a pro . . . The rollicking plot ultimately leads to romance, revealing this witty story's warm and fuzzy heart." —*People*

"[Lipman] has long been one of our wittiest chroniclers of modern-day romance. [Her] writing is brisk and intelligent, and if the plot of this novel is zanier than her usual fare, that too may show just how plugged-in she is to our farfetched times." —*Wall Street Journal*

"A vastly entertaining screwball comedy . . . Witty, dippy, and daft, we have here a genuine, guilty pleasure." —*Washington Post*

"The ultimate V-Day binge read." —*Cosmopolitan*

"Lipman is the easiest writer to read, but she stays with you because she's such a good writer . . . A true pleasure . . . [She] is such a fine stylist . . . [*Good Riddance*] is hilarious, [with] wonderful romantic elements [and] a witty line on every page, in every paragraph." —Bill Goldstein, NBC's "Bill's Books"

"Lipman is a writer to savor. Her wit is at once light and serious, ringing with humanity, and her tangled plots are full of surprises . . . Her writing is reminiscent of the late, fine writer Laurie Colwin."
                                                            —*New York Jewish Week*

"To the many readers who have happily drowned their worries in the sparkling waters of Lipman's fizzy fiction, it is obvious that Lipman was born to entertain us . . . Lipman writes with a light, wry touch that tips a hat to life's many challenges but never throws in the towel."
                                                            —*San Diego Union-Tribune*

"The question of who gets to tell one's own story lies at the heart of Lipman's smart, sassy, and satisfying rom-com . . . Luckily for fans of contemporary women's fiction, the answer is Lipman as she once again delivers a tightly woven, lightly rendered, but insightfully important novel of the pitfalls to be avoided and embraced on one's path to self-discovery."
                                                            —*Booklist*

"A delightful treat readers will want to savor."
                                                            —*Publishers Weekly*

"Fans of Lipman will cheer for a new novel in her signature style: funny, warm, sharp, smart, and full of love for family, no matter how flawed."
                                                            —*Library Journal*

"Au courant elements . . . add a fresh twist to the proceedings. Lipman's narrative brio keeps things moving at a good clip."
                                                            —*Kirkus Reviews*

"It's good riddance to dismay and hello to happiness in this witty romantic comedy."
                                                            —*Shelf Awareness for Readers*

Good Riddance

BOOKS BY ELINOR LIPMAN

Good Riddance

············ *by* ············

ELINOR LIPMAN

MARINER BOOKS

HOUGHTON MIFFLIN HARCOURT

Boston   New York

First Mariner Books edition 2020

Copyright © 2019 by Elinor Lipman

Q&A with Author © 2020 by Elinor Lipman

Recommended Reading © 2020 by Elinor Lipman

For information about permission to reproduce selections from this book, write to trade.permissions@hmhco.com or to Permissions, Houghton Mifflin Harcourt Publishing Company, 3 Park Avenue, 19th Floor, New York, New York 10016.

hmhbooks.com

Library of Congress Cataloging-in-Publication Data
Names: Lipman, Elinor, author.
Title: Good riddance / Elinor Lipman.
Description: Boston ; New York : Houghton Mifflin Harcourt, 2019. |
Identifiers: LCCN 2018006362 (print) | LCCN 2018013818 (ebook) |
ISBN 9780544808287 (ebook) | ISBN 9780544808256 (hardback) |
ISBN 9780358108559 (pbk.)
Subjects: LCSH: Domestic fiction. | Jewish fiction. |
BISAC: FICTION /Contemporary Women. | FICTION / Family Life. |
FICTION / Humorous. | FICTION / Jewish. | FICTION / Literary. |
GSAFD: Humorous stories. | Love stories.
Classification: LCC PS3562.I577 (ebook) | LCC PS3562.I577 G66 2019 (print) |
DDC 813/.54 — dc23
LC record available at https://lccn.loc.gov/2018006362

Book design by Kelly Dubeau Smydra

Printed in the United States of America
DOC 10 9 8 7 6 5 4 3 2 1

For Anita Shreve, perfect friend

Good Riddance

1
....

The Grateful Class of '68

F OR A FEW WEEKS after my mother's death, I was in possession of the painstakingly annotated high school yearbook that had been dedicated to her by the grateful class
of 1968.

Yes, she'd been their English teacher and yearbook advisor,
but that didn't explain her obsessive collecting of signatures and
tributes next to every senior's photo. I could picture her—age
twenty-three, her first job after college, roaming the corridors of
Pickering High School, pen and book in hand, coaxing the shy-
est, least engaged boy or girl to sign—*Write anything. I want to
remember every one of you. Could you personalize it, just a few
words?*

But there would be more—her own embellishments, her judg-
ments and opinions, written next to those photos in her small
legible hand, a different color ink (red, green, blue) for several
milestone reunions, which she attended compulsively, starting
with the fifth and continuing until her last, their forty-fifth.

Her margin notes were coded but easily deciphered: "M" for
married. "S" for single. "D" for dead; "DIV" for divorced. "DWI,"
said a few. "AIDS?" suggested one notation. "Same dress she wore
at 15th" my mother recorded. "Very plump" was one of her milder
put-downs. "Braces." "Pregnant." Occasionally, "Still pretty."
"Looks older than I do" was one of her favorite notes. "Still holds

PHS record for 100-yd. dash," said one. And "danced w. him" appeared often.

Had I known about this project as it was happening? I hadn't. Several reunions were held before I was born, and later ones, attended even after she retired, weren't discussed with her two daughters. After all, we might know some of these graduates as the parents of our friends or our own teachers or custodians or police officers or panhandlers, townspeople still.

A handwritten codicil on the last page of my mother's will said, "My daughter Daphne will take possession of the Pickering High School's yearbook, *The Monadnockian*." And nothing more.

I took it back with me to Manhattan, where it stayed on my shelf for a month until I read a magazine article about decluttering.

The test? Would I ever reread this novel, these college textbooks, these magazines? Did I really need a Portuguese-English dictionary? What about the panini press and my dead Black-Berry? The expert recommended this: Hold the item in question, be it book or sweater or socks or muffin tin, to your chest, over your heart, and ask yourself, *Does this thing inspire joy?*

I hugged the yearbook. *Nothing.* Well, not nothing; worse than that: an aversion. Apparently, I didn't want, nor would I miss, this testimony to the unsympathetic, snarky side of my mother's character.

The best-selling decluttering wizard said the property owner had to be tough, even ruthless. I certainly was that. Good-bye, ugly white-vinyl, ink-stained yearbook with your put-downs and your faint smell of mildew! Maybe it *was* my mother's legacy and a time capsule, but it had failed to stir emotion in my bosom. Possessing too much stuff anyway, in a cramped apartment, bookshelves overflowing, I threw it out. Or rather, being a good citizen, I walked it down the hall to my building's trash closet, straight into the recycling bin.

Okay, Listen

I 'D NEVER MET GENEVA WISENKORN despite our re-
siding at opposite ends of the same hallway. Our introduction came in the form of a note slipped under my door
announcing, "I found something that belongs to you. Are you
home?" followed by an email address and phone, office, and mobile numbers.

My wallet? My keys? I checked my pocketbook. All there. Had
a misdelivered piece of mail or dropped glove been traced back to
me? I went to my laptop and wrote to this seemingly thoughtful
stranger, asking what possession of mine she'd found.

She wrote back immediately. "A high school yearbook. We
need to talk!"

No, we didn't. I hit reply and wrote, "Thanks anyway, but I recycled that," then added a postscript — "It has no meaning or value,
sentimental or otherwise" — in case she was looking for a reward.

"Contact info?" she answered.

My first mistake: I sent it. Immediately, my phone rang. After
my wary "Hello," I heard, "I think you'll be very interested in what
I have to say."

I asked how she knew the yearbook, which I now decided I
needed back, belonged to me.

"Because I found it with magazines that had your name on the
subscription labels."

I said, "I'd never forgive myself if a yearbook with all that personal stuff written in it got into the hands of a stranger."

"Then why'd you throw it out?"

"I thought it would go to some landfill! Or get turned into whatever recycled paper gets turned into."

"I know the rules. If it's trash left at the curbside or at the dump, the possessor has relegated ownership."

The possessor has relegated ownership? Was I talking to this ragpicker's lawyer?

"Finders keepers, in other words?"

"Precisely."

I tried again. "Maybe there *is* some law on the books about garbage rights, but the polite thing, the neighborly thing, would be to return the yearbook, which any jury would see had personal content."

"A jury? Are you going to call a lawyer? Or 911? I'd like to hear *that* conversation."

"Why contact me in the first place?" I asked. "You found the yearbook. Why not just keep it? I'd never know."

"Because I wanted to go about this in the most professional manner possible. Believe me, intellectual property can be a real shitstorm. We should talk—face-to-face, I mean. I want to get this settled before I leave for my writers' retreat."

Get what settled? So far, it was just a question of the keeping or the giving back. In case she thought she had leverage—that she'd expose my mother's poison pen—I said, "You realize that the owner of the book is dead and it's too late to embarrass her?"

"*Embarrass* her? I'm stunned you would say that! Your mother wasn't writing for her own amusement. There's no question she had a future audience in mind."

Did she? What audience? Who else could possibly care? "I don't know what you want from me," I said.

"Permission."

Was I catching on? Not yet. She asked again if we could talk face-to-face. I said, "Is this really necessary."

"Be there in a jiff," she said.

She rang my doorbell forty minutes later, finding me newly annoyed with her interpretation of a "jiff." Her breathing was labored from the short walk, no doubt attributable to her extreme bulk. I recognized her — having shared elevator rides or exchanged nods in the mailroom — due to her colorful, bigger-than-life appearance and persona. She was large, wide, round-faced, with black curls that tumbled around her face, eyeglasses upswept, employing rhinestones. Her outfit could be called a dress if one were kind. It had no shape, only volume, in blocks of red, yellow, and black. She might be forty; she might be fifty. I couldn't tell.

"Sorry it took so long, but I didn't want to come empty-handed." She passed me an open shoebox lined messily with wax paper that contained several layers of cookies. "I figured who doesn't like chocolate chip? They should be cooling on a rack."

No yearbook in sight, however. "Cookies," I said. "Really, you shouldn't have."

"They're Pillsbury slice and bake. I always keep a package in my fridge."

"Come in," I said.

As soon as she stepped into my living room, I could see she was puzzled. *Is there another room? Who lives like this?* She looked around, asked if the hallway . . . went anywhere?

"To the bedroom and bath. And my kitchen, of course."

"It's very . . . cute. What do you do?"

Even though I'd progressed no further than registration, I said, "I'm studying to be a chocolatier."

"Where?"

"Online."

She couldn't have looked less impressed. "Are there jobs doing that? And do they pay?"

With that, I officially categorized Geneva as a boundary-challenged chatterbox whom I didn't want to be chummy with. "Haven't we just met?" I asked.

"I know! Very bad habit, asking personal questions. It's not so much nosiness but a failure to know what's personal and what's just conversation. I get it from my mother, who thinks it's perfectly polite to ask a near stranger why they didn't have children or how much they paid for their co-op or how much they tipped the doorman or, once . . . oh, never mind. I need more people who can tell me when I've crossed the line."

We were still standing. I motioned toward the couch and said I was going to put some of these cookies on a plate.

"No! The cookies are for you," she said. "I have that highly annoying type 2 diabetes. If I lose weight, they tell me I'll shake it. No cookie, but do you have vodka?"

I did. I poured us each a glass and returned. She raised hers, and said, "To your mother, the most committed yearbook advisor who ever lived."

After my half-hearted clink, I said, "I don't understand why you'd want someone else's yearbook from a class she didn't graduate in."

"I ate it up! It's fascinating. It's got a point of view and — what the fuck! — an attitude! I can't wait to hear more about her."

"Such as?"

"Husband, marriage, interests, hobbies, wardrobe. Crushes, boyfriends, lovers?"

"Okay. This just got creepy. I'm her daughter. She left it to me in her will, and now I'm asking for it back."

"Why?"

Why? Did I not just say why?

"It tells a story," Geneva continued. "Correction: It tells a hundred stories. I remember the exact moment I knew this had my name on it: next to one girl's picture, a pretty brunette with a perfect flip, under 'Future,' she had 'beautician.' Your mother drew an arrow across the page to a good-looking guy, thin face, Italian last name, whom she married. What do you think his future was?"

"I have no idea."

"Ballroom dance. Guess how that turned out, at least according to your mother's note. You can bet the 'D' stands for divorced and the 'H' is for homosexual."

I said, "No, it didn't. 'H' meant 'home' or 'here' — that they still lived in Pickering."

The expression greeting that remark clearly meant *Poor you; born yesterday.*

Next I tried, "Let's just say my mother *would* be flattered that a total stranger finds the yearbook so interesting. Fine. You'll read and enjoy it, and when you're done, you'll return it."

"I don't think you understand." Then, as if it explained and justified everything: "I'm a filmmaker."

I swallowed the rest of my vodka and poured a refill. "Are you saying you'd like to turn the yearbook into a movie, because I don't see —"

"Not a feature film. A documentary that explores what happened to the class of nineteen sixty-eight — where are they now? Who's married, divorced, happy, straight, gay, dead, cryogenically frozen? Dreams fulfilled — or dashed!"

"But who wants to watch a documentary about small-town nobodies?"

"People love reunions! We all have reunion hopes, don't we? Go to your reunion, find your old boyfriend, and run off together!"

I told her that it wasn't just my permission she needed but also my father's. I threw in my sister's, too, and my father's cousin Julian's, a lawyer, knowing not one of us would give this cockamamie plan a green light.

She said, "Let me remind you: I rescued this from the rubbish heap. But I'm all about collaboration. Sure, ask your relatives how they'd feel about an award-winning filmmaker putting Pinkerton High School on the map."

"Pickering. If . . . just *if* this went forward, and you found some of the graduates, would they see what my mother wrote about them? Because she'd turn over in her grave."

Her expression said it all: *What a wonderful idea! Hadn't thought of that but wow! Just the tension this project was missing!*

A threat of last resort: "If I told the building super that you picked through everyone's garbage, word would get around."

"Why?"

"Why? Because it's disgusting! People throw away personal stuff. They declutter!"

"And you know what I'd say to that? 'I'm a documentary filmmaker, which makes me a researcher, even a scavenger. More power to me.'"

I asked what these award-winning documentaries were.

"Too many to name."

"Any one I might have seen?"

"Most recently: on TV, last Passover."

"Passover?" I repeated.

"On the Jewish Channel."

I said I had basic cable, which didn't include the Jewish Channel. What was the film about?

"The last matzo factory in Brooklyn." She handed me her empty glass. "I thought you'd be thrilled. The documentary-watching world will get to know a woman who otherwise lived in near obscurity. I'm hoping to find archival footage of her — the teacher all the boys and probably half the girls were in love with! No wonder she kept going to reunions!"

What to digest first—that this woman was going to make a movie about a New Hampshire yearbook? Or that my mother was a sex object?

I said, "I never got the idea from her notes that anything like that was going on."

"Don't get huffy. Of course you wouldn't see that. She's your mother."

I asked if she'd forgotten that New Hampshire was the center of the universe every four years, with reporters flocking there for the presidential primary. Granite Staters are always being filmed. It's ho-hum. Good luck finding people who aren't sick of having a microphone stuck in their faces.

When this seemed to have the desired dampening effect, I added, "Maybe you'll need to find a yearbook from a state that gets less attention."

From a pocket within the folds of her voluminous dress, she produced a phone. I could tell without a view of the screen that she was Googling something.

"I'll admit," she finally said, "that I wasn't factoring in the primary, but it could be just the thing that could get me the money I need."

Money? I told her I didn't follow.

"New Hampshire is one of the original thirteen colonies," she announced.

Was she thinking she'd find yearbooks from the other twelve colonies? "Do you mean a yearbook series?"

"No! I was just thinking grants: *Frontline*. The National Endowment for the Arts. Daughters of the American Revolution. Kickstarter. Dartmouth."

"Dartmouth?"

"New Hampshire, right? I'd release it in an off year just as residents were missing all the attention."

She rose, nodded grandly, turned at the door, and said, "We both know your mother would be all for it."

What kind of bargaining chip did I have? Geneva had the yearbook in her possession. And I, who didn't believe in visitations from the other side, found myself wondering whether this was exactly what my mother would have wanted.

3
....

There's an Ex

I USED TO HAVE A HUSBAND, from a marriage that was a bad idea from the start. Now I can advise others: Never marry a man who proposes too early. I didn't say yes on his first try, of course. I said, "Well, that's very flattering, but I don't know you, and you certainly don't know me."

He explained that he had a special gift, that he could size up a job applicant or a woman on the first date from a gesture or remark, a telling one.

"So what was my telling gesture?"

"Many." His gaze was, I now recognize, faux fond. "Starting with your thanking the busboy for the bread ... Don't give me that skeptical look. To most women, busboys are invisible."

"I waitressed all through college." But instead of shedding light on the topic by revealing how many busboys I'd had summer flings with, I said, "We were all college students. We'd go out after work, the whole crew. It didn't matter if they were waiters or busboys or delivery guys."

"Because you're not a snob. That's what I saw in that gesture. You probably don't know it, but there's an innocence to you."

Yes, there used to be, a big dangerous innocence honed by my six years as a Montessori teacher and exactly why I was targeted by Holden Phillips IV. Despite what I would later characterize as flattery and bullshit, I went on a second date with him. The marriage entreaties were often soft-pedaled in phrases such as "You realize, of course, we'll be married one day. FYI, that's not a proposal, because I know you think I haven't earned you yet."

"Insecurity," the girlfriends said. "Not a good sign. Is he desperate?" They Googled him and saw his photos. Holden was not, as my maternal grandmother used to say, an oil painting.

But he did introduce the unaffordable into my budgeted, between-careers life. He'd order a bottle of wine rather than two glasses and the up-charged desserts on a prix fixe. Yes to that sprinkle of black or white truffle, the chocolate soufflé that required advance notice. And there were orchestra seats to shows that were famously sold out for the rest of any given year.

I was a bought woman — an overstatement, but I deserve it. He called himself an entrepreneur, having cofounded a start-up with a business school pal. Most people didn't ask for more than that explanation. If pressed, I'd add, "It's called Life's Too Short. It helps you hire people to do stuff you don't want to do yourself."

It might sound as if a successful guy would have already found a wife by the time we met. He on the cusp of forty. I was not yet thirty. When I asked if the big rush was about procreating, he scoffed. "Procreating! Who said anything about wanting children! You've had your fill, right? Not even looking for another teaching job?"

"You don't *ever* want children?"

He sensed that he'd gone one selling point too far in the wrong direction. "I just meant I'm not one of those guys whose aim is a young, fertile woman. I mean it's not my first, second, or third priority. I'm not the guy who puts an ad in a Russian newspaper: American male seeking attractive blonde. Wide pelvis a must."

When I looked startled, he said, "I'm joking! At least give me credit for composing a clever fake ad on the spot."

"Of course you were joking. I knew that."

My emerald-cut diamond was huge by New Hampshire standards. And a woman approaching thirty can be stunned into a
yes when a little velvet box is perched on a dessert plate decorated with raspberry *jus* spelling out "Will you marry me?" upon
her return from the ladies' room.

We wouldn't have met in the natural course of either life except for our both going to a CVS for flu shots. We were sitting side
by side. I was wearing a boat-neck, long-sleeved jersey tight in
the arms so it would be easier to expose the required flesh downward from the shoulder rather than work the sleeve north. He
was dark-haired, going gray, neither handsome nor unattractive,
wearing a big lump of a class ring and a camel coat. I said, exposing a bra strap, "Don't look."

He took that as a sexual advance, which might have led to a
conversation if I hadn't fainted the moment the needle touched
my skin. Within seconds, he'd lowered my head between my
knees. I came to, repeating, "I didn't faint, I didn't faint, I'm okay."
The pharmacist, looking stunned, managed to say that a small
percentage of people faint after any vaccination.

Apparently, I started walking toward the escalator without my
coat or pocketbook, giving the impression that I wasn't in possession of my faculties.

"Where do you think you're going?" asked this concerned
citizen, leading me back to my chair. He introduced himself as
Holden and said he was putting me in a cab.

An apparently more senior pharmacist had been summoned.
"You're not going anywhere yet, little lady. We have a protocol."

I shut my eyes so I didn't have to watch Holden getting his
shot. He helped me with my coat and arranged the strap of my
pocketbook over my noninjected arm. Out on the sidewalk, he
hailed a taxi and got in after me. I protested, but he said, "How
else will it be my treat?"

That same afternoon, he sent me flowers care of the doorman on duty when he'd dropped me off. His business card was attached. *Holden@lifes2short.com.*

I could hardly fail to acknowledge flowers, especially ones like these — rare, exotic, out of season, from a shop inside the Plaza Hotel.

I'm only revisiting this to illustrate how occurrences outside the everyday can take on the aura of romance. Fainting is one of those things. I am wiser now, having discovered this humiliating fact: Holden was only acting the part of do-gooder, then suitor, then fiancé, then husband. His marriage motivation was financial: He needed a wife in order to shake free the good-size fortune his grandparents had left him, a condition I deduced from a remark a bigmouth friend let slip in a very careless, frat-boy toast. Had his grandparents seen something in Holden that gave them pause? Or was it their experience that bachelors squander money on boats and fancy cars? Apparently, he'd seen in me an easy mark for a whirlwind courtship and marriage, the kind from two centuries ago, about property and inheritance.

The will and trust that marched me unwittingly down the aisle didn't stipulate that Holden had to stay married. Nor did he have to be a faithful spouse. Everything ended the night he didn't come home because . . . what was his lame story again? He'd had too much to drink at his staff dinner and didn't want to be sick in a taxi.

"First of all, that's ridiculous. Second, I've never seen you get drunk. And where was this staff orgy?"

He named a fashionable SoHo hotel, where ingenues drank martinis at the bar. And here he was at eight a.m., freshly showered, mouthwash rinsed, hair wet, not meeting my eye. I asked, quite dramatically for me, "Who is she?"

"Who is who?"

"The woman you spent the night with."

"I did no such thing. I couldn't go home. The bartender wouldn't let me leave, so he had someone walk me to the front desk, and the next thing I knew, I had a room upstairs."

"Was that someone a woman?"

Now deeply fake-offended, he asked, "What are you implying? That I didn't go upstairs alone?"

"Only an idiot would believe that a bartender sends a drunk guy over to the reception desk."

"Daff," he said. "I should've called —"

"But you couldn't because your phone was dead and the hotel had no landline?"

"I was wasted. I didn't want you to know that. You can be very judgmental about my drinking."

"When have I ever said a word about your drinking?"

More scoffing, and now too casually leafing through the previous day's mail, he said, "It was late, past your bedtime. I didn't want to wake you."

"And there you were, in the bar, no wedding ring, possibly just having ordered an expensive single-malt Scotch. You probably offered to buy her a drink, too. And maybe you told her that you owned the company that was here doing team building. Is that what happened?"

He walked past me into the kitchen and poured himself a cup of coffee. "You're irrational," he finally said.

About this confrontation I was waging: It was the opportunity I needed to end this marriage of his convenience. "Just tell me the truth. I won't get mad," I lied.

He put his arms around me in my homely bathrobe, and asked, "We're good? That was just wifely worry? Now that you know I'm not lying in a ditch —"

"Just tell me: Was it someone you work with? Because sex with an employee can get you sued for a fortune. But I can live with whatever you tell me."

What a good actress this was provoking me into being. He said he was going to be honest. He trusted me, trusted that I was being sincere. Good old Daphne. It won't happen again. Thank you for worrying about rules of the workplace. She was not one of his employees. Hell no; he wasn't that stupid. He had indeed met her at the bar. How did I know that? Not only was I insightful but so fucking understanding as well. He only knew her first name: Amanda. He wasn't going to see her again. She wasn't that bright. He hadn't even asked for her contact information.

"You don't have her contact information? No business cards changed hands?"

"No, I swear—"

I yelled, giving him a shove, "You liar! Of course you're going to see her again. Go back to the hotel. Go live there. You can afford it. Take your grandmother's money and buy yourself a penthouse apartment next to Donald Trump's."

"You tricked me!" he yelped. "You weren't trying to be understanding. You gave me the distinct impression that it was going to be truth without consequences."

"We're newlyweds! I can't be married to someone who cheats before we've gone on the postponed honeymoon."

"That's not fair! I want to take you to New Zealand, but it's winter there. I've been saying that since day one."

"New Zealand, my ass. This is the first time I've heard that mentioned. I will not stay married to a cheater. I have way too much self-respect. Oh, and by the way? I don't even like you."

"Welcome to the world, little girl. You know who's monogamous? No one."

I said, "You're wrong. *I* am. And so is everyone I know."

"Maybe in Picayune, New Hampshire. But not in the real world. Not even animals are! Just some birds, but not us mammals. The sooner you give that up, the better for all concerned."

"*Pickering*, New Hampshire," I spit back. "I never should have married you. You tricked *me*—"

"It's not my fault. Maybe I need treatment."

I was too stunned at "not my fault" to answer in properly flabbergasted fashion. All I could say was "Treatment? For what? Your drinking didn't make you cheat."

"Not that. For sexual addiction."

More stunned nothingness.

"I hoped marriage would cure me. I'm so sorry."

"Sex addict? Maybe that's something you tell a fiancée before she walks down the aisle?" (A figure of speech. There was no aisle. We'd gone to city hall, then gathered at a restaurant with his boisterous friends, his mother, and my father. For brunch.) "Because if you're a sex addict . . ." I raised my eyebrows, implying *Not so apparent in the marital bed.*

"You're right. I should've told you. But it's an atypical presentation—"

"Fine. Get treatment. Go to rehab. You'll probably meet some nice sex-addicted women there and hook up the whole time. I hope you'll be very happy."

Did this seem precipitous? It wasn't. Ever since I'd heard I was merely an inheritance tool, I'd been waiting for him to break a marriage vow so my escape would appear to have means, motive, and opportunity. He did obey my wishes and leave, but not until he'd spent a long time packing his suitcase with too much care, too much consideration of which tie went with which shirt and suit, as if he was preparing for a week of dates with female hedge-fund managers. I finally said, "Just go! I've served my purpose! I know about the will. I figured it out. And I know this for damn sure: You never loved me."

He didn't counter that. Instead, he reminded me that I'd signed a prenup. I'd better not be thinking that his trust fund was mine to share.

Later I looked it up. He'd been right: Except for prairie voles, monogamy was unheard of in mammals.

4

You'll Be the First to Know

I WAITED TO HEAR from Geneva Wisenkorn, who presumably took the yearbook along on her writing retreat, promising I'd get it back eventually. Upon her return, whenever I'd pass her in the hallway, she was in too big of a hurry to talk. The one time I got as far as "Any news?" she looked slightly bewildered as if wondering, *About what?*

After the second unresponsive exchange, I said, "Geneva? You realize I'm asking you about the documentary?"

"Of course I do. I'm still making notes. Rome wasn't built in a month. You'll be the first to know."

I called after her, "But you're still doing it, right?"

"Of course I am. Nothing means more to me than our project."

Our project. I caught that. It had the ring of remuneration.

I didn't have a case with respect to keeping the six-room marital apartment in the divorce since Holden's unsympathetic mother owned it. I considered a move back to Pickering, but my dad said via phone, "No, don't. There's nothing for you here. There's nothing for *me* here. Are you sitting down? I'm thinking of joining you in NYC."

I asked him to define "joining." Did he mean a visit? He'd always be welcome, just not as an overnight guest in my postage stamp of an apartment.

"Maybe I could help. You're newly alone. Maybe if we pooled our resources —"

"Dad! Adult children don't live with their dads unless there's something seriously wrong with them. Or something's off."

"Isn't getting a divorce 'something off'? Or maybe something's off with a parent who lost his wife of thirty-six years and is lonely. For the record? Baby boomers' children certainly *do* live with their parents. It's a movement."

I didn't want to be indelicate. Should I address the loneliness part or the baby-boomer-returns-home part? I said, "I hate to hear you're lonely. Aren't friends inviting you over and leaving casseroles?"

"That's one of the reasons I need a change. Too much mother henning."

Of course that would be true. My father would be a matchmaker's dream once he took the measure of his own five-starness.

"Daff? You still there?"

"Is there no one in Pickering you could see yourself spending time with?"

"Honey, I've sat next to every eligible woman at every awkward get-together that was billed as a casual family dinner. And if I say, 'Too soon,' these hostesses come back with 'Too soon for what? A few hands of bridge?'"

"But you said you're lonely. No one you'd consider taking to a movie?"

"Maybe 'lonely' is the wrong word. Maybe just 'alone.' I want to start this new chapter in a new place. If I don't move now, when would I? I still have my health. I can afford it. If ever I needed an adventure, it's now."

Even though I had no say in the matter, I said, "Let me sleep on this."

I did, and I woke up thinking that I had no right to discourage the very move I myself had made. I called him, and said, "I'm in. You *should* move here. You could volunteer and maybe tutor. Go to concerts and readings. Find bridge partners, for sure. And you won't have to drive to Manchester to see a movie."

"I appreciate that. And, hon? When I said we'd pool our resources, I didn't mean I was looking for a couch to sleep on. I want my own place, a home. I just meant we could get together when you had a free night. For dinner. Or lunch. Your dad could treat you to a play once in a while."

I said, "Sounds great." And I meant it.

"I've wanted to live in New York City my whole life. Your mother was afraid of the city. Well, maybe not afraid, but she hated it. Everyone waving their arms for the same taxi. Long lines for hamburgers that aren't anything special and cost as much as a steak back home. And forget the subway!"

"How come I never heard this before — about your New York dream?"

"Because I thought it would never come true. Your mother wouldn't leave Pickering. Even when I talked about downsizing, she'd say she'd never leave."

Wouldn't leave Pickering. She got her wish. I pictured their double gravestone, the blank half waiting for my father's eventual burial. I couldn't say what I was thinking: that he'd been liberated. Too cruel and untrue emotionally. He'd loved my mother and was still mourning her. Instead, I said, "Maybe the silver lining to losing Mom is that you can fulfill a lifelong dream."

"So you're giving me your blessing? I won't be invading your territory?"

"Highly unlikely in a city this size."

"Three hundred square miles if you count every borough!"

Such enthusiasm. It was almost heartbreaking. What if New York didn't deliver? "So what's the next step?" I asked.

"An apartment, of course."

I said I'd invite him to stay with me for a scouting trip but again — I didn't even have the floor space for a blow-up mattress.

"I'll do that Airbnb thing."

"I'm impressed."

"I'll take the bus in and reserve for a couple of nights. I think I'd like to be near Lincoln Center."

I laughed.

He asked me what was funny about Lincoln Center.

"It's not Lincoln Center. It's you, the Manhattanite already. I never knew this guy."

"What's your neighborhood again?"

"Hell's Kitchen. Aka Clinton. I think you should get closer to a subway, though, especially in this cold spell."

"I'm from New Hampshire! I laugh at the cold."

He came the following weekend and stayed for five days in a skinny duplex, one room up and one down, connected by a spiral staircase I didn't think was safe to negotiate.

He loved the place. Further delighting him was what he called the cornucopia of conveniences: restaurants of every ethnicity, and bodegas and people selling fruit and vegetables on the streets. In winter! He had his hair cut on Columbus Avenue and declared Reuben his new barber. Never had anyone been so sold on a city within the first hour of setting foot in it. And on day five he'd met with a rental agent and signed a lease for a one-bedroom with a loft in the same building he'd Airbnb'd in, four blocks south of me, effective the first of November.

Now that it was actually happening, my worrying set in. I asked if he might be rushing things. Weren't widows and widowers supposed to wait a year before they made any big decisions or lifestyle changes?

"It *has* been a year, Daff."

Oh. So it had been. "Of course. October. I knew that."

"If this isn't hard to hear: After a year, a widower can supposedly keep company with a woman without causing tongues to wag—"

"And that can't happen in Pickering?"

"Let me put it this way: I sat next to Ceci Walsh at church. Remember her? She was the art teacher before the program was cut—"

I heard the grandfather clock clang in the background. I checked my watch. It was on the half hour and had the eerie effect of my mother chiming in.

"I've thought about it," he said. "I didn't want to start up with anyone in Pickering who might be anti–New York and probably make a live-free-or-die fuss about paying state income tax. What I was really asking was if your old dad invited a woman to a show— just being hypothetical here—would that sit okay with you?"

"Yes, of course. You could do more than take her to a show. What daughter wouldn't be okay with that?"

"Holly, maybe."

"You know why that would be, don't you? If you met someone, you might marry her, and she could have children and grandchildren, and what if they were smarter or cuter or lived closer than Holly's two in Beverly Hills? Or, God forbid, a younger woman who'd give you a second family?"

"I don't know if that's fair, Daff."

"Don't worry. When or if the time comes, I can handle Holly."

Was my father a flirt? He certainly went out of his way to open doors for women of all ages. Appraising him through the eyes of prospective partners, I thought, *Yes, handsome in his rimless glasses, his well-cut gray hair, his herringbone overcoat, his cashmere scarf, and his high school principal's dignity.*

I'd told him over wine, our farewell-for-now dinner, that I thought — after seeing him in action — he'd do very well in the dating department.

"Action? Hardly? Good manners, maybe. Well, there *are* a lot of ladies around. And I like the way they look here: smart — in both meanings of the word. Of course, that doesn't mean they're available."

"They'll let you know, believe me."

"First things first. I have to get down here and moved in."

I asked if he was going to put the Pickering house on the market.

"I am. I don't want that responsibility, don't want to worry about who's plowing the driveway and shoveling the walks and weeding the perennials and checking for dead mice in the traps. It's not a snap decision; it's not like I came here on vacation and decided on a lark to relocate."

"I was playing devil's advocate. It's time for the adventure to begin."

"I already called Kevin Hogan. Remember him from Fairgrove Avenue? He's an agent now. I'd promised him the exclusive. He was just waiting for the go-ahead."

I might've said, *Dad, you understand that I'm busy? You'll have to build your own life here, with your own friends and interests and your own activities.* But I didn't. I was relieved, postdivorce, to know that my kind, brave, handsome, lonely father would be living ten minutes away.

I took the bus to Pickering to help him sort and pack. He asked if I could attend to my mother's side of the closet. I shouldn't have given any thought to Geneva Wisenkorn's musings about my mother's wardrobe, but I did. What harm in taking pictures of her most iconic outfits? If this alleged filmmaker found no inspiration in them, maybe I would; maybe I'd have daughters of my own someday, and I could show them pictures of these suits and dresses, and say, "These belonged to your grandmother; this is how a teacher dressed in Pickering, New Hampshire, at the end of the last century."

I hadn't realized my father was watching me as I spread a full-skirted shirtwaist dress out on the bed. "You're taking pictures," he said. "That's nice."

"One never knows."

"What about her jewelry? She liked to wear pins. They're in her jewelry box."

I said that Holly had put in her requests, which was fine with me. I'd already spoken for the pearls and Mom's jade ring. Over there was the pile of things to be negotiated.

"My girls . . ." he began.

"What?"

"In some families, there would be bickering. But with you two, it's been 'You want it? Take it.' No one insisting, 'Mother wanted *me* to have that.'"

He was nearly correct in his characterization. I'd be sending photos to Holly and FaceTiming the flipping of coins over a beaded shawl, three Bakelite bangles, and my mother's dress-up watch.

I wondered if I should tell my father what had happened to the one thing that Mother *did* want me specifically to have. No, not yet. Why announce that her overworked yearbook might get a new life? That documentary would probably never get made, as predicted by every New York acquaintance who'd ever had a brush with Hollywood.

And, worse, I'd have to confess that I'd ditched my mother's prized possession, and a trash-diving documentarian had rescued it.

5

Nice to Meet You

I HAD MET ACROSS-THE-HALL NEIGHBOR Jeremy the day I moved in after knocking on his door to complain about the barking from within. He was tall in a gangly way, with a bony face, a not-unattractive large nose, and a mouthful of braces. He was wearing jeans and a faded *Monkees reunion tour* T-shirt. I stared for a minute because it had the now-deceased Davy Jones on it. I introduced myself as his across-the-hall neighbor, not even having taken up residence, and told him I'd heard his dog since the minute the elevator door opened.

"He's a friend's, only here for one night, and since I was at work, not a happy camper."

"You're sure?"

"That I don't own a dog?" He opened his door wider. "You're welcome to inspect the premises."

I said, "I'm not antidog. I just didn't want to live across the hall from a yappy one."

"What's your name?"

"Daphne."

He smiled. "Like the nymph."

That was unexpected and gave me pause. "Not many people know that."

"I had two semesters of Greek mythology."

"And when was that?"

He smiled. "Is that a trick question? 'How long ago was college?' as opposed to 'How old are you?'"

"Exactly."

"I'll be twenty-six in September."

"That's eleven months from now."

"I'm a very mature twenty-five."

I couldn't agree due to that assertion being at variance with his orthodontics. Behind him, I could see an interior hallway, which meant his apartment was not a mirror image of mine but larger. He must've noticed my surveillance because he stepped to one side. "Care to look around?"

"Another time. Sorry to start off grouchy."

"Already forgotten. Where are you relocating from?"

"Most recently, the Upper East Side. But before that, New Hampshire."

Fresh from the moving van, I was holding two potted plants that I'd liberated from my marital apartment. "Are these for me, a reverse housewarming present?" he asked. "Some quaint New Hampshire custom?"

I said no. I explained that one was mint and the other lavender, both required in my next semester.

"Studying what?" he asked.

"Chocolate making."

He pretended to slump in ecstasy against his doorframe. "Did a chocolate chef just move in across the hall from me or am I dreaming?"

"Right now I'm just a student." Without a free hand to shake, I said, "Well, nice to meet you . . ."

"Jeremy Wynn."

"W-i-n?"

"That, too." Now he was grinning.

"Daphne," I said again. "Maritch."

"And is there a Mr. Marriage?"

"It's my maiden name. Maritch. I'm divorced."

"Sorry about that."

"Don't be. I never should've married him. He tricked me. It was a scam."

"Gay?"

"No. Long story. About a will. He needed a wife to free the inheritance."

"What a douchebag. Who's sorry now?"

"Not him. Believe me."

"Look how close we are already," he said.

It was natural, ten or so days later, after decluttering had brought Geneva to my door, that I would ask Jeremy if he knew her, and if so, did he have an impression of her talents or trustworthiness.

Though he hadn't mentioned what he did for work, I'd seen him leave ridiculously early, a car waiting outside. I left a note. "Knock when you have a minute? Daphne."

He did when he got home that same night. I told him I had a question.

"Shoot."

I whispered, "Can you come in? It's about a neighbor."

He did. "Cozy," he said, looking around.

"It's almost a one-bedroom. What's yours?"

"Two bedrooms. I'll give you a tour anytime." He smiled. The brackets of his braces were sky blue. "You said you had a question."

"I do. It's whether you know Geneva Wisenkorn down the hall. Documentary filmmaker. Maybe forty-five, maybe fifty. Curly dark hair. Crazy eyeglasses."

"Big woman?"

"That's her."

"Sure, but just in passing. Why?"

"She wants to make a documentary about my mother."

"Who's your mother?"

"No one you know. A high school teacher who left behind a yearbook that Geneva thinks tells a hundred stories."

"Do *you* think that?"

"I don't think it tells *one* story."

"What's she doing with your mother's yearbook?"

Why disguise the fact that I'd been careless and coldhearted? "I threw it out and she found it in the trash room."

"She must've seen something in there. Possibly something you missed?"

"I'm thinking . . . maybe."

"Let's go. Eleven what? Will she let me see the yearbook?"

"What for? And what do we say?"

"What we say, Miss Daphne, is that you mentioned to me that she was a filmmaker, and because I'm an actor who'd rather be turning out scripts, you thought we two should meet."

Well, this was a whole new topic. "A working actor?"

"Why do people ask me that? Or the other favorite: 'Character actor?' Is it the braces? Because those are a prop. I play younger. She might even know the show."

"Where? What show?"

"I'm sure you don't watch it—kind of a teen drama: *Riverdale.* Based on Archie Comics, which I say without apology."

I not only knew of the show; I watched it. Or did when I had more channels. "And who are you in it?"

"Random kid in the corridors, in the locker room, sidekick to the dead brother."

"Does this random kid have a name?"

"I got one this season: Timmy."

I made a speech: I'd moved to Manhattan against the advice of everyone who warned that the city was too expensive, too dangerous; there were terrorists in Times Square and slashers in the subway. Didn't I read the newspapers? It was impersonal, a town without pity where neighbors didn't call 911 when they heard you screaming. But they'd forgotten to mention that celebrities walked and lived among us.

"Thank you. It's usually: 'Actor? Alleged writer? What restaurant do you work at?'"

I said, "This could be very helpful."

"How so?"

"With Geneva. You're in the business. You'll get a sense of whether she's a professional or a bullshitter."

"So we exchange an industry handshake, then I ask what she's been up to lately?"

"Exactly. Will you report back as soon as you talk to her? I'm not sure what her daily routine is —"

"Unh-unh. You're coming, too."

"Right now?"

"Right now."

"But you just got home. You probably have lines to learn."

"Ha! This is what I have to sit around all day for: 'Hi, Mrs. Cooper. No thanks. Can't stay for dinner. Bye, Betty. See you at school tomorrow.'"

"Betty's my favorite character."

"Up till now," he said.

I didn't tell him that I hadn't watched season two, having downsized to bare-bones cable. I changed the subject by saying, "Okay. Let's get this over with."

Geneva answered in a plush, floor-length black velour bathrobe, her feet bare and her toes separated by pink foam spacers. Without being asked, she volunteered that she did her own pedicures ever since the *New York Times*'s exposé on nail salons. Slave labor!

Trying not to look at her splayed toes, I said, "I was telling Jeremy—this is Jeremy—that a documentary filmmaker lived on our floor, and he said, 'I should meet her.'"

Geneva, taking in the plaid shirt, the braces, the freckles, said, "Okay. Hello. No jobs on any projects right now."

With a cock of his head, actor Jeremy materialized. "Oh, darn. I was hoping you needed a gopher or an assistant to an assistant."

I said, "He's joking. He's on a TV show."

"Which one?" Geneva asked.

"I'm sure you've never heard of it: *Riverdale*," he said.

Never heard of it? I could see the internal debate she was moderating: Would admitting devotion throw her intellectual bona fides into question?

I added, "He plays Timmy. It's a speaking role."

"Can we come in?" Jeremy asked. "I'd love to hear more about Daphne's project."

Geneva hadn't budged yet. "*Daphne's* project?"

"Based on her mother, I understand."

"Who apparently was everyone's favorite teacher for reasons that aren't very clear," said Geneva.

"Yearbook advisor," I amended. "It was dedicated to her."

"I'd love to hear more about it," said Jeremy. "And to hear what else you've done."

Geneva lifted her right foot a few inches off the floor. "You might've noticed that I'm getting ready to go out." But before we could apologize for the cold call, she said, "Oh, what the hell. I can finish later. Anyway, it's better letting the first coat dry before you apply the second."

Her apartment was a shrine. The foyer walls were a deep red, covered with framed posters of documentaries she'd never told me about. "Yours?" I asked of the first one, then the next one, until I caught on: She had nothing to do with these.

I went into my own acting mode, pretending that she'd brought *Spellbound* and *Is Paris Burning?* and *Capturing the Friedmans* and *Born into Brothels* to the big screen. "Wow. And the only thing you bragged about was the matzo-factory movie. I assume you had a hand in all of these?"

Geneva said, "Ha! I'd be a household name if these were mine. I guess you didn't realize how iconic these titles are."

"I totally realize how iconic these are."

Jeremy asked, "Do you work out of your apartment?"

"Who are you again?" Geneva asked. "In relation to Daphne."

"Across-the-hall neighbor," I said.

"At the very least," said Jeremy, tossing me a look that said, *Play along.*

Geneva plopped onto a nubby upholstered chair and put her feet on its matching ottoman. That left us a sofa that looked like giant upholstered red lips. "Okay. What do you want to know?"

"I understand you found the yearbook in the trash," Jeremy said.

"Not the trash," Geneva said. "The recycling bin. It's found art."

"Lucky find," he said.

I could see that Geneva wasn't sure if she was being teased. "It happened to be sitting on top of a pile of magazines. Anyone would've picked it up."

"And then left it there," I said.

Geneva said, "We've discussed this. I do research. I'm intellectually curious. I'm interested in Americana. I can't imagine who *wouldn't* pick it up."

Jeremy said, "So how's it going?"

"I'm in the note-taking stage. I have a thousand things to absorb."

"I'd love to see it," said Jeremy.

"If there are screenings, sure."

"I meant the yearbook itself."

"I don't keep it here. It's at the bank."

"What's it doing at the bank?" I asked.

"All my important papers are in a safe-deposit box. I have to think of fire or flood. Last year, or maybe it was two years ago, the upstairs neighbor died in the bathtub with the water still running. Drip, drip, drip till he was found. My bedroom ceiling had to be replaced."

Jeremy said, "I remember. I think the building held a memorial service for him."

Geneva said, "I didn't go. It would've been in poor taste because I was suing his estate for the difference between the building's insurance and what the repairs cost."

"Speaking of that, how are you financing the documentary?" Jeremy asked.

Wasn't that a personal question? Apparently not; apparently funding was open for discussion, if not the first question filmmakers and actors asked early in an acquaintance. I made my facial expression match Jeremy's: *Yes, do tell. Where does your money come from and how do you support yourself?*

"Grants. And a family foundation."

"*Your* family?" Jeremy asked.

"Nothing official. It sounds better than 'I have a rich, guilty father.'"

"Guilty?" I repeated.

"Divorced. He left my mother for a series of men. He finally married one. I filmed their ceremony in Southampton last summer as my wedding gift to them. It turned out to be the launch of my business."

"I thought documentaries were your business," I said. "At least that's what I found online."

"My secondary business, wedding videography, doesn't show up on IMDb. But I can send you a highlight reel."

Why did I not welcome that news as proof that she knew how to hold a camera?

Jeremy was kind enough to disparage the brides and grooms who think they can produce a wedding video on their friends' iPhones.

"The contract says that no guest can hold up a phone during the ceremony. The officiant announces that before he or she begins the ceremony."

This is when I said I had to run. I had homework to do. Or maybe I said I was meeting my dad. Neither excuse was true. Jeremy stood and said he had to get going as well.

Out in the hallway, I asked what he thought of our neighbor.

"Rich girl. Grew up on the Upper East Side. Majored in film. Wesleyan, maybe Bennington, maybe USC; tried LA for a while but got no further than assistant. Has to brag because she does next to nothing."

"Wow. When did she tell you all of that?"

"Never. She didn't have to."

6

For Reasons I Never Understood

O NE DAY AHEAD of the moving van, as my father was painting the bathroom of his empty New York apartment a deep, brave midnight blue, I was pushing a sponge around, mostly to keep him company. There was something about our working side by side, our heads covered in matching bandannas, that made me confess, on my knees by the tub, "Mom's yearbook? The one she obsessed over? I had to de-clutter. I threw it out."

Expecting disappointment if not anger, I was surprised to hear "I don't blame you. I wouldn't want the damn thing."

I was swishing tepid water around the tub, which was clean to start with. "I thought you might be upset that I didn't give you the right of first refusal."

"Why would *I* want it?"

"Sentimental value? Because it meant a lot to her. Because she must've thought I'd cherish it —"

"Nonsense! Signing up for every reunion! Joining the commit-tees. She took that advisor thing way too seriously. After the first couple of reunions ... never mind. I promised myself never to speak ill of your mother now."

"Give me a hint ... It won't leave this room."

"I'll say this much: I thought her attending every damn one was unnecessary."

"That's hardly speaking ill of Mom."

"Except that I found it . . . vain. How many times did she have to take a bow? I got that the thing was dedicated to her — but we're not talking about *War and Peace.*"

I asked how many reunions he attended with her.

"Pickering High's? None."

"Really? She didn't insist? Didn't want to show off the handsome Principal Maritch?" — out-and-out flattery, for sure, but it didn't seem to be registering.

"No, never. Apparently, a principal is considered a wet blanket at a reunion. It was her thing, her night out. She used to plan her outfit months in advance." He was now rerolling paint onto the same track of deep blue. "She didn't need me there — that was obvious. And you know how many of these acolytes came to her funeral? Not even a half dozen; not even the ones she had up on a pedestal for reasons I never understood."

I'd heard this sad fact before. After the funeral, after the visitors to our house had left, we'd remarked on the hallowed class of 1968's poor showing. Holly and I had wondered aloud, not in front of our father: Had our mother's devotion been one-sided? Worse: Had it been a topic of ridicule?

I changed the subject by announcing that we had toilet-bowl cleaner but not a brush, so until we did, what else could I do? Should I run out for one?

"It'll be on the truck. I packed everything. So just keep me company. Tell me what else is new? Any prospects in the chocolate field?"

With nothing to report and with my conscience nagging, I said, "I put it in the recycling bin on my floor, and someone found it."

"Are we talking about a toilet brush?"

"No! The yearbook."

"You already told me that. I said I didn't care."

"There's more." I skipped the email overture, the phone call, the cookies and vodka, and went straight to "The someone who found it wants to make a documentary out of it."

The roller stopped. He turned around. Drips of paint landed on the tile floor.

"You said you didn't need a drop cloth," I scolded.

"It's latex. Just explain to me how a yearbook gets made into a movie."

"She, the alleged filmmaker, thinks the world's in love with reunions. And at every one you get the ugly duckling who returns as a swan, the football captain who's never topped his high school glory days, the nerds who founded software companies and show up with trophy wives, the high school romances that get rekindled."

"Are you in love with this notion, too? Because you sound pretty sold."

"No! I told her I'd have to speak to a lawyer. And to you. And I threw in Holly for good measure."

"But can she just show up in Pickering with the yearbook under her arm?"

"She wants to start at the next reunion, whenever that is, and work backward."

"To where . . . ?"

"To high school? To graduation? But we didn't get that far because I kept saying no, no, no."

"So it's over? Not going to happen?"

I mumbled something noncommittal, followed by silence and the running of more tub water, before I said, "Paper towels, sponges, rubber gloves, milk, bread? I'll make a list."

"You didn't answer. Is it going to get made or not?"

Wincing, I said, "I get the impression she can do it without our permission. Finders keepers."

He put the roller back in the tray and slipped the bandanna off his head. "I'll save you a call. Where's my phone? I'm sure I have Julian's number" — his first cousin, the family one-stop lawyer.

"I know what he'll say about a potential movie: 'The odds are it'll never see the light of day.' She's only had one documentary made . . . and it was about matzo."

Not a good sign: that "matzo" failed to deescalate the conversation. "Will it be about the class of nineteen sixty-eight or about your mother?"

"Both, I think. But remember —"

"Even though she's not here to defend herself? Those comments she wrote? *Fat, rude, gay, felon.* How do we know they don't constitute slander? And some members of that class, believe me, could come forward and say things that would slander *her.*"

About what? I chose to believe nothing more than her overwrought devotion to a class full of ingrates.

7

Holiday with Strangers

"WHERE SHOULD I START?" asked Geneva's subject line. The body of her email was blank except for her closing, a six-line signature/contact info/ credential overload.

The haplessness annoyed me out of proportion to its innocent-enough four words. I wasn't going to answer, but then couldn't help myself. "It's your project. You're the filmmaker. And" — the drum I was constantly beating "without the yearbook in my possession, I have nothing to go on."

She wrote back. "That sounded hostile."

Now it was my turn to pick up the phone. As soon as she answered, without preliminaries, I said, "You the professional are asking *me* for advice?"

"I thought you were in the business."

"What business?"

"Acting. Isn't that how you know Timmy?"

Really? Do I even correct this? "Timmy's his character. You mean Jeremy. I know him because he lives across the hall."

"Never mind. Listen, can you come with me to the next reunion? They have a whole website for the fiftieth. All we do is sign up, send a check to the class treasurer, Roland somebody — his address is on there — and show up!"

"Wild horses couldn't drag me."

Undaunted, Geneva asked how one gets to Pickering. Was there a train?

"You fly to Manchester and rent a car."

"Do you think anyone else would be attending from Manhattan?"

"So you could hitch a ride? Unlikely."

There was a pause. "Do you drive?"

"I drive, but I don't have a car. Plus, I'm not going."

"May I say something?" she asked.

I waited.

"If it was *my* mother who had some lifelong draw to this class — correction, lifelong *obsession* — I'm damn sure I'd be running up there to find out the who, what, and why of it."

"There *is* no who-what-why. Obviously, she considered the yearbook dedication a huge honor. And this is a town where there's nothing to do — no clubs or movies or theater unless you count the high school musical every May. This is what she looked forward to, what she bought a new dress for every five years."

"There has to be more. That's all I'm saying. There. Has. To. Be. More."

"If that's what you're counting on, some can of worms, you're in for a long, boring night."

"I'll pay for your ticket," she wheedled.

I didn't think I was agreeing to attend by asking, "Are you sure any random person can go?"

"Absolutely. There's a box you check that says spouse, partner, sibling—"

"I'm not going to go there under false pretenses."

"Wait. And one that says 'other.' We'd certainly qualify as 'other.'"

I tried to sound as grudging as possible when I asked, "When is it?"

"Oh, wait. Let me get the info in front of me . . . Okay. November 30. Thanksgiving weekend, which means you're probably going up there anyway to have Thanksgiving dinner with family."

What was I doing Thanksgiving weekend? Except eating the actual meal with my father, I didn't have a plan, let alone for the dead days that followed. I gave this scenario a few seconds' thought: *Dad over for turkey; no, just the breast cooked in my apartment-size oven. I'd buy or borrow a roasting pan.* I said, "I don't have family up there. My dad's in the city now."

"That settles it," Geneva said.

"Settles what?"

"He'll come with us."

"He never went to reunions with my mother. He's certainly not going to start now. He and I will have a quiet Thanksgiving dinner. Just us two, but that's fine."

"No, it's not fine. Thanksgiving dinner has to be a party. You'll bring him to mine."

"Party? I don't think so."

"I call it that, but it's just dinner. I round up my friends who have no place to go, the ones who eat out or volunteer at soup kitchens. I can fit a dozen around my table with both leaves in it."

I was torn. I didn't want to be with the unmoored and orphaned, but I knew my father would consider such a gathering his coming-out party. I said, "I'd have to ask him. He was widowed not that long ago."

"All the better!" crowed Geneva.

Should I call her on such an insensitive exclamation, or was her diplomacy an unrealistic goal?

"What's better about that situation?" And for added hostile measure: "I think you've forgotten he's dead set against your yearbook project."

"All I meant was that my invitation would be all the more appreciated at a time like this. Is that not true? I order four different kinds of pies. Does he have a favorite?"

"Lemon meringue" popped out.

"You don't think it's a charity invitation, do you? Lost souls for Thanksgiving?" my father asked. We were meeting halfway between our Hell's Kitchen apartments, rather unnecessary when you considered the short four blocks separating us.

"Dad, this is New York. You'll find out how many people moved here when they were young and never went back to Indiana or West Virginia or Baton Rouge. They're actors and choreographers or buyers at good places like Saks and Bergdorf's. They got older. The lucky ones have rent-controlled apartments. Many never got attached along the way."

"Do *you* want to go?"

I admitted that I hadn't made a Thanksgiving plan. And the thought of just the two of us at either his small bistro table, transferred from the Pickering patio, or the rigged piece of wood that hung by a hinge from my kitchen wall . . . no, not that. I could make a reservation somewhere. Restaurants on every block here! Didn't he love that about New York?

"I've never eaten Thanksgiving dinner in a restaurant in my *life*," he said.

I asked if he wanted to think this over: a holiday with strangers. I added the piece of identification I'd failed to provide: "Our hostess is the woman who pilfered Mom's yearbook."

Wouldn't that put a whole new undesirable spin on this invitation? No, it did not. He said, "I can separate those two things. Remember: I was a high school principal. I'd be meeting with a parent who had one great kid and one total pain in the ass."

"Which applies to this situation how?"

"I can compartmentalize. I could run a *workshop* on compart-mentalizing."

Close to giving in, I told him that Geneva had asked what his favorite pie was.

"Did you tell her strawberry rhubarb?"

"That's a summer pie. I told her lemon meringue."

"That'll do. She can't be all bad. I've found that women who cook and entertain are my kind of people."

"She's having it catered."

"Ha. Another new experience for me." He asked if it was pot-luck.

"People don't do that in New York. Somehow it works out. You're the host, maybe you even cook, then they take you to dinner as a thank-you."

"I'm writing that in my book."

"Literally?"

"Not that kind of a book. It's a notepad. When I hear something that sounds like a New York custom or a recommendation for a restaurant or a movie or a doctor, I write it down."

Something about that made me worry about him. A babe in the woods of Hell's Kitchen.

I left a postcard at Geneva's door. The front was a black-and-white photograph of a bakery shop window. On the back, I wrote, "My dad (Tom Maritch) and I accept your kind invitation to join you for Thanksgiving dinner. Let me know the time and what we can bring."

It took a day before I found the same card outside my door. She'd written over my ink scratches in a black Sharpie: COCK-TAILS 6. DINNER 7? WINE RED OR WHITE THNX.

. . .

We went around the table, introduced ourselves by name, and —
at our hostess's request — provided one interesting fact about ourselves. In the previous round, occupations, I'd learned we had two
psychologists, an acupuncturist (Geneva's), a gemologist, an SAT
tutor, a physical therapist (Geneva's), a cantor in training, and a
food stylist.

I almost said, "Pass," when it was my turn because the interesting facts that others were confessing were either too personal or
more impressive than I could come up with: Cancer survivor. Bernie Madoff survivor. Preop transgender. Ice-dancing judge in the
1988 Winter Olympics. Fired by Martha Stewart. Fired by Leona
Helmsley. Taught Woody Allen and Soon-Yi Previn's daughter in
preschool.

Dad and I were last. I'd been watching him take in his tablemates' answers, thinking he might be shocked or awed. But what
I saw was something like a relocation ratification. His answer,
the least glamorous one so far, but a perfect accompaniment to
his bow tie and herringbone jacket, was a simple "I just moved
here from a town with a population of under five thousand. You
could call it a lifelong dream to live in New York." Who knew that
would be an exotic answer? It seemed to me that the whole table
was clucking sympathetically. Geneva let that go on for a few in-
dulgent oohs and aahs, before prompting, "Daphne? Something
memorable to close out this round?"

What did I have to report that was the least bit memorable?
I decided on a truth I didn't have to varnish. "I was bamboozled
into a loveless marriage because my husband wouldn't inherit his
grandparents' money while he was still single."

I meant to say it if not cheerfully then at least with enough
irony to suggest it was behind me. Had I forgotten that there were
two therapists at the table?

"How long were you married?" one asked, overlapping with the other saying, "How'd you find out?"

"The best man at our brunch wedding. Too many mimosas. Something he said made me think, *He knows something I don't know.*"

"But," said my father, "Daphne gave it a chance, didn't you, honey?"

When did I ever have an entire dinner party's full attention? I said, "I gave him every chance until he didn't come home one night."

Geneva was either losing interest in my marital history or really did need to check on the food. She rose, and said, "I'd better see if Rosa needs me."

Only the New Hampshire Maritches asked if we could help. Geneva said, "Absolutely not. I'll yell when the buffet is ready."

"Rosa is her cleaning woman," someone offered.

"Wouldn't she need the day off?" my father asked.

The preop woman said, "She's probably happy to have the extra work."

Back to the topic of my failed marriage. One of the therapists, who was wearing as many necklaces as I'd seen a person manage at one time, asked me if we'd had counseling.

"He didn't want to stay married, didn't need to under the provisions of the will."

"Gay?" asked the figure-skating judge. "Him, I mean."

"Definitely not."

My father said, "Maybe Daphne didn't want this very nice conversation to get stalled on the topic of her unfortunate marriage. The good news is, she got in and out of it without undue suffering. Isn't that right, hon?"

Were we all intimates now? I guessed so because the Bernie

Madoff client, a woman named Suzanne with bangs that appeared to have been shaped over a juice can, said, "I hope you took him to the cleaners."

I lied, and said, "I sure did," with a fake jaunty laugh.

"Soup's on!" came Geneva's bellow.

My father and I exchanged private smiles. We'd never had a buffet Thanksgiving dinner. As the only man at the table, he sprang to his feet first and stood behind his chair until all his tablemates were heading for the kitchen.

There we found, on every available surface, foil serving pans of turkey, sweet potatoes, mashed potatoes, two kinds of stuffing, green beans almondine, Brussels sprouts, coleslaw, cranberry sauce, a cut-glass gravy boat, and (labeled) vegetarian lasagna. Both my father and I exclaimed over the bounty, he more enthusiastically than I because the crinkly aluminum trays, side by side, reminded me of what a shelter's steam table might be offering this day.

Back in the dining room, my father was again standing until all were seated, plates piled high except for the Bernie Madoff client who looked proudly and purposely emaciated. Dad asked, "Do New Yorkers say grace?"

"Why not!" Geneva cried. "Have at it!"

The other therapist, with a shawl around her shoulders and wearing a dress of fabric that had ribbons woven through it, said, "OR we could go around the table and each say what we're thankful for."

I always hated public thanks. There were eleven of us, and my food was getting cold. Geneva, with a drumstick in hand, said, "We can eat while we give thanks. And drink! I'll start right there: I'm grateful for your excellent reds and whites, and the rosé, which ain't easy to find in the fall. And to Deborah for the gorgeous pumpkin pie. You won't believe it, but she made it herself."

"Pumpkin chiffon," Deborah the ex–Martha Stewart employee corrected.

We went around the table, this time counterclockwise. Thanks were variations on the theme of not being alone on Thanksgiving . . . meeting all of you . . . Deborah said she had a new job, was starting Monday at the Food Network. Suzanne was grateful that her daughter was pregnant, knock on wood, after three rounds of in vitro, due in April. I said I was thankful that my father lived only four blocks away and was adjusting to city life like a champ.

He said, "Ditto. How lucky does a dad get?"

The woman who'd been fired by Leona Helmsley said, "Sorry. I have nothing."

"No," my father said. "It can't be that you have nothing to be thankful for? Kids? Friends? Nieces? Nephews?"

She picked up her fork, then put it down. "Okay. How's this: I'm grateful those hurricanes didn't hit New York."

We toasted that and picked up our forks. I soon went back for more gravy on the dry breast meat I'd taken too optimistically. Geneva joined me in the kitchen. "You're coming with me to New Hampshire on Saturday, right? For the reunion? I signed you up. And whoever manages the website wrote back asking if you were June's daughter."

"I never agreed to that."

"Yes, you did! It's the fiftieth, for Chrissake! I mean, how much more do you need as a sign that this fell into my lap at exactly the right moment in time, like it was preordained?"

Back at the table, I dropped the subject. Had my father overheard us? Apparently not; he was looking anything but concerned, conducting a conversation with blue-eyed, pleasantly plump Paula, the woman who needed gratitude prompting.

I asked Geneva on my way out, loaded down with leftovers, "If I went, how would we get there?"

"Car service, of course."

Later, I asked myself if agreeing to go would kill me. The fiftieth would never come around again. Would in-person attendance help me understand why reunions were so magical to my mother that none could be skipped?

I called Geneva in the morning. I said okay, I'd go this once. But please know I was not in any way endorsing a future documentary. I added two conditions: It would be a day trip versus an overnight stay. And that we'd leave New York early enough for me to return two books to the Pickering library that had been overdue for a year.

8

Teacher's Pet

I N THE BACK SEAT, on the cold, dull gray ride to Pickering, Geneva declared, "Your mother didn't have great boundaries."

"Patently obvious," I said.

"At the same time, kind of a snob."

"In what way?"

"Status. Jobs. Successes and failures. Her scribbles made a lot out of what they ended up doing versus their stated goals at eighteen."

This is when I learned that Geneva, dressed in voluminous stiff black silk that fell straight from the shoulders and a fur-collared red coat, had made a study of the graduates' dashed dreams. The class of 1968, she reported, reading from her iPad, had submitted these answers to the question *Ambition?*: Approximately one-quarter had answered either "happiness" or "success." Girls had predicted wife, teacher, beautician, nurse, dress designer, bookkeeper, secretary, stewardess, store buyer, social worker, occupational therapist, one professor, and one opera singer. The boys had higher reaches, among them architect, artist, author, aviation mechanic, foreign diplomat, farmer, doctor, lawyer, Major League pitcher, "take over my father's business," navy, army, air force, forest ranger, hunting guide, traveling salesman, chemist, journalist, draftsman, mechanic, TV technician, aeronautical engineer, foreman at General Motors, director, millionaire. The more philosophical answers included: "Improvement." "To see the world." "To go to Hawaii." "Success in math." "A useful life." "Early retirement." "To be friends with everyone."

"Talk about gender stereotyping. It makes me wonder about the school's guidance counselors," Geneva said.

I agreed, yes, very traditional roles. But at *this* moment, my main takeaway was that the yearbook was no longer in a bank vault. "You brought it with you?" I asked.

"Of course! What's the expression—'You can't tell the players without a scorecard'?"

"And what do you intend to do with it?"

"Get feedback."

"In what respect *feedback?*"

"To the comments, obviously. What else is there? What's my story? Would I have fished the yearbook out of the trash if it were just a bunch of head-and-shoulder shots?"

"No way that's coming with us."

Geneva nudged the briefcase as far from me as the back seat floor allowed. "I don't think that's your decision."

"Really? Then good luck! You'll be like the evil fairy who shows up at Sleeping Beauty's christening: 'Nice to meet you, unsuspecting guy who came looking for a nice time. Would you like to see what snarky Mrs. Maritch wrote about you?'"

"I don't interpret her comments that way."

"Oh, really? *Who's fifty pounds heavier, who's a failure, who's wearing the same dress she wore at the last reunion?*"

Of course, Geneva would have to introduce a mediator. "Sir?" she asked, leaning toward our driver. "Let's say at seventeen your ambition was—I don't know—to head up General Motors, but then reality set in and you ended up as a driver for a car service.

Then an ex-teacher wrote 'drives for a car service' next to your yearbook photo, would you consider that a put-down?"

He turned off the radio but didn't answer.

"I was being hypothetical. I have no idea what you put down under 'Ambition' in your yearbook."

The driver said, "We didn't do yearbooks in my country," quickly amending that America was his country now.

I asked where he'd come from.

"From one of the oldest civilizations in the history of the world!"

"Greece?" I tried.

"Rome," said Geneva.

"Egypt!"

"I've never been," said Geneva. "And I guess it's too late for that now. What a mess."

I thought it best to get back to my anti-yearbook argument since we were now one exit from Pickering. "It's either *it* or me," I told her.

"What's either it or you?"

"*The Monadnockian.* Either it stays in the car or I do."

"Why do you care? You threw it out!"

"I'm not protecting the yearbook! I'm protecting the feelings of the graduates. Good luck enlisting them for a documentary after shoving their faces in it!"

"How else am I going to identify people? What about context? It's going to be a bunch of sixty-something-year-olds —"

"With name tags! That's for sure. And mine will say *Daphne Maritch,* which should be all the social lubricant you need."

"As *if* you're going to recognize everyone and make the connection back to their . . . their pasts! Their former selves now living lives of quiet desperation?"

"That's it, isn't it? All condescension. If they're still here, going to a reunion, they're failures?"

"I need it," she said, almost a whimper.

"That's how you want to present yourself, a stranger who signed up as *other.*"

She turned away and stared out the window. "Factories," I heard her murmur. Even in profile, I could tell she was pouting, waiting for me to negotiate or apologize. I didn't.

"What's your decision?" I asked.

She turned back to face me. "Okay. But here's what I want: Presuming there are name tags or place cards, I want yours to say, 'Daughter of June Maritch.'"

"It'll be obvious. I don't have to announce it."

"Yes, you do. With a Sharpie."

"Which you no doubt brought with you?"

Finally, a grudging smile. "Of course."

I opened the black satin evening purse that had seemed right for an occasion asking for "cocktail attire." I reapplied lipstick in the mirror of the small faux-jeweled compact.

"Looks vintage," Geneva noted. "Was it hers?"

I closed the purse. Before she could spot the JWM, I said no.

A tuxedoed man and a tiaraed woman were checking in guests. I asked them what the round orange sticker on our name tags meant. The woman pointed to her own badge. A gold star, she explained, meant classmate, a silver star was for spouses, blue for plus-ones. Orange meant "other."

I started to write the agreed-upon designation under my name but got no further than "Daughter of..." when an envelope slid toward me. I looked up. The hostess said, "I put you at his table."

"Whose table?"

"Open it," said Geneva, with a nudge.

Handwritten on a note card bearing the seal of New Hampshire, it said, "I saw on the website that you were attending. I hope to talk to you this evening. Sincerely, Peter D. Armstrong."

I asked the woman which table. She tapped my name tag, as if I had never before set foot in the country of catered dinners. "That number there. Table five."

"Do you know this guy Armstrong?" Geneva asked her.

"I know everybody," she said.

"I'm here on something of a scouting trip," Geneva continued. "I'm a documentary filmmaker."

Were these two greeters chosen for their neutrality and frozen smiles, for their New Hampshire election-coverage nonchalance?

Because their badges announced them as Albert Knight and Gloria (Hink) Knight, I asked, "Married classmates?"

"Married now," said Gloria. "Since our fortieth."

"Birthdays?"

"Reunion," the husband said. "We were put at the same table."

"Were you high school sweethearts?" I asked.

Apparently, this was not a polite question. Albert checked with Gloria, who said, "We went to the prom together."

"Then what?" said Geneva. "Broke up? Married other people?"

Gloria said, "No. Just each other."

Albert said, "Twice."

Gloria added, "Not our fault. We were teenagers the first time, which I wouldn't recommend to anyone."

"I'm surprised they put a divorced couple at the same table," Geneva said.

"People knew we were . . . amicable," said Gloria.

"Look who's here!" Albert boomed, seemingly relieved to direct his attention to new arrivals. And to us: "Coat check's to your right. Enjoy the evening."

Gloria tore two tickets from a roll, entitling us to one alcoholic drink per guest. "Cash bar after that. Soft drinks on the house."

Only a few yards from the reception table, Geneva said, "Pregnant straight out of school, I bet. Maybe even prom night. I was tempted to ask if they have a kid who's *exactly* fifty years old."

"Please don't embarrass me," I said.

The woman on coat duty, a gold-starred Beverly Swierczek, was dressed in scooped-neck silver lamé contrasting with her spray tan; her fingernails were dark blue with zigzags of silver.

"Did you pull the short straw?" Geneva asked her.

Her welcome smile faded. "Sorry?"

"This job. I hope you won't be stuck here all night."

"I'm on the reunion committee. I don't mind." Unexpectedly, she winked. "I'm a single gal. Everyone who attends checks his or her coat, emphasis on the *his*."

"Smart," said Geneva.

We entered the function room, which was smaller than I expected, about a dozen round tables draped in burgundy linen. Centerpieces were shellacked gourds and pine cones; at each place setting stood an airline-size bottle of maple syrup. Had I expected a big banquet hall? WELCOME, 68ERS! WE MADE IT! proclaimed a banner hanging from the beams.

"Bar first," said Geneva.

The featured drink was a Tickled Pink, prepoured and lined up, awaiting our ticket redemption. With the pretty drinks in hand, we wove our way to table five. There were four seats occupied so far, two couples, all smiling hospitably. The men stood until we'd shaken hands and took our seats. One wife, coal-black hair in an upsweep, said, "You're the New Yorkers!" She pointed to the name tag pinned to her black lace bodice: She was Donna; her husband was Dave. The other couple, both elfin and white-haired with matching rimless eyeglasses, introduced themselves as Ritchie and Mimi Perry.

I asked if all four had been classmates. Donna said, "Yes, but we winter in Florida now."

"Ritchie and I are both from here," said Mimi. "Though he was born in Laconia."

Ritchie said, "I wouldn't expect you to remember us — arrangements were made with your father — but we are Perry Funeral Home."

"Of course. I thought you looked familiar. You did a lovely job."

Wouldn't this be a good time for someone, anyone, to extol the memory of their famously devoted teacher or at the very least rote-reply about my having their thoughts and prayers?

But then we were eight as two women took their seats. More introductions. They were Roseanne and Barbara, friends going back to junior year when they tried out for varsity cheerleader. Their shrugs and wistful smiles indicated they hadn't made it.

Mimi said, "But runners-up automatically make the PHS pep squad."

"And then we both went to Plymouth State," said Roseanne.

"Where we met the guys we married. And get this: Our husbands worked together at Travelers," said Barbara.

"They're skipping tonight?" asked Geneva.

Both women laughed. "They haven't been to one of these since our — do you remember which one?"

"Tenth," said the other. "That's the reunion where you want everyone to know you got married."

"Interesting," said Geneva, managing to convey in one word that the opposite was true.

Mimi said, "Daphne is Mrs. Maritch's daughter."

"Wow!" said Roseanne. "Is she here tonight?"

There was an intake of breath around the table. Mr. Perry took the reins, explaining in a somber professional tone that Mrs. Maritch had passed away a year ago last month.

"I'm so sorry!" said Roseanne. "Was it on the class Facebook page?"

I said apparently not.

Geneva said, "Facebook page. I'll have to get on that," prompting Donna to ask what her connection to the class was.

"I'll let Daphne answer." She turned to me. "Since you're so worried about what I might say."

Did the others hear the peevishness in that? I said, "Geneva wants to make a documentary about . . . well, *you* explain because I'm not sure."

"Maybe after I've had another drink," said Geneva, fishing the lime slice out of her otherwise empty glass.

"About us?" asked Mimi.

"No," I said.

Geneva fired off a sarcastic *Ha!* followed by "She *wishes no.*"

I took over lest Geneva's amplification point to my mother's poison pen. "Ms. Wisenkorn was inspired by the yearbook, so to the extent it contains your photos, it would include some of you. But right now, it's only . . ." What? Notes on paper? In Geneva's head?

Luckily, something else was distracting her. "Other tables have food," she said. "Fruit cup, it looks like."

Dave said, "With a scoop of orange sherbet. Those are tables one through four. We're next."

"Food committee," his wife said proudly.

It was then that our final tablemate appeared, holding a glass of red wine. He was tall, gray-haired, dressed in an expensive-looking suit. All four women looked happy if not triumphant. "Peter!" I heard. "Pete!"

Was it merely his distinguished good looks and sartorial splendor that made everyone proud to have snagged Peter Armstrong for table five? He asked Barbara, who'd taken the seat next to me, if she minded scooting over one because he had very much hoped to speak with Miss Maritch.

"Sure," she said. "We figured."

I offered my hand. "Daphne," I said rather needlessly.

"I know. Hence the jockeying for the seat next to you. You got my note?"

"Upon arrival."

Now seated, napkin in place on his lap, he leaned in my direction, and said quietly, "We must talk."

Across the table, Dave said, "Congratulations on the landslide. You had my vote. *Both* our votes."

"For what?" asked Geneva.

"Dog catcher," Armstrong said with a wry smile. "Hasn't that news made its way to New York City?"

"He's joking!" said Barbara. "Peter's our new state senator."

"Senator?" I repeated. "Wow. That's big. That's like . . . next stop White House."

"Not U.S. senator. *State* senator. In Concord."

Did Geneva's first question really have to be "Is there a Mrs. Armstrong?"

"Not at the present time."

"Divorced?"

"Actually, never married."

"Broke a lotta hearts, though," said Donna.

"Peter was class president," said Barbara.

"Actually, I wasn't," he said. "I ran but I lost."

"Remind me who won," said Mimi.

"Someone named Duddy," said Geneva. "An Irish last name?"

Shouldn't one of us explain why she knew that? Not Geneva,

who rose and said she was getting another drink. Anyone else? Her treat.

I said I'd have another Tickled Pink, an order echoed by two others, inspiring Ritchie to rise and offer his help. When she was out of earshot and wouldn't hear me drastically underplaying her relationship to *The Monadnockian,* I said, "My mother left her yearbook to me. Geneva's fascinated with it . . . We're neighbors . . . She lives on my floor."

Since Peter's arrival, several classmates had left their own tables to say hello and offer congratulations. During a break from well-wishers, I asked him, "Did you have my mother for English?"

"I did. And I worked on the yearbook. I had her when she was still Miss Winter."

Amplifying needlessly, I said, "It was her first job right out of college."

"We all had a crush on her. She was the youngest teacher in the entire school, at least while we were there."

"And quite the looker," added Dave. "If it's okay to say that to someone's daughter."

Could there have been a more awkward moment for Barbara to have said, "And, boy, you sure look a lot like her. A dead ringer."

Geneva and Ritchie were back, managing three drinks apiece, beyond the orders requested. She took her seat and asked me what she'd missed.

I said in a well-modulated voice, "Everyone remembers my mother. Quite vividly."

"I think she was faculty before your father was principal," said Donna.

"I was at their wedding," said Peter.

What did he just say?

"Teacher's pet!" said one of the women.

"Not as an invited guest. I worked at the club where the reception was held, as a busboy."

"*Were* you the teacher's pet?" Geneva asked.

I noted his political skill when he replied, "She certainly wrote some very nice college recommendations for me."

"Got him into Dartmouth," said Mimi.

"Since when do applicants get to see what their teachers write about them?" asked Geneva.

"Maybe when letters do a great deal for a shy senior's self-esteem," he said.

"I'm curious as to why you asked to be at our table," said Geneva.

His reaction was an eloquent tilt of his head, easily translated as *Our? What our? I asked to sit with Daphne. You are the extraneous plus-one.* "Because I look forward to speaking with Miss Maritch." He didn't add "privately" or "one on one" but did add, "I never had the chance to express my condolences."

That would be the sum of it then. He merely wanted to snag me for his formal expression of sympathy. Had he been one of the handful of grads who'd come to her funeral? Why not ask? I did.

"I most certainly would have, but I was out of the country. I didn't hear about her passing until I returned."

"Do state senators travel a lot, like on those junkets we're always reading about?" asked Geneva.

He ignored the question as waiters were bringing our entrees—breast of chicken with rice and broccolini, apparently obliging Geneva to note, "Broccolini! I wouldn't have expected that!"

"Maybe you were expecting canned peas up here in the boonies," said Donna.

"Or Tater Tots," said her husband.

"Who knows what I was expecting? It just came out. You know what my problem is?"

I said, "I think they do."

"My big mouth. I warned Daphne about it the first time we met. I don't have a filter. Very bad. But you know where this comes from?"

The whole table waited, no one looking the least sympathetic.

"Hollywood!"

"Hollywood?" Roseanne repeated. "From watching movies?"

"No. From working there. The majority of people I dealt with weren't what you'd call diplomatic. In fact, a majority were assholes. And proud of it."

"Oh, right. You make documentaries," said Ritchie.

Would anyone ask the logical follow-up question — What documentaries? — so she'd have to name her prize-winning, if not only, film? Would they even know what matzo was?

There was no music playing, though a deejay had staked some territory behind a table and was fiddling with switches and knobs. I said, "There's dancing?" — a disingenuous question since the yearbook had many references to partners, the desirable and the not so much.

"Any minute now," Peter said. Lucky for him, the music started. I didn't recognize the song, but apparently it was a sentimental favorite: "Three Stars Will Shine Tonight," the theme from *Dr. Kildare*, one of the women explained.

Peter crossed his knife and fork on his plate, removed the napkin from his lap, and said, "I feel it's my duty to break the ice. Daphne?"

I took a sip from my second Tickled Pink, and said, "Why not?"

It's hard to describe what makes a man a good slow dancer. At ease but leading, hands not roving, cheek not docked and unwelcome on the near stranger's. Smells nice.

I said, "Your constituents are staring."

"Let 'em."

"Maybe they think you brought a date."

"It's only a dance," he said. "And I'm famous within this particular constituency for escorting the unescorted." Something of a dip followed, which caused several onlookers to clap.

"I hope you're just being a charming politician."

"As opposed to what?"

"Flirting."

There was a longer pause than I expected. When he finally spoke, his tone was newly formal. "Dancing aside, it would be most inappropriate, in fact, unseemly, for me to flirt with June's daughter."

Not Mrs. Maritch, not Miss Winter. *June.*

"I don't think I want to know what you're about to tell me."

"You've already guessed," he said.

9

Hence the Note

THOUGH I WANTED TO KNOW none of this, I couldn't help asking, "When and for how long?"

By this time, Senator Armstrong and I were outside the function hall, coatless in the cold. He'd offered me his suit jacket, which I batted away. The adulterer!

"I promise you nothing happened when I was a student," he said.

"When? Graduation night? Spring break from Dartmouth?"

"You're really angry," he said. "But I hope someday you'll understand —"

"Understand what?" And this in my old, furious, wronged-wife voice: "That you *fucked* your English teacher — oh, and I forgot — your yearbook advisor."

"After," he said. "*Well* after. I've already said that."

"'Well after' is worse! 'Well after' means she was married. To my father, by the way."

We were both shivering. Armstrong said, "Come inside. I know where we can speak in private."

Clearly, he knew every square foot of the Pickering Knights of Columbus Hall. I followed him grudgingly past the unmanned reception table, the abandoned coat check, around the corner to the handicapped bathroom. I said, "You're kidding."

"No, listen. I've thought ahead. I knew we'd be speaking in private. If we're interrupted, I'll explain that we're discussing the June Maritch Memorial Scholarship, which I'm initiating with this year's graduating class in honor of our fiftieth."

That gave me a moment's pause — did he mean that? I'd appreciate a scholarship in my mother's name, which was about time. But as the door locked behind us, I snapped back to affronted, demanding, "What's left to discuss? Is this when you tell me it wasn't just sex? That it was a great love?"

"Daphne, please —"

"Who started it?"

"It was mutual. We both always acknowledged that."

We both . . . when? During quickies in handicapped toilet stalls every five years? "How long did this love affair go on?"

He closed his eyes as if steeling himself for the attack that was sure to follow the truthful answer. "A long time."

"Until . . . ?"

"I'd rather not say."

"Why do I have to know this? It can't do anything but make me posthumously furious at my mother. It's not like she was unhappily married! My father is a wonderful man. I'm sure they loved each other. He would've moved to New York years ago, a lifelong dream, but stayed here because of her."

What was that pained look I was getting? Grief over my mother's death? Shame? Guilt? Pity for my father? Regret for spilling the ugly beans? I asked again, "Why tell me this? You get it off your chest and I'm stuck with a sickening secret. Anything else you'd like to unburden yourself about?"

"I was afraid of this. I didn't even know if you'd grant me a private audience. But you're a mature woman. You have a good head on your shoulders. I thought it was time for you to know the truth."

"The truth that my mother was an adulterer? Thanks. I needed that like a fucking hole in the head."

"Not that," he said.

"There's more?"

"I thought you would draw the obvious conclusion." He was looking at me with undue tenderness, which made me retreat a step.

"I seem to have miscalculated," he said. "I should've tracked you down, come to New York, met with you privately."

"So you could take me to lunch and regale me with the good times you and my mother had in the sack?"

He cranked a paper towel from the dispenser and blew his nose. "I never married. I never had a family I could call my own."

Looking back, a psychologist would characterize these five minutes as denial of the textbook kind.

Then I got it. Tonight's meeting wasn't about an extramarital affair. It was to announce that he, Peter D. Armstrong, believed he had impregnated my mother and the fruit of that insemination was Daphne Elaine Maritch.

10

What Are You Looking For, Exactly?

F OR ONLY A BRIEF PART of the four-and-a-half-hour trip back to Manhattan, I slept or pretended to after negotiating a long perusal of *The Monadnockian*. Even within the confines of the back seat, doors locked and windows shut, we had to share it across our laps while Geneva maintained a possessive grip on her half of the book.

"What do you think I'm going to do with it?" I asked. "Tear it to shreds? Throw it out the window?"

"All I know is that you want it back, probably more than ever now. I'm just taking natural precautions." She then asked, "What are you looking for, exactly?"

"Same thing you are," I lied. "To match up tonight's acquaintances with the teenagers they once were."

"I bet it's that state senator," she said. "He was certainly on a mission."

I asked why she said that, wondering nervously how transparent our interaction had been — the welcome note, the musical chairs, the dancing, our disappearance and reappearance. I'd hoped all was explained when Armstrong had stood, tapped a water glass with a knife, and announced the creation of the June Winter Maritch Memorial Scholarship, to be awarded to a graduating senior who planned to enter the field of education.

"I didn't see him deep in conversation with anyone else all night," she added. "Odd for a politician."

"We had things to discuss."

"Such as?"

"The scholarship. He wanted my blessing."

"What's not to like about a scholarship in memory of your mother?"

"Nothing," I said.

I went straight to his photograph, as much to see what my mother had written as to inspect the young man he'd been. Like every male senior, he was wearing a tie and jacket. But his photo was different, showing a maturely handsome face and a smile suggesting a dignified future. "Ambition: the law," his entry read. My mother had written nothing, not one stroke of a blue, red, or green pen. My first reaction was surprise, but my second was *Of course; she was being careful.*

Earlier, between bathroom and function room, I'd asked him if paternity had been confirmed, or was it just a guess due to my being born nine months after they'd rendezvoused.

"Your mother knew. I believed her."

I didn't ask the how and what of that, didn't want to picture my mother colluding and swabbing my inner cheek or diaper. Somehow that tipped the scale toward the expanding belief that my mother wanted me to be the child of Peter Armstrong. Which one of them was asking for proof of paternity? Wouldn't most married women live the lie that their own husbands had impregnated them?

"What about Holly?" I'd asked him. "Any claims there?"

"No. Definitely not. Your mother wanted your father to have his own child."

His own child? Had that been what he actually said? I didn't like his mentioning my father at all, let alone as backup inseminator.

Why was I even harping on Holly? She was undeniably her father's daughter, bearing a keen resemblance to two of his sisters. I'd always enjoyed that — those two aunts being no beauties and eventually crotchety housemates we didn't like to visit.

Geneva had fished out reading glasses for a closer study of Armstrong's photo and didn't seem surprised by the lack of editorial comment. "Guess he didn't come to reunions," she said.

I leafed ahead for the sake of appearances to Ritchie Perry. I asked if she'd caught the last name of either Dave or Donna, and she said, "No. And I couldn't have been less interested."

With no more tablemates to research, I moved forward to the group pictures of teams and clubs. First came a full-page photo of the yearbook staff, and sure enough, there was Peter Armstrong in a plaid short-sleeved shirt, posing at a manual typewriter. Next page: the class officers. And there indeed was class president Duddy McKean surrounded by a female vice president, second vice president, secretary, and treasurer.

Geneva yawned and patted the page as if to say, *I've had enough; let's put it away now.* I said, "I'm not through."

I guessed that she let me continue unsupervised because I was respectfully studying rather than vandalizing the book. Another few pages forward, I came to a double spread labeled "We voted!" Here were the seniors deemed best looking, most athletic, best dressed, smartest, class clown, and most likely to succeed — Peter Armstrong, unsurprisingly, next to a tall, bespectacled girl named Martha-Ann Roberts, both grinning and holding briefcases aloft in posed triumph.

I went back to the *A*s and his formal head-and-shoulders shot. With my phone's flashlight illuminating it, I saw a penciled dot, very faint. Then another. Five in all. Dances? Cocktails? Hand jobs? How would I ever know? Did other people get dots? I didn't check every page but leafed ahead, about halfway through the alphabet, seeing none. I'd failed to ask Armstrong if their assignations had happened at a reunion, too stunned and offended earlier to discuss brass tacks. And even fainter: two letters and five digits. It looked like a phone number, old-school, which I had no appetite to memorize.

Geneva, whose head had been lolling against the back seat and whose breathing had gotten noisy, suddenly asked, "Think you'll see him again?"

"Why would I?"

"He gave you his card, didn't he?"

He had. "Maybe."

"At one point in my life, I would've said that he's too old for you, but I've mellowed on that."

I said, "Ugh," for reasons she couldn't know.

"I gave him *my* card, but he only had eyes for you. You wanna hear my theory?"

"No."

"He had a crush on your mother, and you look like the young version of her."

"That's no theory. He announced that as soon as he sat down — that everyone had had a crush on her. Now go back to sleep."

"When you're through poring over that, put it back in my briefcase."

I didn't answer. I found Gloria Hink, hair teased up to the frame of her photo, and — thanks to "Pep squad" under "Activities" — a Roseanne who surely had been our tablemate.

I closed the book. If Armstrong was right, life and paternity as I knew it was a lie. And my mother's fixation on the class of 1968 had gone from silliness to sin. I remembered my father's irritation over the subject of reunions and his unwillingness to attend. He couldn't have known, or irritation would have given way to fury or divorce. And if he *had* known all along that he wasn't my biological father, didn't that make him all the more noble and de-voted a dad?

I owed Peter Armstrong nothing. I was shaken and deeply sorry I'd heard this possible weighty truth. Why couldn't he have fathered an out-of-wedlock child who'd been put up for adoption and would now be thrilled to find a respectable, elegant, seem-ingly prosperous elected official as her birth father? At least, at *least*, this Armstrong hadn't told me of photos, report cards, and locks of hair slipped to him over the years.

Oh, wait. Locks of hair? When did DNA tests start confirming parenthood? I Googled "DNA testing began when?" and learned that it was possible, that tests were around to tell the tale by the time I was born.

Thanks a lot, Peter Armstrong, candidate for most likely to up-end someone's life in an instant.

Your alleged love child never wants to see you again.

11

......

Whatever Works

W AS IT RIGHT AND NATURAL or unfair to as-
sign blame for my agitated state to Geneva? She'd
dragged me to the reunion — more or less — result-
ing in my feeling sorry for myself and the man who would always
be my real dad, biologically or not. Dodging her, I checked the corridor like a sleuth or a cat burglar, nursing my grudge in private.

Well, maybe not strictly speaking in private, because I confided
in Jeremy. The ostensible reason for my ringing his doorbell was
homework in the form of a batch of truffles. It was the Monday
after both Thanksgiving and the reunion. He answered the bell
wearing jeans and a T-shirt that said HATERS GONNA HATE underneath the silhouettes of the elderly hecklers from *The Muppet
Show*. Tray in hand, I told him, "I need a taster with a clean palate."

"My pleasure. Come in." I did, trying not to be too obviously
taking in the surroundings, the handsome deep taupe of his foyer
walls, the watercolors and woodcuts. He selected a truffle, wig-
gling his fingers first, pretending there was a variety to choose
from, chewed it appraisingly, swallowed, coughed. After slap-
ping his chest, he said, "I'm a lucky guy, living across the hall from
someone who bakes. Is this baking?"

"No, they're truffles, which aren't baked. They're just . . . made.
I'm still learning."

"Interesting, though," he managed.

"You can be honest; it won't hurt my feelings. Maybe if a person liked wasabi and raspberry together, they'd be okay?"

He put a hand on my shoulder. "Daphne . . . I love wasabi. I'm kinda famous for my wasabi tolerance . . ."

"But no?"

"Let me put it this way: *Your* garbage pail or mine?"

Then, without segue or preamble, I announced, "I went to the Pickering High reunion. Geneva made me."

"And?"

"Traumatic! I'm trying to put it behind me!"

"I can see that. How about a drink and you tell me what happened?"

I said, "One sec," because the living room was beckoning, revealing a startlingly gorgeous view of the Hudson River. The room was large, book-shelved, grown-up. I asked if he'd done it himself.

"Done what?"

"Picked things out." I pointed upward to a red, black, and yellow mobile, a Calder clone, then downward to the wall behind the couch where three drawings of women's fancy pumps were hung side by side. "Shoes," I said.

"Warhol. From his days as an illustrator for I. Miller."

Warhol. I sighed. I wanted artwork. I wanted walls to hang it on and a view. My ex–marital apartment had some favorite paintings I considered walking off with, maybe just one or two for all my troubles, but my ex-mother-in-law had my departure supervised by a man with a walkie-talkie.

"Martini?" Jeremy asked.

"Gin," I said. "With extra olives. A little dirty."

"You can sit and wait, or you can come and watch."

"Wait? Are you kidding? When I haven't seen your kitchen yet?"

He took the plate of truffles from my hand. "My trash compactor is begging for these," he said.

Why should I have been surprised by an *Architectural Digest*– worthy kitchen? State-of-the-art appliances! A dishwasher and — what was that? — a coffeemaker built into a wall! Not just the counters but the floor tiles were marble, or was it something else black and polished? Before I'd said more than *wow* a few times, Jeremy volunteered, "Thank the previous owner. I got this far on the tour, and I said, 'I'll take it.'"

No counteroffer? No mortgage calculation? Who walks into an apartment like this, and says, "I'll take it"?

"I know what you're thinking," Jeremy said, bringing forth bottles and ice from the freezer, a jar of olives from the refrigerator, then tools from a narrow drawer that appeared to house only martiniware.

"*What* was I thinking?"

"That I'm too young to have a place like this."

"More like you must make a nice living playing Timmy on TV."

"My parents helped. A *lot*. Like they own it. They'll sell it when I move to California to become a movie star."

"Is that your plan — California?"

"I was joking. Now watch. I'll show you how to make a dry martini."

"I've made plenty of martinis in my day. Even chocolate ones."

Faking a truffle-induced cough, he murmured, "Delicious, I'm sure."

Next came the mixing, the icing, the agitating, the garnishing, the presentation in beautiful glasses. I followed him back to the living room to the tufted gray flannel couch where I asked again, "So California's *not* in the ten-year plan?"

Frowning, Jeremy pointed. "Is this the face of a movie star?"

"Could be. You won't always have braces. Do they hurt? Mine did."

"They're fake. I was wired up just for the show. The metal doesn't do anything."

I asked — innocently, not flirtatiously, but in friendly, big-sister fashion, exhibiting interest in a possibly inexperienced young man's social life — "Do they get in the way when you kiss?"

I expected a wry answer. Or, perhaps, for the first time since we'd met, an uncharming, self-conscious one. Or maybe I'd get a casual confirmation of what his Warhol shoe art suggested, that he was gay. I certainly didn't expect nor was I inviting that which followed: He put his martini glass down on the coffee table, relieved me of mine, and kissed me on the lips.

In the past, in this same situation, I'd said things like "I think we got our signals crossed." Or "I'm flattered, but ..."

I said none of those things. It wasn't complicated. He'd kissed me and I liked it.

He served cheese and crackers when we resumed drinking. "You're fine with this?" I asked.

"With what?"

"Kissing your across-the-hall neighbor. It won't get messy?"

"Not with me it won't."

"How old are you again?"

"Almost twenty-six."

"A baby."

Of course, that made him kiss me again to show exactly what kind of baby I was dealing with. Shouldn't I be saying something mature like "We shouldn't. Bad idea." I didn't.

After a few more minutes — it could've been longer — I stood up, and I said I'd get the plate I brought the truffles on. Then, really ... I should go.

"Why?"

Trying not to sound like a bumpkin who thought kissing meant anything more than a pleasant way to pass the time, I said, "More homework."

"More truffles?"

"Bark. Or turtles. I forget."

"You're a terrible liar," he said.

"Okay, here's what I'm thinking: Did you ever make out with someone who lived on your floor in college or was in your eight o'clock class, and you had to avoid each other afterward because, by the light of day, you realized it was a mistake?"

"A. I never took an eight o'clock class. And B. I'm not expecting regrets."

He'd taken my hand by now. "I didn't get the impression that you'd be sorry in the morning, either," he said.

That was true. If any signal was conveyed by me, it was *Yes means yes.*

"How about this as a guideline?" Jeremy continued. "Whatever works. No drama. No avoiding each other in the hall. No buyer's regret. Just enjoying the moment. And the next one."

"Friends with benefits," I said.

Since my unfortunate whirlwind marriage and divorce, I'd considered finding that kind of friend but hadn't acted on it — had not even come close to broaching the subject, let alone kissing anyone. As I was thinking all of this over and considering how Jeremy might fit the bill, he asked, "Weren't you going to tell me what big thing happened at the reunion?"

He patted the couch cushion next to him. I sat down again, closer than the space I'd previously occupied. "I wasn't exaggerating when I said it was life changing."

"Not in a good way, I take it."

"Would you believe that a man asked me to dance, then took me into the bathroom and claimed to be my real father?"

"Wait. You went into the bathroom with a man? Did you know him?"

"No! A total stranger. He'd asked to sit at my table where the ladies were all aquiver because he'd been voted most likely to succeed."

Was that funny? Apparently so, because Jeremy was smiling.

"I'm dead serious. This is horrible! I *have* a father, and I didn't want some random biological one showing up."

"What proof did he have?"

"A long fling with my mother, which makes sense when I look back —"

"I didn't mean that. I meant scientific proof."

"I didn't stick around to ask for proof. Besides, anybody can say, 'I'm your real father and there's a DNA test to prove it.'"

"And who's this guy again?"

"A New Hampshire state senator."

That rendered Jeremy silent. When I asked, "What?" he said, "A politician wouldn't go out of his way to expose himself as a guy who fooled around with a married colleague and had an out-of-wedlock child."

"Colleague? He was one of her students!"

"In high school? Your mother was having sex with a *student?*"

"It started after he graduated, or at least that's the story."

"Still . . . gross. His *teacher?*"

"She was the youngest teacher in the school. And very pretty. There was only five years' difference in their ages."

"*Phhhf.* Five years? Nothing!" He lifted his glass, but I didn't meet the toast.

He asked, "You know what I'd do?"

"Get my own DNA test?"

"No. I'd blow it off, pretend it never happened. Didn't meet him, nothing registered. Sayonara."

"That would be a guy thing — walk away. Ghost him."

"What's the girl thing then?"

"This girl? Obsess."

"I don't mind," he said. "Can we obsess some more?"

I didn't leave because we were back to kissing. I said, "I don't really feel the braces. But what's happening down there?"

"Sorry . . ."

"Now what?" I asked.

"Your choice."

"Did you plan this?"

"Like I knew you were going to ring my doorbell?"

"I mean, had you thought about me in this way before tonight?"

"Of course. I'm a guy."

He asked if I could put off the homework for another half hour or so.

"Maybe a refill? That way I can blame it on being drunk."

"I'm in no condition to make you another martini," he said.

The bold new me asked if he had condoms or should I get my own.

"I believe I do. Want to . . ."

"See your bedroom? Sure."

That was that. Easier than I expected. This was the big city. As a single woman suffering a dry spell, I seem to have decided in the course of one hour that an across-the-hall lover, with no strings, no rules, and an east-facing bedroom that caught the lights of the Freedom Tower, might be just the ticket.

12

Correct Me If I'm Wrong

D ID HE HAVE TO SEND me flowers? No, not Jeremy, but my putative biological father, Peter Armstrong. The kind gesture of sending beautiful, fragrant pink and white lilies might have been more discomforting if his note had been needy and annoying. Instead: "Daphne, please know that I would never intrude. I cannot say how important it was for me to meet you, but what happens now is up to you." With unfortunate timing, my father was visiting when the doorman called upstairs to say, "Flowers for you."

I lied to my dad. I said that the bouquet was from someone I'd met on a blind date.

"He must've had a really nice time. I'd say he's smitten."

I offered some modest, ambivalent syllables, which made him ask if I'd accept a second date.

"Doubtful."

"You should thank him for the flowers. That's only polite."

I said I would. Then, because the very reason I'd invited him over for takeout was conjugal detective work, I began, as planned, with "The reunion was Saturday. Pickering High's."

"You actually went?"

"With Geneva, up and back, a car service."

He said nothing, asked nothing. I volunteered that the theme drink was a Tickled Pink and that the undertakers who did Mom's funeral were at my table.

"The Perrys."

"Right. And there was a Donna, a Barbara, a Roseanne or Rosemary, who didn't make cheerleader."

"All women?"

"No, a couple of husbands." I searched for a vase and settled on a pitcher before adding, "And a man named Peter Armstrong, who announced that he's establishing a June Maritch memorial scholarship."

The dad I'd always known—high school principal, gentleman, and diplomat—would've said, "Isn't that the most decent thing!" But today all my announcement evoked was a grunt.

"I mean, why didn't *we* think of honoring her for all those years of devotion?"

"Is this already in the works?"

"I think he said he'd be putting his contact information on the class's website."

Had Armstrong mentioned the class website? Was there one? I forgot. "Do you know he's a state senator now? Lots of handshaking and congratulations from the time he arrived."

"Scholarship or no scholarship, I don't want to talk about Peter Armstrong."

This was highly uncharacteristic of Tom Maritch and not a promising lead-up to paternal fact-finding. Searching for a question in a range between neutral and pleasant, I tried, "Have you had your museum date with Paula yet?"

"You overheard that?"

I reminded him that it had been a marathon Thanksgiving dinner and she'd been seated on my left.

"As a matter of fact, we went to the Met on Saturday."

"*And . . . ?*"

"And what?"

"Did you have a good time? Was it mobbed?"

"A line out the door! But she was determined to see some costume exhibit that was ending. Very interesting, not something I'd have gravitated to on my own. And then it was my turn to pick, so we went to the Cubism exhibit."

"Did you have lunch or drinks?"

"We had coffee."

"Do you like her?"

"Sure."

"You don't sound gung ho."

"I enjoyed her company. Did I feel a spark? I'd have to say no."

I hadn't meant to delve into his newborn love life, but might that vein get us back on track? I said, "This is nice — that you and I can talk about personal things. And it goes without saying that you have my blessing in terms of dating."

"I haven't heard about any of *your* dates." He pointed to the flowers. "Care to elaborate?"

I said, "Dad. Stop me if this is none of my business. But were you and Mom happy?"

"Why that question all of a sudden?"

We were still standing in my kitchen, leafing through my take-out menus. "Okay. Remember when we were painting your bathroom and I mentioned throwing away her *Monadnockian*? It seemed to touch a nerve — that and when I asked you about the reunions she never missed."

"And that made you jump to the conclusion that we weren't happy?"

"I'm asking for a reason."

"I know what that reason is."

I waited.

"Peter Armstrong," he said. "Peter goddamn Armstrong, golden boy!"

"Wow. Let me go first, then." I fished the accompanying card from the trash. "Here. I lied to you. The flowers weren't from a blind date. They're from him."

After reading its two sentences aloud, he asked, "So? You're your mother's daughter. He met you and he's thanking you for coming to the reunion."

"How about if you sit down in the living room? I'll bring you a Scotch."

He nodded. I told him I'd join him in a sec—just had to excavate some ice.

Alone in the kitchen, or so I thought, I practiced, barely aloud, what should follow the Peter Armstrong paternity confession I had to address. "We're not only father and daughter, but . . . partners. Singles in the city. Luckily, neighbors. Buddies."

Had I not realized he'd never left?

"Totally agree," I heard. "And this new life and new city has been the silver lining to losing your mother."

Losing my mother, that woman of easy virtue? How did *that* square with what I'd learned in Pickering?

I poured his drink and led him back to the living room. "Can you expand on why you inserted the 'goddamn' between Peter and Armstrong?"

He asked what I knew, what Armstrong had told me.

I said, "If I'm being completely honest, my takeaway was that Mom was not entirely faithful."

"He told you that?"

How to elaborate when nothing in life until the past weekend had suggested anything but a happy, faithful marriage between pillars of the education community? I tried a very watered-down version of my mother's betrayal: "Maybe he had . . . a thing for her?"

He shot me a most uncharacteristic look that said, *We're both adults. I'm widowed, you're divorced, must I manufacture retroactive fidelity?* So he said, "At one point, early in our marriage, she confessed to having a crush on him."

Was it up to me to fill him in? "Just a crush?"

"As you must know with two parents in the field, crushes are an occupational hazard."

"Dad! This was a two-way street. This wasn't a student having a crush on a teacher. You just said she had a crush on *him*."

From the handbook of wishful thinking, he quoted, "Your mother maintained that she never violated her professional ethics."

Now what? Stop there? Scrub the truth? I said, "I don't need my parents' marriage sugarcoated. I've become a realist. Do you think I'll fall apart if you told me that all wasn't rosy between you and Mom?"

Eyes closed, he shook his head. "This is not what I want to talk about. I don't want the third degree. I'm sorry, but I'm going home. I'm not mad, but I'm not enjoying this conversation."

I told him I'd change the subject. "We'll talk about . . . me! About movies and politics —"

"Not tonight. I'm beat."

"Okay. I'm sorry I chased you away." I managed to plant a kiss on a fast-moving cheek as he left.

Now what? There went my evening. I picked up his glass, flopped onto the sofa, took a sip.

Without a knock, the door reopened in less time than it would have taken him to reach the elevator. "What did that sonovabitch tell you?" he demanded.

Well, there it was: full vilification. But before I had to confess the gigantic life-changing thing that Peter Armstrong couldn't withhold, my father had taken back his Scotch and was pacing. "You won't believe it — it's such a cliché. It's Peyton Place — you know that novel was based on a real town in New Hampshire?"

"Dad —"

"You want to know how I found out about your mother and that man, the moment I knew for sure that my wife had cheated on me?"

I very much *did* want to know but arranged my face into a look meant to convey *If you must.*

"They rendezvoused at a motel!"

"No!"

"And she paid by credit card! Why? Did she want me to find out? Or because he didn't want a record of it due to his exalted position as an associate in a Nashua law firm? It didn't take a detective to figure out what the charge on our Mastercard bill meant."

What to say in the face of a tirade so uncharacteristic that it rendered me mute? I finally came up with a weak "Are you sure?"

"Of course! And the next time she was out late, 'out with the girls' — how stupid did she think I was? — I was waiting up, Mastercard bill in hand."

"Because it showed —"

"A room charge!"

"And?"

"She told me it was a hen party for somebody's thirtieth or fortieth — who the hell knows? — birthday, anniversary, whatever."

"Are you sure that wasn't true —"

"Who throws a birthday party at a motel?"

I asked when this was — which month and year.

"I don't remember! It's not the kind of thing a husband commits to memory."

"But at some point she admitted everything?"

"And promised it would never happen again, that it was over. That he had a serious girlfriend. That they'd met only to talk, to break up. All lies."

"But you and Mom obviously worked through it. You must've." He shook his head.

"No? You were together for the rest of her life."

"Eventually. But"—and here his voice sounded as bitter as I'd ever heard it—"how humiliating do you think it was? One of my graduates, the most likely to succeed, was bedding the principal's wife! I knew damn well it wasn't a one-time rendezvous. Essentially, I threw her out." He paused, then added softly, "Like a trailer-trash husband except I stopped short of throwing her clothes out the window."

Now I began rewriting my family history for the second time in one week. "You asked her to leave, but she didn't, obviously."

"Yes, she did, that same day, and moved in with her parents."

"For how long?"

"Until she begged to come back. She rang the doorbell one night. It was late. I was weak—"

"You loved her."

"I let her in. She cried. She apologized. Profusely."

"So she stayed."

"She had to. In those days she'd have lost her job."

"Wait. Because she was having an affair? Had it gone public?"

"No. Not that. But if she'd been a woman, separated . . ."

It took a few seconds. I said, "She was pregnant."

"She was pregnant," my father said, and reached for me.

13

......

There's Proof and There's Proof

ONE MIGHT EXPECT that my father and I would spend a few more hours — or at least minutes — discussing reopened wounds and mortal sins. We didn't.

"I'm talked out," he told me, hand back on the doorknob. "I never thought..."

"Never thought what?"

"That all of this would see the light of day."

I had my hand flat against the door, blocking his departure. "One more question, and I'll never ask again: Isn't it possible that you and Mom together —"

"Conceived you? No."

"You know for a fact because you had some scientific proof?"

"I did some wishful thinking that by some trick of the calendar you were mine. But I knew as soon as you were born."

I waited, asked him to sit, to stay, to tell me how he knew from the get-go that I couldn't be his.

The next two words were pronounced so softly I had to ask him to repeat them.

"Blood type."

"Mine?"

"Yours. Your mother and I were both type O."

"So? Doesn't that make you the universal donor?"

"But not the universal parent. We two couldn't produce a child with A blood."

And that was me: type A.

"That was proof for you, but not for"—I now had a title for him—"the donor?"

Another barely audible answer: "There's proof and there's proof."

I asked what that meant.

"Just because you weren't *my* child didn't mean you were his. He's a lawyer. That's how lawyers think. He wanted a DNA test. I said no, but all your mother had to do was swab the inside of your cheek. When I wasn't home. Apparently, she had to prove to him that she was merely an unfaithful wife, not a slut."

The shock of "slut" pronounced by Thomas Maritch testified that this had been festering for possibly my entire life. "Did you think there were others, because that would be too crazy and too"—did "out of character" fit now that June Winter Maritch was a woman I knew not at all?— "unlikely?"

My father said, "I've gone too far," and after an exhausted sigh, "What's the point of this, Daff? I wish you'd never gone to that damn reunion and I'd never opened my big mouth."

Me, too. Could we ever walk this back to the twosome we'd become, the Dad and Daughter Club of New York City? I said, "Stay! How about souvlaki from that place you liked on West Fifty-sixth? I have a five-dollar-off coupon."

"Not up to it. If I'm hungry later, I'll scramble some eggs."

I caught him by the jacket sleeve as he opened the door. "If you're worried that I'm going to make friends with P. A. just because he sent me flowers, you don't have to worry"—realizing and regretting as soon as I'd pronounced the letters that P. A. spelled "Pa."

"He did more in this life than send you flowers."

"You're my father in every conceivable way!"

"You might want to rephrase that," he said.

Was the whistling across the hall meant to broadcast Jeremy's arrival home? Guessing yes, I used the opportunity to dump some trash.

"Long day?" I asked, wastebasket prop in hand.

"Miss Daphne. Fancy meeting you here. Nope, this is standard."

I didn't have anything to contribute with regard to a standard work schedule, so I said, "Maybe we could have another drink some time."

"Sure."

In my new role as a loose woman, I asked, "Such as now?"

"Give me a half hour."

"Not too soon?"

"No. Just a quick shower."

"I didn't mean too soon to come over. I mean too soon since . . ." I completed the thought with a lowered gaze meant to imply *our last intercourse.*

"Your call."

I told him I'd be over after I jumped in the tub and changed from the clothes I was wearing earlier this evening when I told my dad what I'd found out at the reunion.

He had his bike resting on his shoulder and a backpack strap in one hand. "Do you want to discuss this?"

I said no. It was still so raw.

"Clearly."

"He's upset, possibly even mad at me. He's *never* mad at me."

Jeremy had unlocked his door and was waving good-bye, the good-humored kind that translates to *Enough/Shhh/Save it.*

14

Gold-Dome Dirt

I WOKE UP IN JEREMY'S big bed, my clothes a room away, the sun shining from an exposure not available next door. I thanked him for his hospitality and his other talents, said yes to coffee but no to an oversize bagel, and was back in my apartment by 7:30 a.m. I waited an hour before calling my dad, who'd sent a rather stingy good-night text in reply to mine.

"Are we okay?" I asked him.

"I didn't sleep great, but that's not your fault."

I said I think it was.

"Let's not go round and round on this. What's done is done."

But it wasn't. *My* not sleeping great had to do with the ugly breaking news that my entire existence was based on a lie. Shouldn't I have been warned of inheritable diseases that might be down the road? Or told to work harder in high school because I could apply as a legacy to Dartmouth? Such were the 2 a.m. agitations of a dispossessed daughter.

But by the light of day, I was asking, "Can we have lunch? Or take a walk? Or anything?"

"Not today. I've made some plans."

"A date?"

"I have to go," he said.

I was hearing announcements now, a list of towns and cities that sounded loudspeakerish. "Are you at Port Authority?"

"Just cutting through."

"Let me know when you want to get together."

"I will. Gotta run."

I asked, "To where?" but he'd already hung up.

I got my answer by late afternoon that day. After taking a bus north to New Hampshire's capital, he'd walked to the State House and straight to the office of Senator Peter Armstrong.

No, he told the receptionist, he didn't have an appointment. No, he didn't want to take a seat. Was the senator in? Was the senator through that door? Without permission, he rushed past her into Armstrong's office, where he found the senator on the phone, a sandwich unwrapped and sitting prissily on the open square of a cloth napkin.

Senator Armstrong had no reason to recognize this intruder as the cuckolded husband of his old flame. He said into the phone, "I'm putting the receiver down, but stay on the line. I might have trouble here."

He addressed the gray-haired receptionist swatting at the intruder and hyperventilating. "Marie? What's this about? No, stay back."

"I couldn't stop him!" she cried.

"You called security?"

"Of course!"

He asked my father, who hadn't done anything but plant himself in front of the massive wooden desk, if he'd passed through the metal detector at the public entrance.

"Of course I did! Everyone has to."

Backup arrived — one armed security guard and a New Hampshire state trooper whose dull beat was the State House, both wielding metal batons.

"Sir," everyone seemed to be saying at once. "Sir. Please back away from the senator's desk."

My father told them he'd come only to have words with the senator on a personal matter. Still, they asked him to back away.

How did I get every word and detail? From a 603 number not his own. "I can't talk long. I was allowed one phone call."

"You're in jail?" I yelled. "Dad? Where?"

"Concord. Not strictly speaking jail. It's the booking room."

"They arrested you?"

"For criminal trespassing. They took my phone, so if you tried to—"

"Criminal trespassing? Did you say *criminal?*"

"That's the formal charge."

"I'm coming right up!"

"No, you are *not.*"

"Don't be ridiculous! I'll take a bus and be there by..." When? How many fucking stops does a bus between New York City and Concord, New Hampshire, make?

"They need the phone—"

"Do you have a lawyer?"

"Could you call Julian? I don't have his number."

"Are you actually being locked up?"

"I don't know. I think there's talk of a bail bondsman."

A male voice was grousing, "Wrap it up, buddy. I gotta get back on the road."

Now in tears, I demanded, "Wait! Are they putting you in jail?"

No answer because the line had gone dead. How rude! The cop or sheriff or trooper or warden or next criminal in line to use the phone must've lost patience and hung it up.

It didn't take long, only one minute of mental paralysis, to realize there was another avenue to pursue besides catching a plane or renting a car. I dug out Armstrong's business card and called what I hoped was a direct line. When a woman answered, I said, none too calmly, "This is the daughter of the man you sent to jail today. I need to speak to Senator Armstrong immediately."

She didn't answer. Had that snitch hung up on me? I waited until a male voice intoned, "Peter Armstrong."

"You arrested my dad!"

"Who is this?" he had the nerve to ask.

"Daphne! My father called me from jail!"

"I assure you, it wasn't my decision."

"Aren't you the one who pressed charges?"

"He trespassed. And threatened me."

"What threat? What did he say that scared you so much?"

"You don't barge into a government office without permission. He was loud enough to be heard in my waiting area—"

"Oh, boo-hoo. Did you not know he was my father?"

"He made that quite clear. And you'll have to prepare yourself for what this might bring."

"Prison?" I yelped.

"I meant for you. There were visitors out in my waiting area— one was a reporter waiting to interview me about a bill . . ."

I was already appalled that a law-abiding man of impeccable everything would be arrested in his own state capitol. But there was more. What my father had yelled at Peter Armstrong, loud enough to be heard beyond the inner sanctum, was a warning to keep the hell away from me. From Daphne. His daughter. *His!* Do not call, do not write, do not email or send flowers!

The *Concord Monitor* didn't have a gossip column, but the reporter on hand had a blog titled *Gold-Dome Dirt*, which usually carried no juicier scoops than hirings, firings, and snow closings.

But finally, blessedly, this: The state senate's most eligible bachelor had been warned by a furious father, a disturber of the peace, to keep the hell away from his daughter.

15
......

It Still Sounds Fishy to Me

M Y FATHER CALLED from the bus on his way back to Manhattan. After my first gush of relief over his not being incarcerated, I yelled, "What's wrong with you? Since when did you become a guy who breaks into people's offices?"

"Calm down," he said. "This is why I didn't let you in on my plan."

"Plan! So this wasn't just a visit that got out of hand? You intended all along to break down his door and threaten him?"

"You're hysterical, Daff. I did not break down any door. I was released on personal recognizance. Bail was set at $250, so I had to put down $25 to get out of there. Look, I'm getting a low-battery warning. I'll call you when I'm fully charged."

Fully charged in what sense? When he didn't call, I worried on and off for three days, interspersed with nursing grievances over what no one had ever bothered to tell me. Had I missed some subtle hints in the past ten or twenty years? Had I never wondered why I was the hazel-eyed daughter in an otherwise blue-eyed family?

And what was my dad dwelling on now that the truth was finally out? *Legally, she's mine, but there is the shiny object of Armstrong, who'd never grounded her or given her an 11:30 curfew or made her take AP calculus.*

Enough wondering where we stood! I called him. He answered, sounding out of breath. "I'm on a brisk walk!" he announced.

"Tell me where. I'll catch up with you."

"You can't. I'm on the job."

"Did you say *job?*"

"The best one I ever had!" And then, "No, Punkin. Wait. Stay. I have to pick it up."

"Pick what up?"

"Not you — Punkin. A pitbull-Lab mix. She just pooped."

"Did you get a *dog?*"

"No, it's a client's."

I heard more baby talk, presumably aimed at Punkin, and then a monologue with someone named Gizmo. "How many dogs are you walking?" I asked.

"Three. You start with one and work your way up."

"When did this happen?"

"Two days ago. I answered an ad on Craigslist. They liked that I was from New Hampshire, which sounded — who knows what they were thinking? — rural, good with animals. I didn't disabuse them of that."

"Did I know you loved dogs enough to be a dog walker?"

And with that, I got the first near-ironic answer of our unfortunate past few days. "I guess you've figured out by now that you don't know everything about me."

"Everything? How about next to nothing? What do you call running off to Concord like a lunatic?"

"Calm down. I'm having the time of my life. And I've been told by Manuel that dogs can be a magnet for the ladies."

"Who's Manuel?"

"My super's kid. He's in his last year at Bronx High School of Science, which I understand is for only the smartest kids."

What Manhattan lifestyle expertise would be next? I said, "Call me when your shift is over."

"I'll probably take another crew out. You wouldn't believe how well they all get along."

"Come for dinner soon. My freezer can't fit a fraction of my chocolate homework."

After a "Gizmo, no!" and a "Good boy!" my father said okay, soon, but he had to get off—he couldn't handle the phone and the leashes.

"Quick, though: This is a reputable company? They're not taking advantage of you?"

"Very reputable. Look them up: New Leash on Life. Gotta go."

I went straight to my laptop. Sure enough, www.newleashon-life.com featured smiling humans with adoring dogs. I clicked on the tab that said, "We're hiring!" and read their screening questions. "Love furbabies? Like the outdoors and making your own hours? LOVE being greeted with excitement every day? And how do you feel about unconditional love?"

Had an absence of unconditional love and an empty apartment turned Tom Maritch into a professional dog walker? Now I had something new to be answerable for.

A Google alert under "Pickering, New Hampshire" brought the State House noise to Geneva's attention and the person herself to my door. I'd ignored an earlier email marked with high-priority exclamation points and "Whaaaat the hellllll?" in the subject line. Below that, a link to a *Concord Monitor* story, dry and dignified, which had expanded on the reporter's blog.

I answered Geneva's knock. There she was in traffic-cone-orange overalls and a houndstooth sports bra. "Did you read what I sent you? It's about the guy who was at our table at the reunion—

Armstrong? The good-looker. And the man who got arrested for trespassing — his name is Maritch."

Was she so self-involved that she'd forgotten our Thanksgiving dinner, where the Thomas Albert Maritch of the police log had been found charming and adorable by the entire table of ladies?

I could've said, *No, that's a relative.* But I said, "Yes, unfortunately, that was my father, your recent dinner guest."

"They arrested him, you know. Is he in jail?"

I told her that he was released on his own recognizance due to his being a sterling citizen his entire life.

"I want to talk with him. This could be my break."

Her break. How could I stand her? Would I have to move to another building? I told her, as I'd told everyone who'd called or written, that it was all a misunderstanding. Had she noticed how half-hearted, even embarrassed, the newspaper account had sounded, as if reluctantly reporting on a heterosexual bachelor senator's love life? I could imagine the editorial ethics that the *Concord Monitor* had to debate — *we're not the* National Enquirer *so let's keep it as dignified as possible.*

She reached into her bib pocket, removed her phone, and read, "Quote: 'I was not involved with Mr. Maritch's daughter. In fact, we'd met only once, at the most recent Pickering High reunion, where our conversation, if you could even call it that, was limited to establishing a memorial scholarship in honor of her mother, who'd been my yearbook advisor and mentor' unquote."

She touched the screen with a decisive thumb, then returned the phone to her front pocket.

I told her the whole thing was a misunderstanding, that the senator's receptionist had overreacted — you know how touchy terrorism has made all of us — by summoning security. Yes, my father had been agitated, but it was politics. He was lobbying on behalf of the teachers' union — some bill he didn't like. Whatever arguments he was having with the senator were political.

"Bull*shit.*"

Quite rude but hard to refute, since every other word I'd uttered was fiction. She continued in a new, chummy tone. "I came away with a very strong sense that your senator was a lady-killer. And I think you did, too."

"Which applies exactly *how* to my dad?"

"Your father was yelling at him for taking up with his daughter. I'm not so naïve that I don't recognize a cover-up."

"By me?"

"What you just told me — that he was yelling about union stuff."

I wasn't the polished liar I hoped I was. Instead of apologizing for embroidering, I compounded it. We were still in my doorway. I told her I couldn't talk for long, that I had a project in a double boiler, but, okay, if she insisted.

Because I was spinning another lie, an even bigger one, I started with "This is totally off-the-record. Do you understand what that means? You cannot, under the sacred rules of the press, repeat this to anyone. Or put it into a documentary."

I could tell by the intensity of her squint and her moving a step closer that she was all ears. I said, "Okay. My dad was, in fact, warning Armstrong to stay away from his daughter, but it wasn't me. It was a sister I never told you about." And from nowhere, without any premeditated baby-naming effort whatsoever, I came up with "Samantha." Yes, a Samantha who still lives in New Hampshire.

"So he *was* warning him away from a daughter, just not you?"

I told her I couldn't talk. I had chocolate tempering, which was a delicate stage, even a critical one.

"Is this sister married?"

I hadn't thought that far ahead. I combined a look with a half nod and half shrug that might have conveyed *Sort of.*

"If that's a no, what's the big deal if two single people are hooking up?"

"Age difference. Plus, he's a lifelong bachelor. As you and I both know — always a red flag." I repeated, "I have to go. I've probably already ruined the chocolate I was melting," adding for good measure, "You're never to mention this to my dad," at the same time I was thinking, *I'd better clue him in about made-up Samantha.*

"It still sounds fishy to me."

"What part?"

"This is the father you brought to Thanksgiving, right? He struck me as a really sweet guy, not someone who'd get arrested over his daughter's love life."

Her peculiar phrasing, "This is the father . . ." stopped me. Had I, in my state of shock on the ride back from the reunion, revealed something about my newly dual paternity?

"Of course that's the father I brought to Thanksgiving. What an odd question. I can't help it if the truth sounds fishy. Isn't that the way life works? I mean, who'd ever believe that someone would want to make a documentary out of a smelly high school year-book?"

I'd meant that as an insult, but she smiled as if I'd recognized her particular scouting genius. "Do you have Armstrong's email address?" she asked.

"I certainly do not."

"Didn't he give you his card?"

"Thrown out. I'm surprised you didn't find it while foraging in the trash."

"Sarcasm will get you nowhere," she said. She reached into her pocket, withdrew her phone, and tapped the bottom of the screen. "Got it," she said.

"Were you *recording* me? Isn't that illegal? Isn't that like wire-tapping?"

"Your chocolate," she said, with a skeptical sniff of the air. "Better get back to your project."

I wasn't actually tempering chocolate at that particular moment. Face-to-face with Geneva, all I did was fib.

16

Was This My Life Now?

GENEVA WASN'T THE ONLY PERSON with a Pickering, New Hampshire, Google alert. My sister, as ever unapologetic about the time difference between West and East coasts, called just before midnight to ask in condescending fashion, "Did you know Dad was arrested?"

Even half-asleep, my sibling rivalry kicked in. "Of course I did. He called me from the police station. You know how prisoners get one phone call, just like on TV? Well, I was his."

"Good for you. But mainly it's this: Is he losing it?"

"You mean is he getting senile? No! He was wrongly arrested."

"It sounds as if he charged into the New Hampshire State House!"

What to say and how much? I began with "Did I tell you I went to a Pickering High reunion?"

"Don't change the subject! Is he in jail? The article didn't say —"

"No, he's not in jail. And I'm not changing the subject. I went to the reunion because —"

"And Dad went with you? I thought he hated those reunions."

"No, he did *not* go. Please shut up. I'm getting to the senator he trespassed against, Peter Armstrong."

"*And?*"

"So, upon my arrival, I was handed a note from Armstrong saying we'd be at the same table. I'm, like, *Who's he and why does he want—*"

"I don't need the internal monologue."

"Okay. After the first course, he asked me to dance, and next thing I knew, we were out in the corridor—did I say it was the Knights of Columbus Hall?—where he told me he'd been in love with Mom since his senior year in high school. Then on Monday he sent me flowers, and Dad happened to be there when they arrived. Not good."

"And that's why he burst into the guy's office, because he sent you flowers? Unh-unh. Something's missing."

It certainly was, such as my damn DNA. I'd never give up my spot as number one daughter, undoubtedly with Holly's gleeful demotion of me to stepchild. I took a sip of two-day-old water from the glass on my night table before admitting, "I may have left out a critical part—that Dad knew about this crush on Mom, which caused some marital troubles."

"When? And what kind of trouble?"

I needed an answer that wouldn't comport with my exact age plus nine months. "When Mom was young. Before she was married, I think."

"That doesn't sound like Dad—being jealous of a boyfriend Mom had before they were married."

"I think Dad suspected the crush wasn't one-sided."

"And the flowers meant what?"

"A romantic gesture, therefore creepy."

"A romantic gesture toward *you?*"

I didn't acknowledge the incredulity in her voice. "As you well know, I look a lot like Mom. So you can connect the dots—he'd been in love with Mom since he was seventeen, and then I show up like he was in some kind of time warp."

How was that going over? Not well. Holly said, "Dad would've laughed about a student having a crush on Mom. I don't get the anger part."

"Well . . . she went to every reunion that class ever had. And there was that stupid yearbook she had under lock and key."

Did I have to bring that up? Because Holly's next request was for me to overnight it.

"No can do."

"Use our FedEx account. I'll give you the number."

"It's not the postage. I don't have it anymore."

Holly waited. Surely I'd be explaining where it was and how soon I could retrieve it. I said, "I threw it away during a decluttering phase . . . What did you want it for?"

First, a lecture: How could I? Was I *that* unfeeling, knowing Mom wanted me to have it even if we didn't understand why? Finally: "I want to see what Armstrong wrote to Mom."

"He didn't write anything." *Except dots that probably meant something and an ancient phone number.*

"And his picture? Was he good-looking?"

I possessed no compassion for—or loyalty to—the man, but she was talking about half my DNA. "Exceptionally good-looking," I said.

I confess that I'd been picturing myself in a potential documentary, musing about my life, going deeper, interpreting my mother's actions and motives. I wasn't proud of myself for having these filmic daydreams, projecting like a high school glee club soloist crooning into a hairbrush. Even as I resisted Geneva and her cockamamie plan, I'd fallen asleep conducting thoughtful, nuanced analyses of my mother's moral fiber. One thorny contradiction: As I was growing up, she was never anything but devoted and normal, always interested in me, my friends, my homework; willing to stay up late to proofread my book reports, sew my Halloween costumes, bake for the bake sale. Might the documentary include the home movie of her running alongside me, as best she could, straight from school, in a pencil skirt and heels, laughing and cheering the first time I rode my bike without training wheels?

I did have this to contribute under the heading "Negatives": If your mother is a teacher and your father is a principal in a town with one high school, you're going to be crouching in the back seat of the car, begging to be dropped off a block or two early. And it didn't take a psychic to guess that my friends' clamming up when I approached their table at lunch was because they'd been discussing Principal Maritch or second-period American Lit with Mrs. Maritch.

Might this be of interest to an audience—that my mother had grown up in Derry, New Hampshire, where her physician father served two terms as mayor? And would this induce a much-needed moment of levity: that the surname Winter inspired the doctor and his wife to name their three daughters for the months in which they were born? May, called Masie, came first, then June two years later, and finally my Aunt Augusta.

These model daughters went to church, to Sunday school, to Brownies, Girl Scouts, 4-H, ballet, piano, baton. All three went to public schools, which looked good in their father's campaign literature, then to New Hampshire state colleges, with small weekly allowances meant to teach them the value of a dollar.

I debated whether or not I could riff on this possible paradox: my mother's prudishness in light of the infidelity factor. She nursed several grudges related to other people's perceived promiscuity, out of step with the 1960s and '70s. Did I have an example? Yes. There was the college friend with whom she shared a cabin on a three-night cruise to Virginia Beach. My sister and

I were made to understand that the friendship ended because of a shipboard romance— "romance" a euphemism for the friend's enthusiastically losing her virginity.

Why tell her daughters this unless it was a morality tale? We heard that the friend had disappeared two of the three nights, her bed untouched. Unapologetically! It hadn't been a long-term boyfriend, but someone she'd merely danced with the first night. The ship was called the *Alice Roosevelt*, seemingly an important part of the retelling for the rest of my mother's life, adding presidential dignity to the voyage lest we think it was a love boat. Had she ever mentioned that the mayor of Darien, Connecticut, and his wife were aboard? Only about a million times. And that my mother, proud daughter of Derry's mayor, analogous on a smaller, locally elected level to Alice Roosevelt Longworth herself, had dined at their table all three nights?

I'd never say it on the record, but now that I knew about my illegitimate life, I realized what a good actress my mother had been.

Another few days passed without hearing from my dad. Was this my life now, worrying about our relationship, treading lightly or not at all? I reached him with the evening news blaring in the background. "Let me turn the sound down," he said. "There. How's the chocolate business?" he asked.

"So far it's just homework. Still learning. But you sound good. Everything under control?"

"If you mean up north, it's over. Julian sent a nice young woman, an associate in his firm, to represent me in court—"

"Court? You had your hearing?"

"I told you they wanted me back in a week. The judge dismissed the case. Armstrong dropped the charges."

Had we just entered a more relaxed zone where I could work my way toward Samantha the fictional daughter? I decided I could, figuring better me than Geneva catching him off guard with a camera in his face. "By the way, if you get a call from Geneva and she mentions a third daughter named Samantha, just nod and change the subject."

"Whose third daughter?"

"Yours but imaginary. Geneva was snooping around after too much Googling and picked up on the fact that you warned Armstrong to keep away from your daughter. So I made one up to throw her off the scent."

"You can be a little loose with the truth, Daff. Was that necessary? That project of hers will never see the light of day."

Considering the powder keg that was the dual topic of Armstrong and Geneva, I didn't expect his follow-up to be a cheerful "We have ourselves a funny coincidence."

"Which part?"

"The name."

For a worried few seconds, I thought, *Please don't tell me I knew on some primordial level that there really is a daughter named Samantha.* "In what way the name?"

"Okay, a piece of news: I met a nice lady."

"Named Samantha?"

"No! But her pooch is named Sammi, a female; Sammi with an *i*."

"One of the dogs you walk?"

"We call them clients. Yes, three afternoons a week, increasing to five starting Monday."

Was it my job as his romantic consultant to point out that a business relationship doesn't necessarily go off-leash? "How nice," I said.

"She's invited me in for coffee when I bring Sammi back. More than once."

"And?"

"Unless I have another client with me, I stay. And lately it's been a glass of wine or sherry."

"This is good. Not married, I assume?"

"Never married!"

"What's her name?"

"Kathi with an *i*."

"How old?"

"Fifty."

"She volunteered that?"

"She served leftover birthday cake last time. Hers. 'The big five-o,' she told me."

"Fifty's young."

"If you mean too young for me . . . she knows my age."

"Does she know you were recently arrested?"

"She does. I told her the truth after she told me she was worried that Sammi got a substitute walker on Wednesday."

"And that didn't shock her?"

"No! Just the opposite. I told her that my late wife had had an affair and that the man had met my daughter and was making overtures so I asked him to keep his distance. I think she found it a little heroic, especially the arrest part, like it was an act of civil disobedience."

Just like that—a major secret of both our lives, the one he'd bottled up for thirty-two-plus years—now in the possession of a stranger. I asked her last name and he told me, "Krauss. Kathi Krauss."

"Do you think she added the extra days of walking Sammi so she can see more of you?"

I heard a chuckle. "The schedulers are already teasing me. They're all young kids at New Leash. They wouldn't know the meaning of a no-fraternization rule."

"And you're getting a sense that she's flirting. Or at least interested?"

"I wouldn't call it flirting. She's a piano teacher."

A teacher like my mother, the adulterer. How generous and sweet he was — two qualities I might've possessed if not for the missing genetics of it. "Does she know you haven't always been a dog walker?" I asked.

"She does. I worked that in pretty quickly."

"And she's not just looking for a new pupil?"

"Give me some credit, Daff."

By now, I'd made my way to my laptop and was Googling "Kathi Krauss piano teacher NYC." It took me to the website of Kathleen Krauss, MA, where I learned that her specialty was giving piano lessons to adults who "fled the keyboard" as children and were now regretful.

I asked him if Paula from Thanksgiving was officially in the rearview mirror.

"I'll find a nice way to tell her I want to be just friends. Manuel says she'll be cool with that."

"I should consult Manuel myself."

"About the guy across the hall?"

Had I told him about Jeremy?

I asked when Jeremy had ever come up in conversation. "Not ours. I had a brief conversation with him right outside your door. He introduced himself. I picked up a little . . . what would I call it? . . . maybe fond goodwill."

"We can't help seeing each other. I mean, he lives a few yards away."

"I got the sense it was more than that. Or it could be."

"I wouldn't call it dating. It's visits. With no strings attached."

"Which is okay with you?"

"I set the ground rules myself: friends with benefits. Is that hard for a dad to hear?"

"I'm not easily shocked, not after thirty-six years as a high school principal, most of it during the sexual revolution."

Oh, the phrases that were passing between the divorced daughter and the widowed dad these days! "What's your next step?" I asked.

"If you mean with Kathi, I'm taking it one appointment at a time. She says Sammi gets excited even before the doorbell rings, as if she knows it's me and walkie time."

With his sounding happy and optimistic, I risked saying, "One more thing, Dad . . . I don't want to walk on eggshells, don't want the mention of either Geneva's movie or even, God forbid, Peter Armstrong to make you freak out again. I don't want any more calls from booking rooms of police stations."

"We had an agreement," he said quietly. "I had a good reason to, as you put it, freak out."

"Who had an agreement? Us?"

"No, with your mother. And with Armstrong—that he'd never intrude on your life; that if he did, there would be consequences! He had no legal standing. None! Obviously, his word meant nothing. Obviously, he's a man—and state senator and member of the bar—without honor!"

Why had I veered off the cheerful topic of his new lady friend? "When did you say you're next walking Sammi?" I tried.

"Tomorrow!"

"Will you let me know how it goes?"

"I will. Any advice for your old man on how these things should proceed nowadays?"

My old man. Thank goodness he still thought of himself that way. "Okay," I said. "How's this: Over coffee or sherry, presumably as you're enjoying a very pleasant talk, you say, 'Can we continue this conversation over dinner?'"

I heard him rehearse softly. "Shall we continue this conversation over dinner some evening?"

"She'll jump at it. Believe me. She's already told her friends about you."

"I doubt that, but wish me luck."

17

Holden's Willing Accomplice

I WROTE TO MY EX-HUSBAND via his lawyer, requesting the following: an infrared thermometer, two silicone baking sheets, a silicone spatula, a dozen dipping forks and spoons, parchment paper, nesting glass bowls, candy molds, sea salt, superfine sugar, pistachios, dried cherries, and a *bain-marie*, preferably Meltinchoc brand. I knew I'd get most of the things on that list — not because Holden was generous, but because in the same letter, purely for leverage, I asked for a two-bedroom apartment.

The lawyer crossed the edibles, the parchment, the Meltinchoc, and the apartment off my list just to show who was boss and as an unspoken reminder of the get-nothing prenup I'd signed.

Jeremy was proving to be a good audience for both my progress on the confection front and for all anecdotes that vilified my ex. I noticed the funny look I got the first time I pronounced my ex's fancy moniker. He asked me to repeat it, then said if it had been a regular-guy name — a Joe or a Dave or even a Geoffrey with a *G* — he'd be less judgmental. But Holden? So pretentious and lit-ambitious. What was the story there?

I told him it was a family name, that the first son in every generation got it, like it or not, a century before *Catcher in the Rye*.

Further empathic questions: Were these in-laws nice to you? Did they take sides in the divorce? Did they know what he was up to, marrying you to kick-start his trust fund?

I said his father was out of the picture, the apple having fallen
not far from the adulterous tree. His mother was a sharp cookie,
nice enough when I was the shadow daughter-in-law but ultimately possessing a heart of plutonium. Her name was Bibi,
short for nothing. She'd had Holden late; the most personal thing
she'd ever confided was that he was conceived on her fortieth
birthday after a surprise party, after they'd given up hope. At our
first meeting, family heirloom on my ring finger, she stated that
she was relieved that her bachelor son was settling down with a
woman who wasn't . . . well, you know.

I said, "No, tell me."

"A woman my generation would have called easy."

I should've dropped it there, but instead I asked, "Did you meet
many of these women?"

"Some."

"And what gave you the impression they were easy?"

"You can tell. Sometimes it's the makeup or the clothes or the
way they carry themselves."

I saw her practically never during my short marriage. Family
dinners consisted of Holden having Manhattans and not much
else at his mother's apartment, solo. After the first few of these ex-
clusionary suppers, I smelled a conspiracy. Was he unhappy and
confiding in her? Or had I become as unfortunate a choice as the
skanky also-rans? Evidence to the contrary and always reassuring: He'd come home with a beautifully wrapped cashmere cardi-
gan or an evening purse I'd never use, or an Hermès scarf with a
note that said, "For no reason! Kisses, Bibi."

A few weeks into our separation, she called me. Had I received
the German nutcracker she'd sent home with Holdy last Monday? She'd found it in a box with ornaments . . . on and on to news
of her two dogs and their monogrammed Tyrolean winter coats.

"I assume he kept it for himself," I told her.

That provoked only silence until she asked, "Could you put Holdy on?"

"I can't."

"He's out?"

"I have no idea."

Was it my job to fill in the blanks? Because she wasn't my mother, my confidante, my problem, I decided not to elaborate. "When was the last time you talked to him?" I asked.

"Monday. I left a few messages, but I haven't heard back."

"Try a text."

"I don't do that."

"I'll text him and tell him to call you."

She said coyly, "And tell him he's a terrible son! But maybe if he calls, he gets another chance."

Was she clueless? Or perhaps she'd been in on the plot and was only feigning congeniality.

I texted him, CALL YOUR MOTHER & TELL HER ABOUT US!

I gave it thirty-six hours, then called her back, newly motivated to squeal if the coward hadn't come clean about the separation. I suggested lunch.

"What a good idea! You'll be my guest. I insist. Pick a place. You know what I like."

I picked a favorite restaurant of hers that was a doozy, figuring I might as well make it a very expensive, five-star sayonara.

I had to admit she was handsome in an august way, with the white pageboy and bangs of someone who'd once been a natural blonde. She was wearing the pearls, three strands that she'd told me would be mine some day and then, please God, a granddaughter's. I'd planned to tell the story of our dissolution over coffee, but I was having trouble making small talk in the face of my suspicion that she was Holden's willing accomplice. I began with "I know this might be the last time you want to see me . . ."

Did that evoke anything? No. She crossed her knife and fork over her untouched lobster salad.

I started off delicately, or so I thought, with "Things could never be the same after he ruptured several commandments —"

Who was this usually dainty Episco-Republican opposite me, now practically spitting? "Don't talk to me like I'm some . . . some . . . Southern Baptist! Commandments! Ha! You don't think I know that you threw him out!"

I leaned across my own salad, and hissed, "For good reason! Did he tell you that he stayed out all night with a woman he'd met in a hotel bar? I even know her name: Amanda. Because he confessed."

No answer, just an unnerving stare.

"And that confession led to a bigger one: that he'd been having sex with other women from the time we met: when we were dating, when we were engaged, then after the wedding. I think the only time he was on hiatus was our wedding night."

"*And . . . ?*"

And? My face must've registered my incredulity, because her next question had a tinge of humanity. "Is there any chance . . . ?"

"Any chance of what?"

"Any chance he exaggerated his extramarital love life?"

Was that a smile of sisterhood she'd just flashed? "It's not as if Holden is a specimen," she explained.

"Bibi! He told me he was a sex addict. And he'd go to rehab — like drug addicts and alcoholics — in some place like Minnesota."

She had started shaking her head with the first syllable I uttered. "Wouldn't I know that? Wouldn't he have come to me first to say, 'Mother, I have a problem'?"

"'Mother, I'm a sex addict'? I don't think so."

Was Bibi looking thoughtful? Was she summoning a mother-son conversation from their past? I asked what she was thinking.

"You didn't know Holdy's father. No, how could you? He was ancient history by the time Holdy met you. What am I saying? He was gone in many ways by the time I brought Holden home from the hospital as a newborn."

I knew she'd been divorced but wasn't positive which of her ex-husbands had been Holden Phillips III. I asked if by "gone" she meant that he'd passed away that early in their marriage.

"Unfortunately not."

I said yes, now I remembered. Then, just for meanness' sake: "Back in the day when broken homes were rare enough that Holden felt like the only kid in the class without two parents on visiting night."

"I don't like to talk about it." Her voice was now tight. "Of course, when supposed friends in your church are sleeping with your husband, you have to take a stand, don't you? You don't just show up and smile at the two b-words who were having relations with your husband. It's so humiliating."

Whoa. I'd brought out the best or worst in Bibi. I asked how she found out about the women.

"I connected the dots. It wasn't that hard." What followed gave me another glimpse into the very un–New Hampshire, Upper East Side world of privilege and drama: "I hired a private detective. The rest was easy. They know what to look for. He wasn't caught *in flagrante delicto* but in what you might call the comings and goings, the before and after."

"Did he confess once he was busted?"

She actually smiled. "Do you know how I handled it? I told our minister, 'You fix it. You get all of them in here and tell them the jig is up!'"

"Did he?"

"That mouse! No, he begged me not to put him in the middle. I said, 'When I can't come to church because my husband's mis-

tresses, plural, are in the next pew, who else is going to help me?'
And at the time, Dear Abby always told women to talk to their
ministers or spiritual advisors. Have I mentioned they were married women whose husbands went to our church, too? On Fifth
Avenue! Of course, I later found out that the pastor was no angel,
either."

I didn't have to ask if there were only two paramours because
Bibi volunteered, after summoning our waiter for another whis-
key sour, "My divorce lawyer called it Don Juanism — his need to
bed countless women."

"If you're saying this is an inherited vice, it doesn't make me
any more sympathetic."

"Why did Holden marry?" she asked. "Why didn't he continue
sowing his wild oats?"

"Are you telling me that you didn't know about the provision
in his grandmother's trust that he'd get the windfall only when
he married?"

"Oh, that," she said. "That was on his father's side."

"He used me! He thought I was a country bumpkin who
wouldn't notice he was a philanderer, who'd be grateful to marry
someone with, as my mother would've said, means."

"Check, please," Bibi called.

We'd hardly touched our matching lobster salads. I asked to
have mine wrapped up, then forgot to take it.

Jeremy said that this lunch must've been more painful than I was
making it sound and that it couldn't have been that long ago. A
year? Eighteen months? Had there been any follow-up?

"Nope. That was it. I haven't seen her since. Or her precious
son, either. Did I mention that the scarves were hideous? I don't
even think they were new."

"'Holdy,' seriously? Holden's bad enough."

We were watching *Jeopardy!* on his bed, fully clothed, laptop open, contemplating what to order for dinner. "Were you named after anyone?" I asked him.

"If you can believe that my mother admitted this — Jeremy was one of the brothers in *Here Come the Brides.*"

"Maybe she sensed, in utero, that you had a future in television."

"Ah, yes. As Timmy." After a pause, he added, "Which perhaps you recall is the name of my character."

Was Jeremy hurt that I hadn't caught up with *Riverdale?* Why *hadn't* I upgraded my package to include his channel? Maybe because he played a junior in high school and I was having sex with him several nights a week. I said, "I've been economizing on my cable bill, but I'm calling them tomorrow."

"Not necessary."

"I think it is." We turned back to the laptop, to Seamless and our delivery history. When we agreed to hit reorder from our favorite Cuban restaurant, Jeremy said, "This is the third time we're getting these exact things. I wonder if it means we're going steady."

Of course, he was using that ironically. I knew from season one that it was a retro phrase often heard in a booth at Pop's Chock'lit Shoppe.

The smell of coffee in an NYU mug woke me. "I guessed milk and sugar for someone with a professional sweet tooth," he said.

I lifted the covers to evaluate my state of undress. Complete. I told Jeremy I'd wait till he left before getting out from under. The coffee was excellent, thank you.

"I've got to run. Feel free to use the shower."

"No need. I'll slip across the hall." I reached for his retreating hand. "Another plus."

"Along with . . . ?"

What answers did the modern woman give? I mentioned his

coffeemaker, his view of the Hudson, his martinis, and his talented hands.

"Why, thank you. Come back soon."

"You can leave. I'll make the bed and wash my mug."

"I left a key for you on the table by the front door."

A key? I'm sure possession of that didn't have any meaning beyond my being a trustworthy neighbor should an emergency arise.

18

Well, That's a Surprise

AND THERE IT WAS among my bills, catalogues, and circulars, a white envelope of the highest stationery grade, its return address a Concord, New Hampshire, law firm. I opened it slowly, suspiciously, expecting nothing good. It said:

Dear Daphne Maritch:

I am pleased to inform you that our client, Peter D. Armstrong, has instructed me to make this initial distribution of $5,000 to you, enclosed. We shall hold funds that are to pay you this same sum each calendar quarter. The federal income tax status of these payments is not clear at this time. You will receive further information as we know more. Please don't hesitate to call with any questions you may have.

Sincerely yours,

Francis A. Barber, Esq.

Five thousand bucks times four! Should I? Could I? What were the ethics of such a windfall? Had my benefactor died? Should I call him or call Francis A. Barber, Esquire? Return it? Cash it?

Be reasonable, I told myself. Five grand every three months

would be a shot in the arm for someone living on subpar alimony checks.

I knew whom I'd *not* be asking for advice: Tom Maritch, who would surely consider this the buying and selling of my affections. Not to mention a violation of the promise Armstrong had allegedly made not to butt into my life. And the last thing I wanted to hear was my widowed dog-walker father saying I should return this and every subsequent check because he'd match it.

So I did nothing except walk the three blocks to my bank and deposit the check as fast as the ATM could take it. I chose print receipt not just for security but for show-and-tell, to say, *Not only am I going for the Select and Silver cable programming, but I might even buy a flat-screen TV!* I was sketching that whole high-fiving, glasses-clinking scene when, back in my building's lobby, I spotted a fur-coated Geneva. Usually, I ducked into the mailroom to avoid her, but today I was feeling up to the task.

"You're looking pleased with yourself," she said as we watched the elevator readout descend to *L*.

Was that any way to greet a neighbor? I didn't think so. I said only, "Life is good."

"Ditto," she said.

To engage or not to engage? I waited until we were in the elevator before asking, "Anything new with the documentary?"

"Which one?"

Oh, really — which documentary of the many you've been juggling? I said, "I forget. Either *The Sorrow and the Pity* or the one about my mother's Pickering, New Hampshire, yearbook."

"The latter. It's moving forward. In fact, it's on the front burner."

What would that mean in the Geneva world of sketchy, underachieving work? "How so?"

"I've been talking to your mother's students."

"In person? On the phone?"

The familiar thud of the elevator meant we'd reached our floor. "Do you want to hear more?" Geneva asked.

Without waiting for an answer, she followed me to my apartment. I looked at my watch. Five minutes to 4. "Tea?" I asked.

"Well, that's a surprise."

I knew what she meant: a surprise to see a show of hospitality from hostile me. Without removing her coat, she took a seat in the living room while I put water on to boil. When I returned, she was on her phone, holding up a finger to ward off an interruption. How rude was that, silencing the host? Back in the kitchen, I entertained myself by rereading the letter that had accompanied my check, posted on my refrigerator until my dad's next visit.

"Okay!" I heard.

I didn't join her. "You're free now? Because I'd hate to interrupt."

"Do you have green tea?" she asked.

Back in her presence, having grabbed a dented box of generic supermarket tea bags, I asked, "No. This okay?"

She shrugged.

I asked in more neighborly fashion what she was learning from my mother's students.

"It's still being tallied," she said.

Tallied? I asked if that meant she'd taken some kind of count? Or a poll?

"I sent a questionnaire."

"About what?"

Her nonanswer: "I had it printed up at FedEx for the ones who don't do email."

I asked if I could see a copy. She twisted her mouth this way and that as she frown-scrolled through attachments, then handed me her phone. I read:

1. Did you know Mrs. June Winter Maritch? Yes ___ No ___
2. If so, in what capacity? Teacher ___ Advisor ___ Other ___
3. On a scale of 1 to 5, how well did you know her? 1 2 3 4 5
4. Did she sign your yearbook? Yes ___ No ___
5. If so, please quote what she wrote: _____
6. Do you still have your copy of *The Monadnockian*?
   Yes ___ No ___
   If inscribed, would you be willing to lend it to Gal Friday
   Films? Yes ___ No ___
7. You are Male ___ Female ___
8. Which of these reunions did you personally attend:
   (Circle all that apply) 5th, 10th, 15th, 20th, 25th, 30th, 35th,
   40th, 45th, 50th
9. If you did attend, did you see Mrs. Maritch or speak to her?
   Yes ___ No ___ (note which reunion) _____
   If yes, please describe your exchange(s)_____
   _____
10. Do you have any photos of her teaching ___ coaching ___
    chaperoning ___ dancing ___drinking ___ other ___
11. Did you ever hear rumors regarding her personal life?
    (Even if just student gossip) Yes ___ No ___
12. If so, please describe: _____
    Other impressions: _____
    _____
13. Do you recall her husband attending reunions with her?
    Rarely ___ Always ___ Never ___ I don't know ___
    Did you meet her daughter, Daphne Maritch, at the Novem-
    ber reunion? Yes ___ No ___
    If so, can you briefly describe that encounter?
    _____
    _____
14. Did you attend Mrs. Maritch's funeral? Yes ___ No ___

If you have other memories, comments, or observations, feel free to attach an additional sheet. Please provide your name, email, daytime, evening, and cell phone numbers. Thanks!

Geneva Wisenkorn, Gal Friday Films

Good thing I wasn't holding mugs of hot water when I read this. I managed to ask if she'd distributed the questionnaire yet.

"Why?"

"Because I hate it! *Asking* for rumors and gossip? You don't think that's leading the witness?"

Geneva sighed at my obvious filmmaking naïveté. She said her work had a point of view. And a POV didn't just appear without digging.

"You didn't think to run these questions by me first?"

"This is basic research. This is how I find people to interview and ultimately film. And there's a script that needs to be written. It isn't all camerawork."

I went back to the kitchen and made tea for one—me. And while it was steeping, I had an idea of how to frustrate, annoy, and torment Geneva in her quest for what was behind my mother's overinvestment in a mildewed *Monadnockian*. I'd tell her outright that my mother had been having an affair for decades. I might even modify "affair" with "torrid." But not until I uttered the phrase "off-the-record," driving that home since Geneva was anything but a real journalist. She couldn't use it! My reasoning: By swearing her to secrecy, I was handcuffing her. In the confines of my kitchen, it seemed logical: It was better to hand her the juicy missing link up front, accompanied by a gag order, than have her snooping around, reading between the lines of the questionnaire's answers.

I returned to the living room. "I've given this serious thought, and I've decided to tell you something that is key."

"About?"

"My mother. It would explain everything."

Geneva visibly perked up. "Should I get my camera?"

"No. Because what I'm about to tell you is off-the-record. As I've explained before, it means you cannot repeat it, quote it, and — most important — you can't put it in the documentary, should that ever get off the ground."

"Ever?"

"Ever."

"This better be good," she said.

"This is strictly off-the-record. Do I have your word?"

"Yes! I get it! For Chrissake, just say it."

"It's come to light that my mother and one of her students —"

"Girl or boy?"

"Boy. But what difference does that make if you can never use it?"

"I bet it's the one who was at our table, the senator."

"Do you understand that none of that matters, not that I'm confirming a single thing, because it's off-the-freaking-record?"

"Can't I be interested? Is that against the law, too?"

I hadn't yet told her anything. It was then that I came to my senses. I could not tell her something juicy on the theory that she'd drop the whole project if her hands were tied. So I said, "Oh, it's nothing. It was about me."

"But you were going to tell me something about your mother and one of her students."

"Well, it was about her, but now I realize it was nothing, a stupid little story about" — What did I have? Oh, right, the Josh and Jason O'Rourke caper — "a set of identical twins in two different English classes, and she found out that the one who had the test in the earlier class took it all over again in his brother's afternoon class!"

"That was it? Then why that buildup about off-the-record, never use, never film, never think about it?"

"I was babbling. I have nothing. Nada. Your questionnaire isn't going to produce one juicy thing."

"Even if it doesn't, I have the yearbook. And I picked up a vibe at the reunion."

"What kind of vibe? From whom?"

She said too smartly, "Oh, how about a former male student?"

Had my voice sounded strained? It must have. I tried reverse psychology in the form of "This is going to be the most boring biopic ever filmed."

How was that working? If I thought that had deflated her, I was wrong. Just the opposite. What I heard was "You're an open book. Your mouth is saying 'most boring biopic ever,' but your face is saying 'I'm terrified.'"

"No, it's not! You never met my mother! She was a stick-in-the-mud! She might've had a yearbook thing, but she certainly did not cross a line with any students if that's what your questionnaire is trying to root out. I'm sure she didn't even cross any lines with my father before they married! They had to be role models. They had to be discreet. They —"

"Trusted each other?"

"Of course. They taught together. They had two kids together. They were together until she died."

"I met him, don't forget."

What was that smug smile for? "You had Thanksgiving dinner with him."

"And all the eligible ladies — which was everybody, now that I think about it — were making a play for him."

"Was that his fault? And even if he went out on a date with one of them, he was entitled."

"New widower and all?"

"It was over a year since my mother died! Plus, I don't like this line of questioning. My father is the dearest man. And a true gentleman. I can't believe you're implying that he did something wrong. You know what I think? I think you're finally facing the truth: that all you have is a story with no payoff about a New Hampshire English teacher with a yearbook fixation."

Did she just wink at the end of my tirade?

"Before this . . ." she began.

"What? Before what?"

"Before this, you struck me as a logical person. Someone who thinks before she speaks."

I huffed that I always thought before I spoke.

"Daphne," she said, sounding weary and charitable. "I've distributed the questionnaire. If anyone sends it back, hinting at some kind of hanky-panky, I'm off and running. There's my story. I'd be quoting that person on deep background, not you. And maybe you don't know the whole story. You're the daughter. But I can find someone who's been waiting decades to squeal."

I said no, no, no, she wouldn't. "People in New Hampshire would never speak ill of the dead."

Who was I trying to convince, Geneva or myself?

19

Suddenly There Are Girlfriends

I HAD TO SEND PETER ARMSTRONG a thank-you note, didn't I? More than a week had passed since the check for $5,000 had arrived. I'd been mulling over how to express my gratitude without sounding effusive or daughterly due to the grudge I was holding for his arresting my father.

Finally, I wrote, "I've received and cashed your first check, which was most welcome and generous. Thank you. Sincerely, Daphne."

So why did it come back with "Return to Sender" scrawled in purple felt-tip pen? The envelope had been opened and taped shut. Inside, attached to my note, was a Post-it rudely demanding, "Oh, really? 'FIRST check?' Who are you?"

Who the hell are *you?* I might ask. Did Armstrong have a gatekeeper/secretary/girlfriend/boyfriend/live-in accountant who opened and passed judgment on his private correspondence?

This was hate mail, I decided. I found his business card and called his direct line. After dozens of rings went nowhere, he picked up with a brusque "Armstrong!"

"It's Daphne," I said, then plunged in with "I wrote you a thank-you note—thank you, by the way, for the check—but the note was returned in a manner I'd describe as crazy."

"Wait," he said. "Start over."

I summarized: A note I'd sent him came back defaced—rudely and anonymously.

I'd expected shock and outrage, but his question was lawyerly. "You wrote me an actual letter on paper, and then what happened?"

I quoted my own innocent dispatch and the uncalled-for counterattack.

"Go on."

Go on? That much wasn't offensive enough? "Who opens your mail and writes in purple?" I asked.

"I have to take this call. Can you hold?"

I waited. Just before giving up, I heard, "That would be Bonnie."

"Just now? Calling you?"

"No. The person who mistakenly returned your note."

"And who is Bonnie?"

"My partner."

"What kind of partner?"

"I think you can guess."

"Girlfriend?"

"Correct."

"Is she a secret girlfriend?"

No answer.

"A live-in girlfriend?"

"No—"

"Yet she intercepts your mail?"

"Force of habit."

"Force of whose habit? Isn't opening other people's mail against the law?"

"Not in this case." Then, reverently: "Bonnie was my office manager at the firm."

"Is that why this is hush-hush?"

More silence.

"Is she married?"

"Not anymore."

"Kids?"

"Two."

"How old?"

"Ten and thirteen? Something like that."

"And Bonnie herself is how old?"

"Daphne. I don't think you realize that you're giving me the third degree as if . . . Oh, never mind."

As if I were a real daughter who'd earned the right to interrogate and judge. I knew the answer anyway: Bonnie was young. And nuts. I tried to imbue my next question with a modicum of concern, a more psychiatric "Is she a stable person?"

"There's a vote happening downstairs. Let me get back to you."

"You should tell her she made a terrible first impression."

"Clearly."

"And inform her why you're sending me quarterly checks."

"Gotta run. I'll get back to you if there's anything satisfactory to report."

"She's trouble," I told the dial tone.

Speaking of girlfriends who suddenly materialize, Kathi the piano teacher sent me an email dinner invitation with the subject line, "From Sammi's mom." Three upcoming dates were proposed. I chose the middle one, Thursday of the following week, asking what I could bring. She wrote back: "I've heard about your culinary talents from your greatest fan! Would it be rude to ask you to bring one of your famous desserts?"

Famous where? Never mind. I said yes, happy to do that. Was she allergic to nuts?

No. She was not. I deduced from a heart emoji that she loved them.

A good guest does her homework. I suggested to my dad that we get together for a pre-dinner-party briefing. I chose a Swedish film at the Paris Theatre about a curmudgeonly suicidal widower who is rescued, literally and figuratively, by a lovely young Iranian neighbor. Waiting in the theater lobby for the earlier show to empty, he said in the direction of two smiling older ladies, "This is my daughter. Aren't I lucky that she wants to see a movie with her old man?" *Adorable*, the women's expressions seemed to say. Once seated, I said, "That could work for you."

"How so?"

"They'll assume you're seeing a movie with me because there isn't a wife or girlfriend in the picture."

"Not on the market," he said, shushing me with a finger to his lips.

"Because of Kathi?"

"It seems so."

On the walk home, under too much scaffolding, past skyscrapers under construction on West Fifty-seventh, I brought up my own social life, thinking it would encourage him to mine a similar vein. "You remember Jeremy — across-the-hall neighbor? It's a nice thing. And you can't beat it for convenience."

"And that's okay with you? Just convenience?"

"A little more than that. I'm having fun. And he's good company. Isn't that what we're all looking for?"

"If you say so."

We reached Ninth Avenue. I told him that here on this corner, come spring, there would be a farmers' market Wednesdays and

Saturdays. No bargains, but he'd like it. Then, in as airy and neutral a voice as I thought was needed, I asked whose idea it was to invite me to dinner.

"Kathi suggested it, which I thought was very nice, especially since she isn't much of a cook. But who in New York City is? So many restaurants. I've heard people say they eat out every night or get food delivered. A woman in my building told me that it's cheaper to go out than to cook at home."

I said I didn't know how eating in restaurants could be cheaper, especially with a glass or two of wine.

"Well, by the time you buy a package of chicken, or a couple of lamb chops, a bag of onions, potatoes, a stick or two of butter; or have you noticed that every hunk of cheese costs seven dollars? And maybe a carton of eggs, a green pepper—"

"Dad—I get it."

"Look around"—he gestured to an empanada take-out joint as we passed it—"a world of cheap food. I mean when you think about Chinese places in Pickering, just that one on Highland."

He sounded so contented, so enthusiastic. I said, "Yup. And the miracle of delivery."

"Even my dry cleaning gets delivered!"

"I bet your clients say, 'And I don't even have to walk my own dog!'"

That made him beam, effectively granting me permission to return to the subject of number one client, Kathi. I asked if their friendship had gone beyond sherry and tea.

"We've had a couple of dinners, and we went to a chamber-music concert at Alice Tully Hall. I think I told you she's a pianist. Did you know you can go to rehearsals of the Philharmonic for hardly anything?"

Topic hijacked again, I said, "I was hoping to hear something more relationshippy."

"Such as 'I enjoy her company very much, and she seems to enjoy mine'?"

"No. More like 'After the concert, we go back to her apartment and take off our clothes.'"

"Daphne! You've gotten very bold. Is it the actor's influence? Or you think it's how a sophisticated New Yorker talks?"

We'd reached my corner. "None of the above. It's just that you and I never spent this much time together so you didn't know what a badass I am." I kissed him on one cheek. "See you Thursday. I'm bringing dessert. Any requests?"

"Yes! No smirking. No jokes or questions that have a sexual connotation."

"I'll try!" I was walking backward, smiling and waving.

He motioned *Come back*. I did, to where he was pointing at a menu board in front of a dingy bar, "happy hour 5 to 8." He checked his watch. "Are you in a hurry? There may be something I should mention before Thursday. Nothing bad, just a possibly sensitive topic."

I said sure. I even had time for — I checked the board — truffle fries. We sat at the near-empty bar and ordered two glasses of the house red. "This might come up," he told me. "Kathi lost both her parents within a short time of each other, and it's still raw. The mom went first and the dad had a heart attack driving down to Florida, where he was going to start his new life."

"Just since you've known her?"

"No. But recently enough. The dad about a year ago. He might've survived the heart attack except for the crash. Or maybe it was vice versa."

"Siblings?"

"A brother who lives in Hoboken. Commutes to the city by ferry."

"Nieces? Nephews?"

"Does he have kids? I don't think so. Never met him. But you can ask him yourself on Thursday."

Oh dear. I worried until the night arrived that it would be a setup. But the brother, Denny, brought his fiancée, whose name I had a hard time catching, which turned out to be Alissa after I asked her to spell it. I gathered from the congratulations being offered that the engagement was new. He'd lived at home with his parents and suddenly had a house, its contents, no rent, no mortgage. The engagement ring had been his mother's, in need of a professional polish, but I still faked an admiring gasp.

Kathi's apartment was a loft in what was once a soap factory, with charmingly scarred floors and the biggest grand piano I'd ever seen except on a stage. Doors off the main room suggested a bedroom, maybe two. There was a giant worn Persian rug, two mismatched couches that were clearly dog-friendly, and a wall of pretty sunsets and crashing waves painted by her mother. "I was lucky," she confided. "Not Denny's taste."

Speaking of pretty, Kathi herself: fair-skinned, blue-eyed, dark hair threaded with gray, in a bob with bangs. She was wearing a midcalf skirt, boots, a black turtleneck, and a lacy scarf. When I admired it, she said "Don't look too closely! I made it years ago, and it was the last thing I ever knit."

She served something I thought went out of style before I was born: chicken à la king over rice. Sure enough, the recipe was her mother's, which made all five of us nod in sympathetic appreciation. The green peas, Kathi told us, were her own addition. On the side, steamed carrots, attributed to the helpful peeling by my father, who'd arrived early.

I asked in the manner of a friendly, interested guest what everyone did.

"You mean for the meal?" Alissa asked.

"No. In life. Jobwise."

Alissa said she was going back to school, working toward a degree in accounting at Fairleigh Dickinson. Denny, she continued,
was an accountant already, a CPA, with a master's degree. They'd
met at a firm where she'd been interning but didn't start dating
until that rotation ended.

"HR has eyes in the back of its head," said Denny.

"Some people think being a CPA isn't glamorous," Kathi added.
"But they love their work, and some of Denny's clients — is this vi-
olating any confidence? — are theater people and actors."

Proud sister? Check. Generosity of spirit? Check.

My father said, "I had the same guy do my taxes my whole professional life. Then he passed, and I left Pickering."

Kathi gestured toward her brother with an open hand.

Denny said, "Might be too close for comfort," then asked where
I worked.

"I'm studying to be a chocolatier."

"Are there jobs in that?" he asked.

I said I hoped so, but it might end up being nothing more than
a hobby.

"Is that true?" my dad asked. "Because there aren't jobs in that
field? Or because you're disenchanted?"

"It's too early in the semester to think about placement." And
then to the table at large, "He worries too much about me. Sometimes I think it's the real reason he moved here."

"You know that's not true! I've always wanted to live in New
York!"

I waited a beat, then asked, "Even if he's exaggerating, even if
I had nothing to do with it, how many here think I won the dad
lottery?"

Kathi's hand shot up. She waved her arm strenuously, impersonating a teacher's pet to excellent comic effect.

What had I prepared myself for? Not this woman. I must've been expecting her to possess a number of unattractive qualities based on my old piano teacher who was sour in demeanor and ever scolding due to my lack of talent and insufficient practice. My father asked what I was thinking; what was that dark cloud that had passed over my face?

I pointed to the giant piano as if that had been the trigger. "Remember Miss Gagnon?"

"Oh, God," he said.

"She was my piano teacher — very scary," I explained. "And her house smelled funny. I dreaded my lessons."

"I hate to hear that," Kathi said.

I asked her if her adult students practiced as much as they were supposed to.

"Either they practice, or they're sad they haven't practiced more. Don't forget: no parents pushing them to take the lessons or stick with them when they want to drop out. They really want to be here."

"Do you make them have recitals?"

"No recitals. A few, sometimes four or five of them, get together here once a month, very informal, wine and cheese, and whoever wants to play plays. It doesn't feel like a performance, more like 'Oh, I loved that piece. Can I learn it, too?'"

"It sounds so . . . pleasant," I said.

"Did we do this to you?" my father asked. "Because I don't ever remember forcing you to practice, let alone take lessons."

"It's not as if I had any talent, but she could've been a whole lot nicer. We never talked during my lessons! No conversation ever."

"She wasn't what you'd call an affable woman," my father said.

"It has to be social," Kathi said. "People don't learn well when they're anxious."

"Maybe it's time to take it up again," my father said.

My lack of enthusiasm must have been plainly visible, inspiring Kathi to say, "Her chocolate lessons probably keep her busy enough."

I was grateful for that, since it ushered in the topic of what I had in the oven, a flourless molten-chocolate cake. I said I'd better check on the dessert. Kathi asked, "Can I whip the cream?"

Was I being too proud by saying, "I do it by hand. Won't take long. I kind of enjoy it."

"She's a professional," my father said. "Almost certified."

I didn't contradict him. I would be mailed a piece of paper that could pass for a certificate, though merely issued by the educational packager I'd paid for my online course.

And, truly, the cake was delicious — hot, melty, semisweet. I complimented Kathi on her oven, that it heated evenly at the correct temperature. Rare! Alissa asked if I'd consider making a wedding cake.

"Yours?"

She launched into her list of favorite cakes, favorite frostings, favorite brands of boxed cake mixes and how she doctored them before I cut in with "I wouldn't be right for the job. You want a real wedding cake, which is a whole other specialty. This is just a dessert. I don't even have the right pans."

Denny said, "Plus, we're getting married in New Jersey. It's going to have to be a rum cake."

"He means I have three Italian grandparents," Alissa said.

"Do you have a date yet?" I asked.

"No," said Denny.

"Except . . . Denny? Remember? The thrombosis?" Alissa said.

"One of her grandmothers might not make it if we wait too long," Denny said.

"Then go for it," I said.

"I know it takes months and months of planning. The wedding

dress, the venue, the caterer, the florist," Kathi said. "Not to mention booking the church."

"Not to mention is right," Denny mumbled.

I sensed a sore subject.

"He may not have told you that I was married before," Alissa said. "I was very young. It only lasted two years."

I said, "I can top that. I was married for under *one* year. It was a sham from start to finish."

My father said, "Daff—let's not get into that."

Kathi helped change the subject by freeing Sammi, who came bounding out from behind one of the closed doors, doing laps between the table and the door, then lying down, ecstatic to see his mistress and my father, her underbelly offered for his attention.

I said, "It looks like she enjoys Dad's company as much as he does hers."

Kathi said, "We're up to five afternoons a week. She can't believe her good luck."

"It's mutual," my father said.

Sammi lifted her head and was sniffing the air with such dedicated twitching that we all laughed. "She smells the chocolate," Kathi said. "And she's thinking *Don't tell me you finally used the oven!*"

Once again, it struck me that I hadn't expected to like this woman. When she'd been only a name and a concept, she was too young, too cute with her spelling of Kathi, too eager to meet me, and certainly too eager to rope in my socially naïve father. But here she was: kind, hospitable, good-natured.

Lost in my character analysis, I wasn't paying attention to the conversation about chocolate being toxic for dogs until I heard Denny ask my father, "So you walk dogs for a living?"

"Not exactly. I'm retired, so it seemed a good idea, to indulge my love of dogs without getting one of my own."

"Retired from what?"

I waited for the answer that never failed to subdue any man who'd ever been assigned to detention. But what I heard from the most earnest man I knew was "Carnival barker. Why?"

Would Kathi jump in to assure her brother that her suitor had a bachelor's in education and a master's degree in secondary-school administration? She didn't. "I think that's what drew me to him in the first place," she said. "I'd gone out with doctors and lawyers but never a carnival barker. Imagine the stories he has to tell."

How could I resist adding, "My mother was a trapeze artist." I closed my eyes and bit my lip. *So tragic.*

Denny said, "We should probably head back."

Wouldn't this be Kathi's cue to say, "We were joking! Tom was a high school principal in a district consistently rated one of the top ten in the state!" But all she said was a sprightly "Thanks for coming! Thanks for the wine."

She retrieved their coats, and we three plus Sammi walked Denny and Alissa to the industrial-size elevator. When its doors closed and we heard its lumbering descent, I said, "That was great, especially the improv." And to Kathi: "You're a quick one."

"He deserved it," she said. "No imagination. None. And no curiosity. What if your mother really had been a trapeze artist and that's why your dad is widowed?"

I said no worries; they were nice enough.

"Good time?" my dad asked me with a glance toward our hostess.

"Can't you tell? I'm leaving you two alone now. Oh, wait. Dishes. I should offer."

They said no, no. You go. Have a nice evening. Thank you for the cake. Oh, that's right — the bowl and the whisk and the pan. We'll wash and return them next time we see you.

I said something uninspired like "Till then" or "No problem." They both kissed me good-bye. I walked to the E train deep in daughterly contemplation. If I were a person who spoke to the dead, I'd tell my mother that her husband, who had loved her and forgiven her, who hadn't been especially rewarded for that, was, on this cold December night, as lighthearted as I'd ever seen him.

20

......

When Did I Get So Mean?

I T MIGHT HAVE BEEN a more thoughtful notification if Geneva's update ("Oh, Daphne — hi; I have something to run by you.") hadn't been delivered nonchalantly when we crossed paths in the trash room.

"About . . . ?"

"The documentary. Yours and mine. It's not going to happen."

Just like that, unexpected and hugely welcome news delivered as if I had only a glancing interest in whether it was dead or alive. Trying to match her bloodless delivery, I said, "What a pity. Can I have the yearbook back now?"

"No! I need it more than ever."

"For what?"

"Phase two."

I waited. She busied herself rifling through several issues of someone's discarded *New Yorkers*. "A whole new project?" I prompted.

"A whole new *medium*. Do you know what a podcast is?"

"Of course, but —"

"Maybe eight episodes. Maybe six."

"About the yearbook, still? And my mother?"

"Most definitely. From all angles. Do you subscribe to any?"

"I do —"

"Everyone does! They're hot. I'll need a sponsor or two, but I have some leads. Would you be willing to be interviewed for the first episode where we talk about how I came into possession of the yearbook?"

"No."

"Just a few minutes: You'll say, 'My mother left it to me. Even though I threw it away, I wanted it back. I fought it. Intellectual property blah blah blah' so the listener immediately gets what I was up against."

"You were up against my wanting what was rightfully mine."

"So you say. I want the push-pull that you brought to the project. Every story needs tension."

"Did you get questionnaires back from any of my mother's students?"

"A few."

"And?"

"Off-the-record, as you would say."

"'Off-the-record' is then followed by the goods, which is whatever you don't want to be made public."

She smiled in a way I didn't like. "Stay tuned. I hope to have the first episode up and running by March first."

"Episode one being me saying, 'I wanted it back. I still do. You stole it.'"

"Along those lines, for sure. It's not only backstory but the *why* of the whole thing. Why it meant so much to her that she left it to a daughter in her will." Hugging the preowned *New Yorkers,* she smiled proudly. "I already have a name for the podcast, and I think it will grab everyone who ever graduated from high school and had one signed."

"Let me guess: *The Yearbook?*"

"Wow," she said. *"Exactly."*

. . .

A Google alert I'd set up to monitor the fortunes and possible wedding vows of my ex-husband led me to a fine-print paid obit in the *New York Times*. His mother, the disagreeable Bibi, had died suddenly, no cause stated. The funeral was in two days at the Episcopal church where her husband's affairs had taken root. Only a masochist would attend, I told myself. But wouldn't an appearance attest to the evolution of my self-esteem?

I texted my dad. "Don't suppose you want to go to my ex-mother-in-law's funeral. It's Tuesday, 11 a.m."

He phoned, out of breath, which was how he sounded when managing multiple leashes. "Hell, no," he said. "As if she'd ever come to mine. And why are *you* going?"

"Because you raised me right."

"Still—above and beyond. You're up to seeing your ex-husband?"

"From afar, sure."

Throughout our short conversation, he was exhorting the dogs to keep up, or stay, or stop doing whatever they weren't supposed to be doing. I asked if Sammi was among today's clients.

"Sammi I do alone."

"Do you charge extra for private walks?"

"No. New Leash is good that way. If you tell them she has issues with other dogs, then a solo walk is fine."

"*Does* she have issues?"

"You met her! None. It's my personal preference."

"She's very nice."

"She's nine years old, but she has the enthusiasm of a puppy, don't you think?"

"I meant Kathi."

"Oh. Of course. She is, indeed, very nice. Sometimes I can't believe what this job has led to."

I told him I was happy for him.

"Good to know," he answered, but I could hear in his tone a reprimand; I'd missed some boat in reporting my favorable impressions.

"You could tell I really liked her, right?"

"She liked you, too."

"If I had a real table, I'd reciprocate."

"You can't afford a real table?"

Now I could. I had a few thousand unexpected dollars in my checking account, and the next installment from Sponsor Armstrong due in March. I said, "I just might do that."

Between my hat, bought just that morning, an unseasonable black organza with a floppy Kentucky Derby brim, and the oversize tortoiseshell sunglasses, I hoped to achieve a look between incognito and conspicuous-attractive.

I took a seat midchurch on the aisle to facilitate a fast escape. I could see Holden in the front row along with, presumably, relatives. Bibi's gleaming coffin was decorated with nonfloral cascading greenery that someone whispered was copied from Jackie Onassis's casket embellishments.

A female priest read from the *Book of Common Prayer* and gave the eulogy. Bibi, she told us, was philanthropic. She loved her dogs, who were her second children. She had a way with orchids and African violets, and was famous for her porcelain vegetable forms—that eighteenth-century cauliflower! The nineteenth-century asparagus server! I looked around to see if this was registering with any other visitors as oddly impersonal. I saw nods: *Ah, yes. The cabbage tureen! Those wily salt and pepper shakers shaped like artichokes!*

Holden spoke next. "My mother was, as most of you know, smart, stylish, even—some might say—charming. She was politically astute and generous when it came to a few pet charities, emphasis quite literally on 'pet.' She was passionate about this city, about her home and its furnishings and, yes" — he looked toward the priest — "its knickknacks. She liked to travel. She could take a cruise that lasted six months, or so it seemed to me as a child. And what made that all right? Modeling Princess Elizabeth, who left her children behind when visiting her subjects all over the globe. I think you know where I'm going with this: Bibi wasn't the most maternal woman in the world. She had me at forty in the last gasp of a marriage and, as she liked to say, with her last egg." He surveyed the room, eyebrows arched. "Dad? You here? Apparently not," which got a nervous chuckle in the room.

He continued, "If you're doubting Bibi's capacity for great love, just ask any one of the champion French bulldogs who worshipped the ground she walked on. By the way — anyone need a dog?" More nervous chuckles.

I was half-appalled, half-thrilled, wondering if Holden was drunk. The priest seemed frozen. A white-haired man in the front row stood, walked up the altar stairs, met Holden at the rostrum, and said, "If I may."

"Be my guest," said Holden. He flipped through the notes he hadn't yet consulted. "Oh, right. I forgot to say that she graduated from Vassar and was proud of that, though Smith was her first choice." He shrugged. "In her own way, she loved me." He nodded. "Yes, I think that's an accurate statement."

The man now had his arm around Holden's shoulders. He identified himself as the husband of Bibi's younger sister, Mary Jane. "I think our nephew suffered a shock — we all did. Bibi was fine one day. And then the call came from the hospital." He tilted his head toward Holden, a silent acknowledgement of *It's the shock talking.*

Holden softened his unwanted-son expression long enough to say, "Thank you. I'm good now." Meaning: Go back and sit down.

He closed with "I hope I didn't make a fool of myself up here." He started his descent, then darted back to say, "Thanks for coming."

Was that *it* for Bibi's good-bye, two lame eulogies? The mourners were stirring, whispering. The priest read the Twenty-third Psalm and said that the family would form a receiving line in the vestibule. And please don't forget to sign the guest book.

How to escape? Only one of the aisles led to the receiving line. I excused myself across a row, and headed for the front door that was farthest from Holden. I ignored the guest book, but once past it, I stopped, backtracked. I'd come, hadn't I? Politicians attended the funerals of their mortal enemies. Estranged children and long-lost friends turned up after decades of not speaking. I might as well go on record.

I was the first to sign. As I pondered whether I should set an example and write a word or two of condolence, I heard a male voice calling my name.

Holden's. He was gesturing toward the meager line of mourners. "You should be here, too," he shouted.

I pointed to my own breastbone. *Me?*

More motioning. Here. Come *here.*

Does one argue with a man in shock, who pays you alimony, who is alone in a receiving line except for Aunt Mary Jane and Uncle Reg?

I did look the part this day, slightly mournful and dignified in my big black hat and dark glasses. My coat—also black, part cashmere, with mother-of-pearl buttons as big as Ritz crackers—had been purchased by its first owner at Bonwit Teller. As soon as I stood next to Holden, my inner actress came to the fore. "Thank you so much for coming," I said to the mourners. Or "I'm Daphne" with no further designation.

When the last mourner had either embraced me or shaken

my hand, and his baffled aunt and uncle had departed, I said to Holden, "Didn't see that coming."

"Cardiac arrest. No history of heart trouble."

"I didn't mean your mother. I meant your pulling me into the receiving line. Why confuse people? They might think we're back together."

"So? I never see them."

"But—"

"Hardly anyone knows we got divorced."

"Well, this could've been a good time to catch them up, don't you think?"

"No, I don't. I was married and divorced in the space of—what was it—nine, ten months? My mother didn't advertise that, and I don't think she ever forgave either of us."

Instead of pointing out that I was innocent of any wrongdoing except stupidity, I said, "That was some eulogy you delivered. I could've done better and I didn't even like her."

"That's cruel. People know me. And it did get a few laughs, didn't it?"

I said something quasi-kind along the lines of "I'm sure many found your honesty . . . refreshing."

"Maybe I should've talked about the good times. Like a birthday party instead of her abandoning me for six months. Well, not abandoning. I had a nanny. I was no worse for the wear. I probably didn't even notice she was gone."

"It's never easy, even when they're not candidates for mothers of the year."

He must have thought we had entered a confidence-sharing zone because he volunteered, "I'm seeing someone."

"Lucky her."

"She knows what happened between us—you and me. After I

told her, she refused a second date, and a third, because of what it said about me. She thinks I used you."

"I'd like to have been a fly on the wall when you made that confession. Why would you even do that on a first date? Oh, I know — twelve steps? Rehab inspired you."

"Except I never made it to rehab."

The funeral director had entered the vestibule, had collected the guest book, and was standing by in obsequious fashion. "Sir? Are you coming?" he finally asked.

"Do I have to?"

"Have to what?" I asked. "Because I hope it's not the cemetery you're skipping."

"No, the crematorium."

The funeral director said, "Not at all. Most don't."

Holden said, "Okay, thanks. You'll drop off the ashes?"

"Of course."

When the funeral director had bowed his way out of the church, I said, "You forgot to tell him not to bother you; just leave the ashes with your doorman."

"Don't be mean, Daff."

I had been mean. I touched his forearm. "Okay. Finish what you were saying about the girlfriend. Obviously she agreed to give you another chance."

"I'm seeing a shrink. That was one of the conditions to reestablish trust with Julie."

I was tempted to mimic his "reestablish trust" as both psychobabble and a fib, but all I asked was "If everything is so fine with Julie, why wasn't she here today?"

"I told you. I couldn't show up with a new woman by my side when hardly anyone knew about our divorce."

"So they'd find out right here in the receiving line. 'Yup. Single again. Didn't my mother tell you? No, don't feel bad. It was never meant to be. Say hello to Julie.'"

"You know why Mother kept it under wraps? She thought people would talk, might say, 'Like mother, like son.'"

I had to ask, didn't I, before parting; before never crossing paths with him again, "Is everything going to you?"

He looked up from whatever text he was writing. "Are you asking about my mother's will?"

"I am."

"I have no idea. Nor would it be any of your business."

"It's kind of my business, because I didn't know when I signed the scroungy prenup that I'd be out on my ass and living on paltry alimony payments. You do realize that I'm struggling?"

"Like you were when I met you. And that was struggling without an alimony check every month."

"I think a raise is fair, considering your new circumstances. And as Julie pointed out, you used me."

"You really think this is the time and place?"

I looked around with some stagy gaping. "What place? An empty church right after I did you the giant favor of standing next to you and accepting condolences for your mother? I was duped into marriage. And when a woman signs a prenup, she doesn't think, *This is what I'll be living on.*"

"Because you thought this—us—was forever?"

"I certainly didn't expect I'd be out on my ass in a year."

"Correction: You threw me out."

Technically, he was right, but why litigate that now? "I'm assuming you're getting everything—the apartment, the money, the furnishings, the artwork, the ceramics. You need to do some deacquisitioning. I can help, in a way."

"What way?"

"After you liquidate all that, you can give some to me."

He expelled a *Ha* that was pure scorn. "As compensation for coming today?"

"No. Out of fairness and to help clear your conscience. You knew from the get-go that the prenup would be my living wage until I got back on my feet. *I* sure as hell didn't. I signed it under false pretenses." I added, for good measure, "A jury would award me damages for pain and suffering. You're going to be richer than ever while your only ex-wife is living in squalor. We could be the plot of a tragic opera."

"You stand by that—pain and suffering and squalor?"

"I live in an apartment that could fit into"—I gestured around us—"this vestibule, no, two-thirds of it."

"Didn't I buy you that apartment?"

"See? You have no idea what my situation is. No, you did *not* buy me the apartment. I rent."

"I have to talk to my lawyer and the trust attorney—"

"Those tightwads? They'll both say no. And let me say on Julie's behalf—hire someone with a heart to draw up your next prenup."

"That's a leap. I've only known her for a few months. And I'd prefer to leave Julie out of this—"

"Fine. Do you have a check with you?"

"Who would hit up a man at his mother's funeral?"

"Don't change the subject. I didn't know this would come up today. But carpe diem."

That was true. My demand wasn't premeditated. I'd planned nothing more than slipping into a pew and leaving before any condolences needed to be expressed. I seemed to be making progress, though. "I don't see any reason to wait until your mother's assets are distributed. We can end this conversation right now if you promise to put a check in the mail—"

"Jesus! I'm not writing you a check."

I took off my sunglasses to achieve more penetrating eye contact. "Did you want to follow that with a 'but'?"

"But . . . I'll consider a cost-of-living raise."

"I'll need it in writing," I said, pointing to his phone. "Send me an email. Twenty percent raise okay?"

"Don't be absurd. Five percent."

"Don't *you* be absurd."

"Seven and a half percent."

"Ten percent." I dared him to guess what his Scrooge accountant was direct-depositing into my checking account every month, usually late. He didn't know and, to his credit, looked surprised to hear what he was underpaying me. "Eight and a half percent, take it or leave it," he said.

"That is bullshit. I could go public, you living in splendor, me in a garret. I'm going to be telling my story in a podcast soon. Make it ten and you won't have to worry."

"This is blackmail. In church, no less."

"Not that again. How about ten percent till I get a full-time job? That way I get a cushion and you get to tell Julie you're a new man, making amends. Win-win."

"Don't think you're coming back next year asking for another raise. This is a one-off."

"Ten percent?"

"Until a job comes through."

What a good and distant deadline that was going to provide. "Deal," I said.

21

The Reevaluation of Daphne

GENEVA'S PATRON, her wealthy father, once again came through with enough money to get the podcast off the ground against my strenuous but fruitless objections. She proudly announced this on a formal visit to my apartment. Green-lit! She'd found a recording studio on Eighth Avenue willing to do one episode at a time with a real sound guy. She'd direct, and I'd be the first interview — a piece of news she delivered as if I'd be honored.

"Count me out," I said.

I could see she'd come prepared for my lack of cooperation because her follow-up was "Fine. I'll ask your father to kick it off."

"Nice try. Do you even know his name, let alone how to contact him?"

"Tom."

"Tom what?"

"Maritch, like you."

"Well, you're not going to reach him through me."

"I can't?" She raised her eyebrows.

As I was reviewing the possible ways she had of contacting him — Was his number listed? Would she stalk him on Facebook? Would the internet yield his address? — she said, "Your polite father sent me a thank-you note after he came for Thanksgiving. On paper. With a return address."

Of course he would have. "Please don't involve my father. This whole thing could be very painful."

That might not have been the smartest approach. Painful? In a way that made good copy?

"I'm not ruling anyone out. You have to go first. Or do you want it to open with that valedictorian, the one who started the scholarship in honor of your mother? Didn't she write him college recommendations?"

What did she know? Had her offensive questionnaire yielded some link to Armstrong? I had to say okay, I'd let her interview me about the yearbook, the literal, physical one. Don't ask me questions about the people in it or about my mother's comments next to the pictures. Okay? I'd do it as long as she promised not to involve my father or Peter — I caught myself — "what's-his-name, the valedictorian."

So I went to the Eighth Avenue studio, where Geneva was waiting, looking officious, trying to impress me with producerdom. Episode one, she instructed, would supply background; she wanted me to start with a physical description of my mother at her peak. She'd have her photo on the website —

"What picture? What website?"

"Every podcast has a website so listeners can donate. The picture from the yearbook — don't tell me you didn't know they gave her portrait a whole page?"

I reminded her that it had been ages since I'd laid eyes on the damn thing. And what did she mean by donate?

"Money."

"To the scholarship in her name?"

She checked her watch, tapped a pencil on the table between us, and reminded me that she was paying for one hour and didn't want to run over.

A disembodied voice asked if we were ready. He wanted to do

a sound check. Would I say my name and something else? I said flatly, "Daphne Maritch. I'm here against my will."

"Ready," he said. "And don't forget, if you stumble, don't sweat it. Just repeat it. I'll edit it."

Geneva told me that she'd recorded an introduction to the whole thing.

"Which I'd like to hear."

"You will when it's aired." She scribbled on a notepad and slipped it toward me. *The chip on your shoulder — good.*

"Happy to oblige."

Now in interview mode, she asked, "Your mother, June Winter. Can you tell us why this yearbook, this class, these graduates, meant so much to her that she devoted her life to them?"

"That's not true. She devoted her life to her children and then, secondarily, to teaching."

"Is that so?" Geneva asked. "Pardon me for questioning your truthfulness, but what was this *thing* she had for this particular group of students?"

"That's easy. She taught there. And was the yearbook advisor. This one was dedicated to her."

"And how old was she in relation to the graduates?"

I knew this figure by heart but pretended it was nothing I'd had any reason to calculate before this moment. I said, "About five years' difference."

"Older?"

"Yes, of course, older. She was their teacher."

"What else was she to them?"

"*Excuse* me?"

"I think you know what I'm driving at."

"I don't have a clue."

"What else was she to them in a personal sense. Outside school?"

I said, "I wasn't born yet when she was their advisor. I only know that the dedication was a great honor for her."

I wrote on the same scratch pad, *Stop it.*

Of course she had to report that I'd scribbled a note. "What do you want me to stop, Daphne?"

She wanted to play dirty? I said, "You stole this yearbook! I've been trying to get it back for months!"

"I stole it? Or did I find it in the trash?"

"That was my mistake. I recycled it, but as soon as I found out you'd absconded with it, I wanted it back, and don't say 'Finders keepers,' because I don't think that would hold up in court."

Next, Geneva was talking to her audience. "Why would the family be so afraid of it falling into the hands of a producer—"

That provoked me to yell out, "Who calls herself a producer on the basis of one documentary!"

"We'll edit that," she said. "Aaron?"

"Got it," said the voice in my earphones.

I had to sound calm. I had to stay on message, my own.

"Shall we go back to your mother's appearance? Would you be willing to say she was stunning?"

I said, without any affect or feeling, "Okay, she was stunning."

"And young when she started teaching."

"We already covered that."

"What are you afraid of?" Geneva asked psychiatrically.

"Nothing. I'm pissed off. I'm only here so you wouldn't drag my widowed father into this."

Whoops. I shouldn't have brought up my father. Geneva pounced. "Why do you suppose she left the yearbook to you instead of her husband? Were there notes she didn't want him to see? Or some symbols—those checkmarks and dots I haven't yet translated—that were in code?" And then to her imagined future audience: "Totally fascinating."

"Maybe to you it was. To my father, it was just a hobby of my mother's. Like her gardening. And his following the UNH Wildcats."

"Were they happy?" she asked.

A not-utterly-truthful "blissfully" flew out of my mouth. Still, I had to expose Geneva as a woman who couldn't keep her word. "I agreed to be interviewed only if there were no personal questions. And that's a very personal question."

"Bliss-full-y," she echoed. "I see. Do you need water?"

By now, I was feeling such a rush of hatred for Geneva that my voice went squeaky. "You'll live to regret this thing, this stupid soap opera!" And then to anyone listening: "I come from a long line of educators. Before I moved to New York, I was a Montessori teacher! This isn't right. You never met my mother. You can't judge a person by the dots and adjectives she writes in a yearbook!"

To Geneva's credit, she didn't cut my final diatribe. She also left in the sound of my chair hitting the floor as I charged out of the booth. "Are you wondering, like I am, why June Winter Maritch's daughter is so angry?" she mused. Then she repeated her own theory that my mother had a dying wish, unconscious or not, to share the yearbook with the world.

22

I Took It Upon Myself

O F COURSE, I KEPT LISTENING to the episodes, one per week, airing on Sunday nights. Geneva managed to enlist a woman from our fiftieth reunion table. Geneva added sound effects, pages flipping. "Is this you?" she asked. "I see that your yearbook wish for your future says surgical nurse. Did that happen?"

"Let me see that," the woman said. I deduced it was the sharper of the two pep squad members. Barbara? Rosalie? No, Roseanne. Geneva doesn't use her name. "Now, about Miss Winter — do you know what the selection process was for the yearbook being dedicated to her? Was a vote taken? Was it the whole class or maybe just the yearbook staff?"

"I didn't work on the yearbook," said the woman.

"What's your best guess?"

"Why does it mattah?"

"It matters because I'm researching every aspect of this puzzle. Was there a relationship between the yearbook staff, possibly an individual, an editor of the yearbook, and Miss Winter?"

"How the heck would I know?"

Yay, pep squad member, I thought. And what pathetic preinterviewing Geneva had done, if at all.

"Let's move on," I heard. "Miss Winter, now Mrs. Mah-RICH . . ." Did Geneva just pronounce my last name like that, Mah-RICH?

Roseanne doesn't correct her. The question being asked is whether this classmate can decode the dots and checkmarks that appear next to certain graduates' pictures. Geneva added, "These symbols are only next to boys' pictures. Well, they're seventeen and eighteen. I should call them 'men.'"

Next question: "Was there ever gossip swirling around the school about Miss Winter and a student?"

Now I *am* going to sue her. She had no scruples, no journalistic ethics. And my big mouth was entirely to blame.

The know-nothing Roseanne said, "There's always gossip about teachahs. It doesn't mean where there's smoke there's fiah."

"Let's get back to these symbols. I'm noting that different years have different color pens. But why are some of the dots in pencil? In fact, very faint pencil. Possibly a code?"

"You're only showing me a coupla pages. I haven't looked through the whole thing. I nevah saw this before. I mean, I have my own copy, but I nevah saw Miss Wintah's."

"Do you know this young man?" Geneva asked next. "And please remember that we're not naming names."

Of course, she had to be pointing to Peter Armstrong. The woman said, "Sure. He was our valedictorian. Can I say that? Funny he didn't write anything."

"Funny why?"

"Because he was a big shot in the class. And I'm positive he came to the reunions."

"How odd then. Don't you find that odd?"

"The whole thing's odd. Who writes all ovah a yearbook that's not your own? I'm trying to remembah if she had the thing tucked under her ahm when she came to the reunions? If not, she went straight home and wrote this stuff down."

"Look closer. Not next to his picture but above it. Tell me what you see."

"A phone numbah. That was our exchange: ELwood, then five numbahs."

Geneva let that marinate in case the presence of a phone number didn't register as out-and-out adultery. "I can tell you this: No other graduate got a phone number above, below, next to his picture," she continued. "What do you suppose it meant?"

"Why don't you ask him," said Roseanne.

Except for the occasional polite exchange of emails acknowledging receipt of my quarterly checks, I didn't stay in any kind of daughterly touch with Armstrong. Besides my own confusion as to what we were to each other, I wanted to respect my father's Armstrong aversion. But I thought I should warn the former class valedictorian by email that Geneva, who'd big-footed her way to his reunion, would surely be inviting him to appear on her podcast.

"She did say she was going to do something with our class, as I recall," he wrote back.

That was too neutral, too calm. So, without sugarcoating what was surely ahead, I replied, "She's portraying my mother as a floozy who preyed on her male students."

Was that not attention-getting enough? When there was no answer, I wrote again two days later asking if he'd gotten my most recent email, the one containing the word "floozy."

"Received and noted," he answered. "I won't go on the show or whatever it is. Take care, Peter"—a kiss-off I attributed to his busy job, law practice, and my clinically cold correspondence up to now.

Next was episode three, not featuring an unnamed valedictorian, nor classmates of his, nor members of my family, which had been another worry. But the innuendo continued with the introduction of a woman, an alleged substitute teacher at Pickering High School, who claimed to be a workplace bosom buddy of my mother's.

Wait. What was I hearing? What did she just allege? I was scribbling furiously on a notepad, which was how I listened, ready for slander. The bosom buddy had the nerve to say that she and the young June Winter sneaked "off campus" for a sushi lunch—impossible because no one was eating raw fish in Pickering for another few decades. Nor did they chaperone field trips together to the Boston Museum of Science because Pickering High School field trips were always to Canobie Lake Park the last week of school.

And then this: "Every single boy had a crush on June. She was very attractive, and believe me, she used it."

She used it? And every single boy had a crush on her? Talk about hyperbole. Wouldn't I know this alleged bosom buddy?

"But harmless crushes, right?" Geneva asked her.

"How would she know?" I yelled at my phone.

"You'll have to ask those boys," said this anonymous bigmouth. "In those days, we didn't have the rules that are in place now."

"Rules?"

"Pretty basic: no sexual contact between students and teachers, ever."

I texted Geneva furiously: WHO IS THE WOMAN WHO SAYS SHE WAS A SUB @ PHS?

I DON'T DIVULGE MY SOURCES, she wrote back.

Next, I called her, dumped into voice mail. Do I spell out how furious I am or save everything for a courtroom? "It's Daphne; call me" was all I said.

After an irked sleep, I strode to her door in the morning, rapped first with the ineffectual knocker, then with what might be considered a pounding.

"Whahh the hell?" I heard from within.

"It's Daphne. I need to talk to you."

"About what?"

Seriously? "Your horrible podcast! Who's that woman who says she was a sub at the high school?"

"Jesus Christ. I thought someone was going to say the building was on fire. It's gonna have to wait. What time is it?"

It was a few minutes past eight. "It's eight-thirty," I yelled back. "I have a job interview at nine and I might be gone all day."

"What kind of interview takes all day?"

"That's beside the point. I meant this can't wait."

"Hold on. I'm naked. Let me get some clothes on."

A neighbor I'd never seen before, to the right of Geneva's apartment, a skinny tattooed man with earrings up and down his lobes, opened his door shirtless. "People are sleeping, for fuck's sake."

I repeated that it was the wholly decent hour of eight-thirty. "The city's awake. It's full of people rushing off to work."

"Is that so? I go to work at five and get home at three if I'm lucky. And that's three freaking a.m."

"Oh. Sorry. I guess that's why we never met. I'm Daph—" But he'd slammed the door just as a bathrobed Geneva was opening hers. "You never heard of having a conversation by phone?" she asked.

I didn't say that I wanted to see her face-to-face, to catch her in a lie, to read her unprincipled mind. To sucker punch her if words failed me. I said, "You don't answer my calls."

"Is this how you dress for a job interview?"

I said it was at a Montessori school, so dowdy was fine.

"You'd do this full-time? What about your chocolate thing?"

"Don't change the subject. The woman in episode three? Where did you find her?"

She retreated but didn't close the door on me. I followed her into her electric-lime-green kitchen, where she put a pod into a coffee machine without asking me if I'd like a cup.

"That woman who said every boy was in love with my mother? First of all, that's ridiculous. If she and my mom were bosom buddies, I'd know her. Did you check her employment records—"

"What for? The episode has already aired. It's out there in the universe." Geneva's hands made otherworldly circles in the air.

"You don't seem very worried that she might not be who she claimed to be."

"Want a cup? It makes tea, too."

"Who the hell is she?"

Was that a sigh of annoyance over me being me again, resisting and challenging at every turn? Or was it capitulation? "I probably have it in an email, but I don't have time to find it now."

"Why? If you do a search, you'll find it pronto."

"I meant you don't have time to wait for me to do a search. And how do I search when I don't remember her name? Plus, I think she had one of those cute email addresses—like her cat's name. And you have a job interview"—she checked the microwave clock—"in less than an hour. Casual or not, I'd change into something more professional."

"Okay. But I want a name. I think she could be an imposter."

Shouldn't she say something like, "I can assure you that I double-check every source"? But there was no reassurance, no pushback. She merely raised her cup in a half-hearted toast, as if she'd, of course, be complying with my request.

I changed into a skirt and sweater because I actually did have an interview at a Montessori school, an opening created when a pregnant teacher's ob-gyn prescribed bed rest. Even with my new, unearned, male-sourced income, or maybe because of it, I felt that life above the poverty line was suddenly within my grasp.

I wanted a paycheck again; I wanted enough to shop at Whole Foods, to hail the occasional taxi, to save some money, and eat in a restaurant not just when my father was treating. Why had I waited this long? It was time to admit I occasionally missed sitting in a circle with toddlers who wrapped their arms around my legs in wild enthusiasm over not much: *my* little clients dispensing unconditional love; my own little peeing and pooping clients; *my* New Leash on Life.

After the interview I was observed, which in Montessori terms meant pretty much my observing the little bees at work, using, then putting away the tools I knew by heart. I was well practiced in guiding, consulting, hanging back, and speaking calmly. The Manhattan children were better dressed and more racially diverse than the Pickering three- and four-year-olds, but otherwise it was all so familiar. I was told by the head teacher they'd decide soon, surely by the end of the week, but when I returned home, my phone was ringing. I'd been hired. They'd reached my old supervisor in Pickering. My new chocolate-making skills were a bonus — well, not the sugar or the allergens or the double boiler, but knowing my way around a kitchen. Skill building!

I texted Jeremy, who had encouraged me to apply on the basis of my leaving the apartment and getting out in the world.

GREAT NEWS, he texted back. WE NEED TO CELEBRATE. YOU FREE FOR DINNER?

I said yes. His place?

NO, OUT. IN STYLE. ANY PREFERENCE?

Joking, I named the swanky place, impossible to book, where I'd last lunched with my deceased ex-mother-in-law. Adding, JUST KIDDING. ANYWHERE.

He texted me a half hour later. PUBLICIST GOOD FOR SOMETHING. SEE YOU THERE, 7:30.

. . .

The maître d' greeted Jeremy in sycophantic fashion and me not at all. We were led to a table that seemed the opposite of Siberia—in the front of the restaurant by the windows. The place looked different at night, sconces dimmed, votives lit, china gold-rimmed. Jeremy insisted we both order the four-course tasting menu with wine pairings and the Grand Marnier soufflé that required advance notice.

Settled, napkins unfurled and practically tucked in by our waiter, I looked around. I was glad I'd worn my navy blue silk honeymoon dress, the one I'd chosen anticipating venues such as this one in married life. Did those glances from the next table with accompanying titters mean TV's Timmy was being recognized?

"I think those women know you," I whispered.

"You sound surprised."

"I meant . . . I guess . . . I wouldn't expect patrons at a place like this to be *Riverdale* fans."

He rattled his tall, newly minted menu, and said from behind it, "Clearly, you don't understand the demographic. These patrons, unlike some people I know, have an adequate channel lineup."

"I apologize. You are 100 percent correct and I'm a snob." I told him I'd upgraded and had been watching the show and finding him a very convincing Timmy. "Not that you're convincing as a junior in high school. Just that you make Timmy a real person."

He smiled. "Did you notice his pals are calling him Tim now?"

I hadn't. "On purpose? Or is that just what slips out?"

"Some of us think he may be getting a girlfriend."

What was that follow-up? I was quite sure he'd said, "Like in real life." He raised his glass of the champagne that came with course number one, which were frilly greens and a lot of paper-thin raw vegetables. "To the fans," he said, "and their prying eyes." He meant a newly seated party of women, one of whom was wearing a cardboard crown. They were staring in a way that made me rise to the challenge. I leaned over and kissed Jeremy lightly on the lips, as if we were two self-conscious, modest celebrities mindful of smartphone cameras.

Have I mentioned that New York City is a small village? I say this after Jeremy's attention was drawn to an approaching pin-striped stranger whose hair was slicked back like a Trump son's.

"Daphne. How nice to see you," Holden Phillips IV, now tableside, lied. "You're looking well."

Although his mother's funeral had been only a few weeks before, I was startled and unrehearsed. Maybe I was looking well, but was I looking *good?* The truffle oil that was dressing the frisée had surely dissolved my lipstick.

I introduced Holden to Jeremy as the man I was married to for five seconds.

Holden wasn't sure how to react, which gave me more nerve. "Are you here alone?" I asked, then spotted a fiftyish dreadlocked Caucasian woman at a table for two, intently studying this very interaction. "Is that Julie?"

"No! I'm here with one of my new partners. Did you hear about the buyout?"

"No. Why would I?"

Jeremy was wearing as neutral an expression as an innocent bystander caught between enemy exes could.

"But still with Julie?" I asked Holden.

"Since I saw you, like, a week ago? Of course we're still together."

"I forgot to ask if you were dating her while we were married?"

Was I showing off in front of Jeremy? And did Holden really have to take the high road by ignoring my rude question?

"I was just trying to do the decent thing, coming over here," he answered, then nodded with unnecessary dignity before leaving.

"Well, well," said Jeremy when the coast was clear. "So that's Holdy."

"I can't believe he was here!"

"Isn't this his mother's favorite restaurant?"

Oh, that.

Jeremy was shaking his head in a way I hoped wasn't the re-evaluation of Daphne — from sexually compatible neighbor to mean girl.

I knew a cooler conversationalist would move on, but I couldn't resist asking, "Is he back at the table? And can you tell if he's whispering about how rude I was?"

Jeremy glanced over and back. "They're laughing at something —"

"Laughing like one of them made a joke or laughing like *My ex-wife is here. Do you believe my bad luck?*"

"Hard to tell."

I knew such blathering didn't show me at my best. Thus, I didn't voice my twin worry: that the first time I ran into Holden socially I'd just kissed a man young enough to wear braces. And on the back of my chair, in case I felt a chill, was a sweater that had been a gift from the coconspirator I used to call my mother-in-law.

23

Hit Play Again

MPOSTER?" JEREMY ASKED. "Is that what you're think-ing?" We were back in his apartment, in bed, listening to *The Yearbook*—an inevitability after my obsessing over dinner about episode three.

"I knew all my mother's faculty buddies," I said for the second or third or hundredth time. "They came to dinner. They slept at our house after a bad breakup. I babysat their kids."

"And you don't think it's possible that your mother had a close friend on the down low? Before you were in high school or after you graduated?"

I was forced to admit that, yes, okay, my mother surely had lots of secrets and, yes, this woman might have been a confidante.

After listening hard, diagnostically, eyes narrowed, he asked, "The woman's voice . . . is that a New Hampshire accent?"

"No, but she could've come from somewhere else."

"She sounds . . . modulated."

"I noticed that, too. But toward the end, you'll hear her say that she taught public speaking and drama."

With that, he went from looking merely thoughtful to forensic.

"What?" I prompted.

"I'm remembering something she asked me."

"Geneva?"

"It's probably nothing . . ."

"Out with it," I said.

"Okay. We passed in the hall . . . maybe a month ago? Then she called, 'You're an actor, right?'"

I waited.

"Her follow-up question was did I have any actor friends who might want a gig — not for scale. Off the books. I said no —"

"Did you ask for what?"

"I must've, because she said it was for those wedding videos she makes, her sideline — sometimes she needs voice-overs."

"And that sounded right?"

"I was in a hurry. I just said no, sorry. Everyone I know is either Screen Actors Guild or Equity. In other words, 'I'm not going to help you stiff my friends.'"

"A voice-over in a wedding video? Whoever heard of that?" I reached for my phone. "I'm calling her!"

"Hold on. You think she'll tell you the truth? Or even answer her phone?"

"So I do nothing and let her get away with it?"

"She won't. Besides, is anyone even listening?"

"I'll tell you who's listening! Every single person in Pickering, New Hampshire, who knows what a podcast is! This is a really juicy scandal by their standards. New Hampshire isn't big on adultery. They went blue last election because they didn't like Donald Trump grabbing anyone's pussy! Are you too young to remember *Peyton Place*? Because that was set in New Hampshire!"

"Really? That's where this took you? To Donald Trump?"

"And *Peyton Place,* which is not irrelevant! Some idiot is going to call my father, and say, 'Wow, Tom. I guess Pickering High School is the new Peyton Place.'"

"I think you have to chill over this. It's one person, an actress saying, 'All the boys had crushes on June Maritch.' Hardly what you'd call a scandal."

"One person? This could be the rest of the podcast — all fiction, all actors playing BFFs."

"Wait. Just because she asked if I knew any cheap actors doesn't mean it was for the podcast."

"Yes, it does! Boom! It explains why I didn't know this dame and why Geneva wouldn't give me her name or her email."

"How many episodes have you listened to?"

"All three."

Jeremy touched the screen of his iPad, which took him to *The Yearbook* feed. "No, there's a new one. It was posted yesterday."

"Play it," I said.

He tilted the screen away from me, gave something a quick read, then said, "I'd skip this one."

"Is the imposter back? Or worse?"

"What would be worse?"

I hadn't actually given this any thought, but it was easy enough to answer. "Some actress pretending to be my sister. Or — wait, no — Armstrong!"

Was Jeremy looking even unhappier? "Why did I tell you?" he groaned.

It was easy enough, with a quick grab, to see what he was looking at. Episode four was titled "The Men in Her Life." I said, "Tell me it's not my father."

He said, "It's not your father."

I waited until I was in my own bed, which Jeremy recommended so he wouldn't have to witness my meltdown. After having taken a homeopathic tranquilizer, I opened my podcast app. First there was music, the same song that opened every episode so far, Elvis crooning, "Are You Lonesome Tonight?" — surely its rights not paid for. Next there was Geneva saying that *The Yearbook* was brought to you by Gal Friday Films, memorializing "your weddings and commitment ceremonies so sensitively that you'll cry every time you watch them."

Then a male voice, seemingly borrowed from the introduction of every audiobook I'd ever listened to, intoned, "Actor Robert Jaffe will be speaking the lines of the graduate we're calling John Doe."

I waited before panicking, since half the graduating class were males. It could be the funeral director or class president Duddy McKean or the guy at our table who served on the food committee.

But then there was the introduction. Geneva claimed that the following conversation was a reenactment of an interview with a prominent member of Pickering High School's Class of 1968. The actor was reading from a transcript, we were told. Geneva would play herself, asking the questions.

Could I bear it? I decided to listen first, get worked up second if warranted.

"Yes, I graduated in 1968 from Pickering High School. Yes, I knew Mrs. Maritch, who was Miss Winter when she was our yearbook advisor." Geneva interjects, speaking to an alleged audience, "You'll note I started with baseline yes-or-no questions, like the warm-ups in a lie detector test."

But then this one: "Several sources have confirmed that you and Miss Winter had a personal relationship. Could you comment on that?"

Well, of course, the publicly respectable member of the New Hampshire bar I knew would never answer that question, would never have agreed to sit down with Geneva. But this faker said, "When you work on a yearbook, especially as the deadline ap-

proaches, you're there all hours. And sometimes, when the cus-
todial staff knocks on the door, and says, 'You have to wrap it up.
I'm locking up the school,' then you move to someone's house."

"Whose house?"

The actor read aloud what must have been a bracketed stage
direction. "Long pause." Then reluctantly, "Miss Winter's. Her
apartment."

Apartment! What apartment? More evidence of this as a put-
up job.

Next, Geneva asked if anything physical had taken place between student and teacher on that visit.

"That visit? No."

"But that wasn't the last time you and Miss Winter met privately at her apartment, was it?"

"Inaudible," read the actor.

"Mr. Doe? It wasn't the last time was it?" Geneva the prosecu-
tor repeated.

The actor emitted a guilty no.

"How old was Miss Winter at this time?"

"Young."

"Were you in love with her?"

"I was. I still am."

Okay. This was now officially and blatantly false. *Still in love
with her?*

"You didn't even go to her funeral," I yelled at my phone, then
reminded myself that this was not — nor had it ever been — the actual Peter Armstrong.

"How long did the physical relationship last?"

"Just till graduation. I went off to college and she got married."

"Today, you realize, even in New Hampshire . . . this would not
only have gotten Miss Winter fired but also prosecuted and no
doubt jailed?"

Insult to injury: *even in New Hampshire?* That backwater where we chew tobacco and intermarry?

"I was eighteen," he said. "Maybe she'd be fired, but she wouldn't have gone to jail."

Okay, this was complete garbage. But what nerve! What unmitigated gall to make up a story about a real, named person even if not named. Peter Armstrong would never have admitted to an affair, nor would he have agreed to talk to the obnoxious woman he was barely civil to at the reunion.

I texted Jeremy. I'M GOING TO KILL HER.

My phone rang. "No, you're not. You're going to let nature take its course."

"What does that mean?"

"Someone such as myself will give her a no-star rating and write under comments, 'This is total bullshit.'"

"I'm trying to think of the best way to tell John Doe Armstrong that Geneva the sociopath has made up a story about him and my mother having sex in the yearbook office."

"Made up? Isn't it the truth that he and your mother —"

"Later! He was already a lawyer, remember? It was thirty-one years and nine months ago! The school crush never got acted on. I mean, in its own way, it's almost honorable. Well, no, it's horrible because my mother was married to my father when it happened."

He asked if I wanted to come over. Though I had never turned down that invitation, I did tonight. I said I'd be railing nonstop. "I mean, who was next? My father?"

Jeremy didn't answer, which was entirely uncharacteristic. I found out soon enough that it was delicacy that made him go silent because when I hit play, the fakester after John Doe was indeed Tom Maritch, cuckolded husband, referred to on this sickening project not by name but by "Husband."

I called Jeremy back. "My father! You should've warned me! How can I sleep now? I want her to end up in jail for ... human trafficking! Wouldn't that fit in some bizarre way?"

"You need to be a little zen about this," he said.

How? And, for God's sake, why? Even my scalp and hair follicles felt overheated. Could blood actually boil? Is wanting to bankrupt, sue, and murder Geneva zenlike enough?

24

It's Nothing

I WAS NEVER SOMEONE to let things go, and I wasn't going to start now. Besides being furious and impatient, I was worried that word would have gotten around Pickering. What if some bigmouth wrote to my father with misguided congratulations about how his late wife's yearbook had made the big time?

I gnashed my teeth for a few days as I watched the little ones at their tasks — polishing silver, pouring water from vessel to vessel, folding mats, raking sand, cutting, serving. Which path to take? Didn't I value what I tried to teach daily, to have my students think critically, work collaboratively, and act boldly?

I emailed Cousin Julian after he hadn't taken an earlier phone call. Could he send a letter asking Geneva Wisenkorn, producer and director of a podcast lame-named *The Yearbook*, which was filled with falsehoods, to cease, desist, and retract?

Attorney Cousin Julian wrote back somewhat formally, reminding me that he was a tax lawyer and didn't practice the various kinds of law that my branch of the family often needed. It wasn't very cousinly; between the lines, I thought I was reading *Note that the pro bono work I do is for the indigent and underserved who need help with tax preparation.*

Had Geneva picked up some vitriolic vibe emanating through my front door, inspiring her to knock one evening? No, it was not sensitivity or emotional intelligence that made her come calling. Her visit was inspired by a casual, fair answer by Jeremy when she'd asked him in the elevator one morning if he'd seen me lately — off-base again as to what Jeremy and I constituted — and if I still lived in the building.

"I said of course you were still living here and that you'd gotten that teaching job."

"Did she ask anything about how I liked the podcast — as in 'Is Daphne consulting a lawyer?'"

"Nope. I wasn't going there." He then asked if I'd listened to the entire alleged-dad interview.

"I couldn't."

"Maybe you should."

That caused a new shrinkage to the heart and stomach. I asked why; what was left?

"Because it's so ridiculous that it's nothing. I mean it's terrible writing. Oh, and you'll love this — I'm positive that the guy who played John Doe also played your dad."

Did that count? Hadn't she announced at the beginning that an actor would be portraying the men?

I had to ask, despite my revulsion, "What did she have the fake husband say?"

"Here's the part you'll love — the deal breaker: He talks about his three daughters."

"Three?" I repeated. "You're sure?"

"Three daughters," said Jeremy. "It's over. Good-bye, crappy podcast. Farewell, Gal Friday Films and heartbreaking wedding videos."

"How do you know that? When I tell her there's no Samantha, no such third sister, she'll say 'So what? It's art. It's the way Hollywood takes a real life and does whatever it wants with it! They make it up! And win Academy Awards!' She'll be proud of it. She's impossible to humiliate."

I called my sister — finally the time difference was on my side. Holly hadn't known about the podcast but promised to get off the phone and find all four episodes. I said, "This has become my personal nightmare, so if you're going to yell at me, please don't."

I waited in bed. I tried to read. On my new TV, I watched an episode of *Law & Order* I'd seen at least once before. When the phone rang, I'd dozed off. It was Holly, the logical, dry-eyed younger sister who'd done one year of law school before switching to motherhood. "I'm on it," she said.

"You're on the podcast? Where? I didn't hear —"

"No, I meant I'm going to fix this."

"How?"

"I'm suing on behalf of the family. Doug and I will take that on. He listened to the podcast with me. I can't believe you didn't tell me about this before!"

Too much *Law & Order* maybe, because what I was hearing, her "We'll take care of it," had a hit-man flavor to it. I said that sounded ominous.

"Don't be ridiculous! I meant we'd hire and pay for a lawyer. And we know someone who won a libel case against the *National Enquirer.*"

"*Is* this thing libel? Because she'll call it an adaptation. A work of fiction. Poetic license."

"He'll send a letter, that's it, and believe me, she'll recognize his name. It'll threaten that we're going to sue her for a couple of million if she doesn't cease and desist. Doug?" she called. "You have the lawyer's cell, right?"

Doug apparently said yes, he'd call him early tomorrow.

"But the damage is done. It's been up for weeks. No lawyer can turn back the clock. Plus, it'll only generate publicity *for* the podcast."

"But someone in this family has to show some muscle."

I pointed out that I'd been showing plenty of muscle. "I never cooperated with her. I never told her one word about Mom or Dad or the class of 1968 —"

"You may not have told her things about Mom and Dad, but you effectively put the stupid yearbook in her hands. And I know from her blog—"

"Blog?" I coughed out.

"You didn't know she had a companion blog to the podcast? She announces it at the end of every episode."

I could've hung up and found the blog myself, but I didn't have the stomach to read one word of it. "Does it mention me?"

"She said you took her to a reunion and you introduced her all around to members of the class, which was her way in."

"Oh, shit."

"You didn't take her to Pickering?" Holly asked. "Did she make that all up? Because there were several selfies of her with mom's ex-students. Maybe she photoshopped them."

"I did go. She dragged me." I couldn't confess that at that point, in the earliest planning stages, after she'd thrown around the executive producer title but before I'd come face-to-face with Peter Armstrong, I might've considered myself to have been . . . on board.

Holly asked, "You don't think there's a chance that Dad really did have a third daughter with someone else? Is it possible that Geneva hired a private detective and found someone for real?"

I began uttering no, no, no as soon as I heard "third daughter." At least that much I could take credit for, the big fib about Samantha the imaginary sister.

"One more thing," Holly said. "Dad needs to know. Should I tell him or will you?"

Just like that: *Dad needs to know*. I stuttered, "I can't. You do it. No, let me. No . . . he's the last person I can discuss this with . . . It might do terrible damage to our relationship. He'll withdraw. He might never speak to me again."

She didn't jump in to say anything to dispel that fear. It could have been a distraction at her end or the favorite-daughter contest — that she could live with my father's alienation of affection as long as it was directed toward me.

"I'm sure that could never happen," she finally said. "By the way, Doug and I thought the episodes stunk."

And then, as easy as you please: "You know who I heard from?"

"Who?"

"Remember Sheila McDonough? She babysat us a few times and lived over on Sullivan Terrace? We're friends on Facebook. She heard the podcast and wanted to say hey."

"And you're telling me this . . . why?"

"No, just an update. She's living in Mendocino, and her house is an Airbnb."

Okay, now I'd officially lost faith in anything my sister and her husband advised, friends or not with a famously badass lawyer. I thanked her for listening to the episodes and wanting to help. Now I had lots to think about. "Don't do anything until we talk again, okay?" I said.

I hung up. I'd sleep on it. Maybe tomorrow I'd figure out how to tell our dad that his dirty laundry was being aired. Or maybe I'd punt. Must I announce to a man who didn't even own earbuds that an obnoxious podcast was awaiting his subscription?

25

Miss Daphne

THANKS TO THE UNWAVERING TENETS of Maria Montessori, the towns of Pickering, New Hampshire, and New York, New York, were never so closely aligned — with their natural-wood furniture, their white and beigeness, their floor mats, their strict order and placement of every learning material for every life activity. And I was Miss Daphne again, advising, supporting, facilitating without overhelping.

Montessori had started to wear on me in Pickering, and Manhattan earnestness soon reminded me why. On my third day, a little boy was turning four. Would it be the same ritual we observed in New Hampshire? Indeed: His parents had packed, in lieu of any confection, pear slices with tofu brie. The birthday boy, Beckett, selected a helper, Finn, who asked each child sitting in the circle whether he or she wanted the alleged treat. If yes, Finn gave the child a plate, just the plate. Then Beckett followed, placing his pears and "cheese" on each waiting vessel. After snacking, we sang "Walk Around the Sun" while a teacher named Miss Inez lit a candle representing the sun. Then Beckett picked up a miniature earth and walked around the candle one time for each of his four years. Science! Astronomy! Self-esteem! I found it tedious and a little creepy, which made me wonder how many birthday observations I could endure.

My dad was too pleased to hear about the job. "I knew it," he crowed. "You were bored. That chocolate thing — where was that going? Not that you weren't talented in that arena, but you always seemed to love your teaching job back home. In fact, I always thought it was a little rash — moving to Manhattan without asking for a transfer."

"It doesn't work that way. It's not like I worked for Proctor & Gamble and wanted to move from Cincinnati to New York. Besides, I needed a break from the family business. New York was me rebelling."

He laughed at "rebelling," and I let him. I confessed that when Holden's friends had asked me what I did, and I said, "Montessori teacher," it stopped the conversation cold. None had children. Their expressions seemed to say, *How quaint, how minimum wage.* That was when I stopped applying for teaching jobs and embraced stay-at-home bride.

Over the phone, Dad's relief and enthusiasm were rendering him tone-deaf. "This is what I call progress, hon, even if you think it's not a step forward. You went into teaching because you loved it, not because it's what your mother and I devoted our lives to. I'm like you — I hate being idle. I'm not sitting around watching cable. I'm walking dogs! I get to be these little creatures' favorite human for forty-five minutes. Sometimes I wonder if their own parents are kind enough or attentive enough. It's extremely satisfying."

I said, "I know one doggy parent you don't worry about being kind enough."

I expected him to chuckle or convey the verbal equivalent of a blush. "You mean Kathi?" he asked without the affectionate tone I was expecting.

"Is something wrong?"

"I'm not sure."

"You're still seeing her?"

"Of course I am. I walk Sammi five days a week."

"That's not what I meant. No more coffees or sherries or dates?"

"That hasn't happened in a while."

I asked exactly how long a "while" meant.

"For the past week. Something's not working."

Uh-oh. I hope he didn't mean you-know-what. I pretended it didn't. "Then *ask* her what's wrong. You're not shy. I saw how she looks at you. It's hard to believe she's cooled off."

"Maybe she realizes that a younger man would be more suitable," he said.

Do nothing, say nothing, let my father sound defeated and unloved or get to the bottom of it? I emailed Kathi, asking if she'd like to meet me for a late-afternoon coffee. She didn't answer for a whole day. Finally, an email reply said, "Late afternoon is tricky. Let me check with your dad to see if I can switch Sammi's walk earlier in the day. Back soon."

I wrote back quickly, "Actually, I wanted to talk to you about my dad, so can we keep this between ourselves?"

My cell phone rang instantly. "What about your dad?" Kathi asked. "Is he okay?"

"He's fine. It's just that when I spoke with him last night . . . he sounded a little down. He thinks something's amiss between the two of you."

When she didn't jump right in to contradict that, *I* became the worried one. "Is it true?" I asked.

There was a call-waiting click on her phone, and I almost said, *Don't take that! Answer me first!* at the same time thinking like a jealous lover, *It's him. The competition. The interloper. The younger man!*

"Sorry," she said, back with me. "Habitat for Humanity — well, this is awkward. Your dad thinks I'm upset about something, but I'm not."

"So he's just imagining things have cooled off?"

"I'll be blunt," said Kathi. "I know what's bothering him, why he thinks I wouldn't want to be with him . . ."

But nothing followed that. Was she waiting for a prompt? I said, "He mentioned the age difference. Is that what's bothering him?"

"It's related to that . . . I think he's embarrassed and avoiding *me*. Not the other way around."

Later, I realized I shouldn't have asked reflexively, "Embarrassed about what?"

"It's personal" — pronounced in a whisper that automatically translated "personal" to "sexual." Which is when this soft-spoken, never-married — virginal, for all I knew — teacher of piano studies whispered, "ED. Could you talk to him?"

Now it was unmistakable: She was talking about my father's penis. I said, "He thinks you're backing away. Talk to him! And tell him either you don't care or there are pills to take!"

I heard a meek "I know I should've."

"And don't tell him that you discussed this with me!"

"Can I tell him you wrote me? Because I'm really touched that you reached out —"

"No! Because he'll figure out that you confided in me and that's why you're speaking up."

"Then I won't," said Kathi.

I'd regained my equilibrium enough to say, "He was married for a long time. It's probably scary to be with a brand-new woman. Not that you're scary. No, just the opposite. And who knows, as a widower, he might be feeling guilty on some level, like he's breaking his marriage vows."

"Oh, God. I hope it's not that."

I was already sorry for saying such a thing. I asked when she'd be seeing him again.

"Tomorrow. When he picks Sammi up and brings her back."

"Which is what time?"

"Between four and four-thirty."

"Will he have other dogs with him?"

"No. He does Sammi solo."

"And you're alone then, no student there? Not teaching?"

"I don't teach on Fridays."

"Okay. Here's what you do: Make the place dark. Light some candles. Greet him in something slinky. Do you have anything slinky?"

There was a longish pause. I could hear soles clicking on the hardwood floor, then the squeak of a drawer being opened. "I have slips," she said.

"Close enough. Do you see where I'm going with this?"

"I do. But I don't want to give him performance anxiety."

"It's not about that. It's to say, 'There's other stuff. Closeness. Warmth. Affection'..."

"You don't think I have to tell him first, about not caring what happens once we get...you know?"

Newly anointed sex therapist Miss Daphne said, "This isn't necessarily leading to bed. This is your making a gesture that says, *I want to be with you. I'm not backing away.*"

"This is good," she said. "I'm not sure, though, about the slip. Won't that be a weird way to answer the door?"

"Okay — then how's this. Pretend you just got out of the shower. How about a bathrobe? Do you have one that's not quilted or a big terry-cloth job?"

"I do somewhere. A kimono. I hardly ever use it."

"Okay, so the doorbell rings, you buzz him in, the big cargo elevator doors open, my dad sees the room is dark, candles lit, and you're in a silk bathrobe. PS: nothing underneath it. And remember: You never talked to me."

"I'll try my best," Kathi said.

A good day's work straight out of Maria Montessori's book: Provide a nurturing environment to teach social interaction and emotional skills. I knew it by heart: Education is not a chore but a joyous exploration of life's mysteries.

Pretty close, except for the founding principle that children teach themselves.

26

Nine-One-One

B Y NOW, I KNEW Geneva's slothful schedule: She slept late, made no appointments before noon, ran no errands because she had everything under the sun delivered. It was a Monday holiday, no school for me. She was home for sure because the delivery man from the Turkish restaurant had mistakenly knocked on my door with her order.

I'd sent him off in the right direction and given her just enough time to eat that bag of food, then made it my business to knock on the door, prepared to—what? Negotiate? Threaten? Throw myself on her mercy?

There was no answer. I knocked some more. She was home and clearly avoiding me.

After another bang, I put my ear to the door. This time I did hear something, a muffled noise. Was she in the bathroom? I yelled, "It's Daphne. I need to talk to you."

A noise came back, and I swear it was a "Help!"

"Are you all right?" I yelled back. I tried the doorknob. Locked. More *helps* from within, louder. "Can you let me in?" No, of course not. Why even ask! Now I was scared in the way of a daughter whose mother had collapsed from an aneurism and had been found by her walking buddy after not showing up at their appointed time and corner. I yelled that I was getting someone to open the door for me — the super, a doorman, anyone! I'd be right back.

I ran for the elevator, then realized, *No, faster to call him.* I patted my pocket. Oh, shit. Nothing! I ran back to my place, got my phone, yelled into it that Geneva Wisenkorn in 11-J couldn't come to the door, maybe an accident, maybe — who knows! — shot, stabbed, being held hostage.

"Calm down," said the super, whom none of us liked.

"Please get up here with a key!"

"I'm on my way," he said wearily.

"Fast! She could be bleeding to death. Or having a heart attack."

He did come, and brought his wife, name now forgotten, who explained as he tried various wrong keys, "He brings me when it might be a woman who fell getting outta the tub — like the way a doctor has a nurse in the room when he examines your privates."

Finally, the right key and the click of the lock. "Okay. You're in now," he said.

"I'm not going in alone! What if she's dead? What if those two guys who escaped from prison upstate are in there?"

"Oh, sure. With doormen around the clock? That makes a lotta sense."

"Geneva?" I was yelling, now inside the foyer, down the hallway, past the bathroom, toward the wounded-animal noises. And there she was, splayed on the bedroom floor, blood on the carpet and dripping down her forehead. She was fully dressed, caftan over flowing pants, barefoot, toenails painted a startling emerald green. The super asked her, "What happened? Did you break something?"

"My head, you idiot! Look at me. And my arm is killing me."

"Did you fall?" asked the super's wife.

"I don't know. I must have."

"You must've?" the super's wife repeated. "How does someone not know if she fell?"

"Sometimes you just fall! I hit my head on the corner of the goddamn bureau. I need stitches!" She explored her head and screamed at the sight of the blood that came back on her fingertips.

I said, "I'm calling 911. Can you get up?"

"Would I be flat on my ass if I could get up?"

"What if we each took you by the arm —"

"I broke it! Or some part of it!"

"You're not supposed to move an injured person," said the super's wife. "You could do something to the spine and she'd be paralyzed for life."

I said that settled it: I'm calling 911 and getting a facecloth. I'd be right back. Not to worry. Everything would be fine. Head wounds bleed a lot. You probably won't even need stitches.

"Want us to stay?" the super asked when I returned.

"Oh, is your lunch getting cold?"

"No need for sarcasm," said his wife. "It's not like we can do anything."

Geneva's eyes were fixed on me, and maybe I was projecting, but they seemed to be asking, *Why did SHE have to find me? I'm in the hands of the enemy.*

"Did someone do this to you?" asked the wife. "Like a boyfriend?"

"Jesus! I fell! I passed out and fell, or I fell and got knocked out."

What to do but wait for the ambulance, stroke her arm, issue reassurances, convey that I would do no harm.

"I'm going with you in the ambulance," I told Geneva. "Oh, wait ... your handbag. You'll need that." And to the super, "Stay with her while I look."

"What do you need her pocketbook for?" asked the wife, immediately identifying herself to me as someone who couldn't be trusted with another person's purse.

"Her insurance! Her keys! Her wallet! Her phone! Did you think I was going to help myself to some cash?"

"Just do it already," said her husband.

"Do you know CPR?" I asked them. "Just in case?"

Geneva was now swearing in a way that wasn't pain-filled, but in indignation over our discussing an imminent downhill slide. I said, "No, no, you're going to be fine. I don't know why I asked that. I'm sure the emergency room doc will just write a prescription and you'll be on your feet as soon as I can fill it. I'll be right back. Do you have insurance cards in your pocketbook? And your keys?"

"I don't know where the hell my phone is. The kitchen? My study? Just get it."

Her shoes were next to the bed, one of them under her torso. I freed it gingerly and handed the pair to the super's wife. "Here, put these on her." And repeated to Geneva, "I'm not going anywhere, I promise. In the meantime, you guys listen for an ambulance" — which in this city was as logical as saying, "You guys listen for a horn to honk."

It would reflect quite badly on me to admit exactly when the opportunism arose, but it could have been as early as hearing the first cry for help. But hadn't I done the right thing? Answered her distress call? Got the door open? Called 911? As promised, I ran out to the hall, and I did flag down the attendants as soon as they stepped off the elevator. But between leaving her side and climbing into the ambulance for the thankfully short ride to Mount Sinai, I'd had time to enter her study, rummage through her desk, find the yearbook, and repossess it.

27

Who Are You Again?

BORROWING HER THUMB, I unlocked her phone, called all the numbers listed under Wisenkorn despite her protests from the stretcher. I figured out the one named Myron was her father and the "Mom" listing was her mother, whose 802 area code suggested she lived too far away to be of help.

I was relegated to the waiting room because I'd flunked the sister test — apparently a ruse used by every friend posing as next of kin. I said, "Okay, we do have different last names. I'm just her half sister. I'm the product of her mother's second marriage. Doesn't that count?"

"Her emergency contact is Myron Wisenkorn."

I asked how they knew that.

"It's on the computer. She's been here before."

"We'll tell you as much as we can," said the desk each time I inquired.

I also called Jeremy, who promised to get to the ER as soon as possible. I said no, not necessary, just an FYI. She'd be released after she was stitched up or x-rayed or whatever was taking so long.

After I left three messages for her father, he finally called back. And, after battling the Long Island Expressway, arrived two hours later. He was just what the situation needed, a take-charge guy, maybe seventy, tanned in winter, camel coat over high-end dad jeans, used to yelling and demanding the best doctors that money could buy.

"Who are you again?" he asked, finally taking a seat next to me.

"Just a neighbor. I live on her hallway."

"You found her?"

"I did. I'd come over to talk to her —"

"About what?"

Yes, that kind of guy, illuminating in a bad way, deficient in manners when talking to a nobody. I continued, "I knocked on the door and she didn't answer. Then I heard 'Help!'"

"So you went in?"

What he implied with that, judging by the accusatory tone, was that I had trespassed. I said, "Are you familiar with the term Good Samaritan? Because I probably saved your daughter's life. I did *not* go in. I didn't have a key. I called the super. He opened the door and I rushed" — I put a Florence Nightingale spin on *rushed* — "to the back bedroom where she was lying prostrate on the floor in a pool of her own blood."

Despite my protest that he did not have to meet me, Jeremy arrived, in makeup, in the middle of Mr. Wisenkorn's cross-examination, which he paused only to bark, "Who's this one?"

"Another neighbor," I said.

"Named?"

"Jeremy Wynn."

He didn't seem to approve of that, either.

I said, "I'm sensing you think we had an ulterior motive. It's very insulting. By the way, where's your husband? Why isn't he with you in a family emergency?"

Was I suggesting that he couldn't be such a tough guy if he'd married a man and might be a tad more human and gentler than the heterosexual asshole he was portraying? No. My point was that I wasn't some stranger who'd helped myself to a crisis, but that I knew Geneva well enough to have chatted about her father's same-sex wedding.

"What did you have to discuss with her?" he asked.

I went right to the war Geneva and I were waging. "Her podcast, *The Yearbook.*"

"What about it?"

"She stole that yearbook, which belonged to my mother."

Apparently, one did not use the verb "stole" in the same sentence as a family member of Myron Wisenkorn's. Without asking me to explain, his whole demeanor changed from merely grouchy to bellicose. "You'd better watch what you say, young lady. You keep that up, and —"

"You'll what?" asked Jeremy, now on his feet, looking none too scary. "Because if you use that tone with her, I'll call security over here and tell them you just threatened my girlfriend."

"Calm down! I didn't threaten anyone. I'm trying to find out what's wrong with my kid and I've got this one here telling me about some goddamn program I don't watch."

Finally, a nurse or aide or someone with a stethoscope wrapped TV doctor–style around her neck came toward us. "Mr. Wisenkorn?"

"What?"

"I can bring you in to see your daughter."

Jeremy and I sat there, me trying to look absorbed in the medical emergency while thinking what I'd do once Geneva discovered my heist. Maybe we should slip away right now while the coast was clear. "I took back the yearbook. She doesn't know," I whispered.

"How? When?"

"She was lying on the floor, and the super was watching her, making sure she didn't die. I ducked into her study and stole it — right off her desk! Whoosh!"

"Where is it now?"

I gave his arm a nudge with my elbow. "I had to run into my apartment for my coat and bag, didn't I, before jumping into the ambulance?"

He smiled.

"I know. She'll kill me."

Whatever his reaction was, it had to wait because her father was walking back toward us. We reset our expressions to Good Samaritan. I asked, "Good news?"

He seemed to have acquired some manners, perhaps due to relief. "They stitched her up here" — tapping his own scalp — "keeping her for an EKG. Also, they're x-raying her elbow. So thanks. You can go. How about if I get you an Uber?"

I said yes he could, that would be very nice.

Jeremy asked if they were keeping her overnight.

"Doubt it. They don't keep anyone overnight anymore. I had a cabbage and I stayed for one night! Jesus! You'd think they'd want the business!"

"Cabbage?" Jeremy repeated.

"Coronary bypass surgery," Wisenkorn said. "Which, by the way, I came through like a man of forty. That's what they told me."

"Did you get to talk to her?" I asked.

"About what?"

Could the man *not* answer the most logical question? "About what happened to her — whether she fainted and hit her head or slipped and knocked herself out on the way down?"

"I don't know if I'm supposed to tell you," he said.

"It's safe with us," I said.

"Okay, but this is as far as I can go: It's a condition she doesn't like to talk about."

I said, "As her neighbors, we should know in case this happens again. I think we would be, like, a safety net —"

"Daphne's a teacher. She knows first aid," said Jeremy.

Mr. Wisenkorn seemed to be weighing caretaking versus the wrath of Geneva. He sat down again. "Okay. She has a condition. We used to call them petit mal seizures. She'd just go blank, stop in her tracks, once in a while lose consciousness. It's why we never let her get her driver's license. Now they call them" — he fished out a small square of paper and opened it — "absence seizures. Whatever."

"So this has happened before?" I asked, earning me a lecture on Geneva's productive, healthy, accomplishment-filled lifestyle. "She's making a film right now," he said. "Working day and night. About a yearbook."

Jeremy and I went silent. I refrained from saying, *Oh, really, like I didn't tell you fifteen minutes ago that I was dragged kicking and screaming into a stupid podcast titled* The Yearbook?

Jeremy took over, asking in born-yesterday fashion, "A film? Did she tell you anything more about it?"

I felt this was my cue to add, "Jeremy is an actor. When he hears 'film' his ears perk right up."

I could see Jeremy weighing his options: either go along with Daphne's riff on film or set the record straight. He said, "A slight correction: Your daughter's project may've started out as a documentary in her mind, but that went nowhere so she started a podcast —"

"And you're producing it!" I said.

"I am? *Me?* I'm the producer?"

"It just means you bankrolled it."

"I thought 'podcast' meant 'documentary,' but what the hell do I care? She asks me to fund her projects and I usually say yes."

"Even without asking for the details or who it might hurt —" I started to rant.

"Uber? Now would be good," Jeremy said.

Mr. Wisenkorn took out his phone, tapped to unlock it, and handed it to Jeremy. "Here. You do it. Andrew calls them for me."

"Andrew's your husband?" I asked.

His yes was delivered warily, as if unsure of my sympathies.

"Good for you," I said. "Belated congratulations."

Jeremy said, "All set . . . We have Zahid a block away."

I asked Mr. Wisenkorn when he thought Geneva would be released. *Would be back in her apartment, discovering the larceny.*

"Now. Today. But she's coming home with me for a day or two at least."

"Which is where?"

"Woodmere."

"Will you be stopping by the apartment for her things?" I asked.

Fortunately, that sounded to her father like another caring gesture, an offer to gather and pack what Geneva might need during her Long Island convalescence.

"Thanks, but she keeps stuff at our place."

He surprised me with a hug and a thank-you that finally, apologetically, had some warmth to it.

We ran out the door to Tenth Avenue. Zahid was already there, double-parked and asking "Mr. Myron?" We said yes, close enough. I wondered aloud on the short ride back to our building what would happen when Geneva discovered that the yearbook was missing.

"Why? You didn't take it." He smiled. "She probably misplaced it. It's hard to keep track of things after a whack on the head, right?"

"You're saying I'll deny it?"

"Sure. *She* would. And when she keeps accusing you, you tell her to come over and search your apartment. Ransack it. See what she finds, which will be diddly-squat."

"Because I've burned it?"

"No. Because it'll be at my place, where she's never set foot and never will."

I kept watching for signs of her return, bracing for the pounding on my door, demanding the return of her property. I wasn't the world's most skilled liar, so I practiced in the mirror, assuming a look of, by turns, surprise, then shock, then umbrage at being accused of theft. After three days, I asked two different doormen if Ms. Wisenkorn had returned. Each said no with an unconvincing shrug.

I woke up on day four to an email from her sent at 1:05 a.m. the previous night. "Still on Long Island. My dad told me you and Jason (?) stayed in the ER for a couple of hours. Thank you for helping me after my stupid fall. I'd have been able to get up myself except for what I did to my elbow. I'm getting work done here so not rushing back. G."

Thus I knew: not back yet so still in the dark. Nor was she admitting that a seizure caused the accident. Her father must have nagged her to write and thank me for my life-saving help. What a brat. Would it have killed her to mention that she might still be lying in a pool of blood if I hadn't fortuitously come by that very hour to knock her block off?

28

Happy Hour

NOW THIS, SAD TO SAY: Neither Jeremy nor I expected permanency as a couple, and I regret suggesting otherwise. Even though he'd rushed to my side at Mount Sinai five days earlier, even though the words "girlfriend" and "boyfriend" had been used, when does that ever advance to a commitment when one of them is male and under thirty and gets fan mail? Shouldn't I have seen that we were merely sexual placeholders in a city filled with eligibles? Other people come along. Perhaps one of them is named Tina and she is too young to have worried aloud about creeping infertility and the quality of her eggs, which were already beginning to deteriorate.

Jeremy didn't take up with Tina in a sneaky way. What he wanted to discuss with me in a dark corner of a bar on Ninth Avenue, ironically during happy hour, was that he was thinking about seeing other people. "I still want to be friends," he told me. "I know that's a cliché, but I mean it. I'll still be across the hall. We can still have martinis and we're still partners in crime, right?"

I asked which crime, thinking he might mean off-the-record sex.

"Geneva related. She's not going away anytime soon."

"And that's your problem how?"

"I didn't say 'problem.' I meant — and please don't take this the wrong way — that you can get worked up in a way that isn't totally productive."

"So you'd be the steady hand making sure I don't go off the rails? How charitable of you."

"It's not charity. I'm invested in this."

Invested? What kind of left-brained thing was that to say in the middle of a breakup? Borrowing a scene from my own marriage's unraveling, I asked, "Who is she?"

"Who is who?"

"The woman you'd like to go out with."

That's when he told me he hadn't acted on it yet. Well, there *was* someone who'd asked *him* out, but he wasn't going to accept the invitation before talking to me.

"What kind of invitation?"

He made the face that any theatergoer would have made, which was helpless, innocent incredulity. "Two orchestra seats to *Hamilton*," he said.

"And she's asking a total stranger?"

"Not exactly a total stranger."

"Let me guess: She's a fan."

"No."

"Another actor?"

"No, she doesn't watch the show. Which I like —"

"Do you? Hooking up with someone who's not steeped in popular culture."

"I meant that it makes her overture not, you know —"

"Star fucking?"

"She wouldn't even know what that means. She's an adjunct professor."

I must have repeated the "adjunct" with something like disdain because Jeremy asked, "Something against adjunct professors?"

Besides the obvious, her interest in you? I said, "'Adjunct' means she pops in once or twice a week to teach one class and borrows someone else's desk for her office hours. What's her field?"

"Sustainability."

I gave that a good smirk, though I didn't know what that field was. "How does an adjunct professor afford tickets to *Hamilton*?" I asked.

"She didn't say."

"How'd you meet this millionaire?"

"Why'd you say that?"

"Do you know how much those seats cost? Like a thousand bucks apiece."

I knew this wasn't going as he'd expected. I tried a somewhat more neutral "How'd you two meet?"

"Daff—what does that matter?"

Only my beloved nonbiological father was allowed to call me Daff from now on. "Tell me it wasn't through online dating."

"Since when am I online dating?"

"You mean why you, the famous star of the small screen?"

He was doing some agitated shredding of his napkin instead of answering. What a brat I'd suddenly become. "Everyone does," I continued. "Maybe your membership was up for renewal and you thought, *I'll see what's out there.*"

"You know I've never done online dating."

"I knew no such thing. You could've been swiping right and left next to me in bed." I added "naked" for extra weight.

"Wow . . . Daff . . . I didn't expect this."

I repeated, "How'd you meet her?"

"She lives in the building."

"Which building?"

"Ours. She keeps her bike in the rack in the basement."

"Well, that's convenient," I said. *"Again."*

When he looked puzzled, I said, "Like us. Geographically compatible. Only now you might have to take the elevator to have sex. What floor is she on?"

"Two. But—"

"So you ran into her one day and you welcomed her to the building—"

"Like I know who lives here and who's new? No. She had a flat tire and she'd seen me leaving with my bike, so she gave the door-man a note asking if I knew of a local place where she could have her tire patched."

"Patched," I said. "How touching."

"You're mad. I'm sorry. Nothing's happened yet."

Why *was* I mad? Hadn't I been using him to forget my humili-ating marriage and build a case for my being a woman with big-city sexual mores?

So I made a weak effort to pivot, to show how coolly this cos-mopolitan woman, me, could conduct herself. I said, "Let's start this conversation over. You want to see other people. So do I. This doesn't have to be awkward. Certainly not between us. And you know what? Even if I see you and Tina together, I'll be civil. And from now on, when I ask if I can borrow a cup of sugar, it'll mean an actual cup of sugar, not code. I'll have my panties on."

When that didn't evoke anything but a pained expression, I asked, "Does she know about me?"

"Not specifics—"

"Not anything?" I prompted. "Not my name?"

"Just that I was involved with someone."

"When's the show?"

"Saturday."

"Matinee?"

"Nope. Evening."

"Well, good for you."

"I mean it—I want us to stay friends."

What was that proverb? Good fences make good neighbors? If it had been wise to apply that to Jeremy and me, shouldn't the same go for Tina? I said, "I think it's best if you gave me back the yearbook."

"Not a good idea. It shouldn't be in your apartment. Geneva's crazy enough to hire some guys to turn your place upside down. Like the opening of *The Big Lebowski*, where these thugs ransack—"

I said I'd never seen that. But, okay, keep it. Just be sure to notify me if you're moving.

That earned another disappointed, possibly hurt, look. I knew how I was sounding, but I couldn't stop myself. And though the waiter had already slipped the check between us, I said I'd have another glass of the pinot.

I didn't speak until the refill arrived. "Okay if I hate you now?"

He slipped the check to his side of the table. "You don't mean that."

"I want to," I said.

29

I Thought I Knew Everything

OF COURSE IT WOULD be now that my father suggested a double date. I accepted, opting for mañana to tell him that Jeremy couldn't make it — this night or any other.

I asked if he'd like to come for dinner.

"You mean at your place?"

"Sure."

I waited for a delighted acceptance. Instead, I heard a wary "Would that have to be on tray tables?"

I said no worries! I'd found a table on Craigslist. We'd christen it.

"Can Kathi come, too?" he asked.

I said, "Of course she's invited. This will be my chance to get to know her better," hoping to imply that she and I had never had a conversation about his erectile dysfunction. I added, "I guess that thing you were worried about, her cooling off, was just a misunderstanding."

Because we were speaking by phone, I couldn't see what I hoped was relief on his face or, still better, his blushing over where Kathi's entreaties had led. He said, preceded by a *heh-heh*, "Your old man hasn't had much experience in the dating world, don't forget. Kathi is definitely on board. I don't know what you said, but it must've helped her express her feelings."

Oh, God: busted as sexual therapist. I said, "She didn't need any coaxing. She hadn't realized that maybe there was a way to reassure you that her feelings were as strong as ever."

On my end of the phone, I was making tortured faces that only a discussion of one's father's love life could induce.

"Is Saturday good for you?" he asked.

I said yes. I was free. Quite. Seven? Seven-thirty?

"You know your old dad. Six?"

"Perfect," I said.

Now I could reassure Holly, who'd been calling more than usual, that in exactly five days I'd be seeing Dad, and under the right circumstances, I might confess that the Geneva thing had metastasized into a podcast featuring an actor pretending to be him.

I reached her in her car, in traffic, on her Bluetooth. She told me that she and Doug had talked to their friend, the famous attorney. Unfortunately, it wouldn't be a slam dunk.

"Which means what?"

"The intellectual property part. The slander or libel part. The invasion of privacy. Not much to go on."

"Did you tell him the producer made up stories and had actors pretending to be" — I almost said, "Peter Armstrong," but caught myself — "students and friends of Mom's and Dad's without a warning label saying, 'The following story is bullshit. I totally made it up.'"

Then, gravely, Holly asked, "*Did* she?"

"Did she what?"

"Make it all up."

"Yes! You know she did. She has no scruples!"

"Having no scruples isn't actionable."

"I didn't have a year of law school like you did. I guess I thought

ethics might count when it comes to ruining a dead woman's rep-
utation."

Whatever show tune she'd been playing stopped. "Maybe
there's more to Mom's story than you realize."

"Like what?"

"It's not my place to tell you."

Another power play. Holly had the goods and I never would. So
I took the plunge, trying to sound world-weary and in the loop.
"Are you talking about Mom's affair?"

There was a most satisfying gasp at the other end. "You *knew?*
When did you find out?"

"I've always known. I sensed it. Call it intuition. I didn't need
anyone to spell it out for me." *Only the perpetrator himself, shock-
ing me to the core at the Knights of Columbus Hall.*

"You couldn't always have known! I only found out the night
before my wedding."

Wait. *What?*

"Mom told me. Well, not in so many words. She came to my
room and sat on the edge of the bed. You know what a goody-
goody she was. I thought it was going to be the honeymoon
talk. So I said, 'Ma. C'mon. You think Doug and I have never
done it?' She looked puzzled, so I said, 'This isn't about what to
expect on my wedding night?' She actually laughed. And it was
like—I don't know how to describe it—like there was this sophisticated woman sitting on my bed laughing at how clueless I
was. About *her.*"

"Go on," I whispered.

"This was after the rehearsal dinner, so she'd had a few drinks.
She said, 'Don't make the same mistakes I made.' I said, 'What
mistakes?' She said, 'There are temptations around every corner.
It's not worth the immediate gratification.'"

"Mom actually said 'immediate gratification'?"

"Maybe not, but something like that—maybe 'not worth the thrill.' Plus, she was in her party clothes, looking flashier than usual. Do you remember that dress? It was a navy blue taffeta or something that rustled—"

"Holly! What else did she say?"

"That Dad was a wonderful man."

"Meaning?"

"Meaning he didn't cheat on *her.* Or that she loved him even if she fooled around."

"Or that she was sorry?"

"To me, it meant, 'Your father isn't capable of such a thing, but *I* am.' Quite a thing to lay on your daughter the night before her wedding!"

"Did you ask her why she was telling you this?"

"No! I was so mad! I was getting married in, like, twenty hours. I needed my beauty sleep, and I get socked with that."

And now I was the one being socked with new examples of my mother's bad judgment, bad timing, unnecessary unburdening, and infidelity. "Did you ever ask her why?"

"Why she cheated or why she was confessing?"

"Both."

"I tried the next morning, just the two of us in the breakfast nook. I said, 'The stuff you told me last night—about temptation, about staying faithful to Doug—what were you really saying?' She just cocked her head like she didn't know what I was talking about. I said, 'Don't give me that look. You more or less told me you cheated on Dad. I need to know if your lover is going to be at my wedding.' She said, 'No, of course not.'"

And now Holly's voice was all chummy. "But I have a theory." She stopped there.

"Can I hear it?"

"You ready?"

I was, on one hand, entirely ready because I knew the answer, yet not ready because my sister would be guessing Peter Armstrong, so obvious from the podcast, and I'd have to confirm, deny, or plead ignorant.

But what I heard was "Lyman Roundtree."

I repeated the name, laughing.

"Hear me out: the North American Scrabble Championship in Springfield? They drove there together."

"So? They were colleagues." Lyman Roundtree was a guidance counselor at Pickering High notable for the odd reason that he wore only brown suits, shoes, and ties, and had a very amateurish toupee. "What led you to that conclusion?"

"A letter I inherited."

"Mom specifically left you a letter from Lyman Roundtree?"

"In a way. It was with her stuff—"

"What stuff?"

"Her photo albums. Her grading books. Cards and letters she kept."

"We went through her stuff together. Why didn't I see it?"

"I didn't know what I had till I got everything home. You signed off on the albums because you thought it would be nice for my girls to have them. The rest looked like nothing."

That was true. I remembered that gesture of mine, meant to seem aunty and altruistic, but it had more to do with the limited storage space in my apartment. "When did you find it?"

"What does that matter? At some point, when I was back home, I went through everything."

"And you found a letter from Mr. Roundtree?"

"No. From his wife."

"Saying what?"

"Saying, very angrily, leave him alone."

"Holly, don't you remember that his wife was crazy? She was in and out of a mental hospital. She thought every woman who ever talked to her husband was in love with him."

"Why'd Mom keep the letter if the woman was crazy?"

"As evidence. It could be exhibit A in a court case if Mrs. Roundtree ever got sprung from the state hospital and came after Mom."

"I think there's something to it. I think he could've been the man Mom had an affair with."

"That's the best you can do — Lyman Roundtree? I'm almost offended on Mom's behalf."

"I think the whole idea of Mom's cheating on Dad horrifies you. You don't want to go near it."

Hmmm. How to play this? I decided to plead guilty to protecting my innocent mother's virtue. I said, "I think you're right. I'm bending over backward to keep her memory . . . pure."

"The podcast sure wants us to think she fooled around with some students. Do you also want to leave that unexplored?"

I said yes; to what end, what good, would it serve otherwise?

"Because if it's true, Mom and Lyman Roundtree, it explains why she was fired."

"She was never fired! She was teaching the whole time I was at Pickering High."

"The union got it fixed. I can't believe you didn't know this."

That again, the favorite/better-daughter competition. I couldn't admit that I'd missed something so major, so I said, "It's a little fuzzy, but now I remember Mom and Dad whispering about something job related." I followed up that lie by asking who had fired her. Surely not Principal Maritch.

"The school board *tried* to fire her. In executive session."

"You're quite the authority on all things Mom."

Her answer was a nonresponsive, overly breezy "I have another theory: Peter Armstrong."

Uh-oh. "What makes you say that?"

"Dad getting arrested in his office? C'mon. Dad was angry at something. Does he live in Concord or still in Pickering?"

"I don't know. Why?"

"I'd like to talk to him."

"Why? What possible good would that do anyone? And who's going to admit to a daughter that he fooled around with her mother? *If* he's the one."

"I'd be fact-checking. I don't want to get sued for reporting something that never happened—"

"Report to whom? What are you talking about?"

"It's public knowledge now, Daff. Our mother's love life has been turned into a podcast. Which reminds me: Weren't you going to overnight the yearbook to me?"

I told her no, never. I had enough trouble getting it back into my possession. It was in a secure location, locked up.

"I'll need it eventually. There's a lot of research still to be done, and I want the original source."

Had I not caught on yet? "To give to Doug's lawyer friend?"

"No! For my project!"

After additional backs and forths, purposely vague on Holly's part, increasingly agitated on mine, I finally got a concrete answer: My sister, who'd dropped out of law school specifically so she'd never have to pick up a pen again, thought she'd witnessed enough dysfunction and scandal to write a memoir.

30

Further Confusion

I'D SENT JEREMY a purely informational email announcing a dinner at which I'd be telling my dad everything, laying my soul bare.

Jeremy called immediately even though it was 10:55 p.m. "I think I should be there," he said.

"Do you mean now?"

"No, the dinner."

"Why?"

"Can't it just be for moral support?"

"A little late for that," I said.

"Unfair and off topic. Deets, please, the when and the where."

"My place, six o'clock, but —"

"I can do six."

"On a Saturday? You don't have tickets to a sold-out Broadway hit?"

"C'mon, Daff."

"C'mon what?"

"You still sound pissed."

I didn't say, *You're right, I'm beyond pissed. How could you do this to us? What a bumpkin, what a romantic fool, thinking that fate and real estate were the things we'd be toasting at . . . Oh, never mind.* What I did say was "Why should I be? I always knew our thing came with an expiration date." Before he could answer, I pivoted to the dinner he wouldn't be attending, asking, "Do you think I'll need to play episodes of *The Yearbook* for my dad or just kinda outline them?"

"*That's* your dinner party, playing the podcast? Without some kind of warning? You can't just have a nice dinner?"

"No. Because if I don't tell him, my sister will. She thinks it's better if he gets a heads-up before the *Concord Monitor* and *Union Leader* call him for comment."

"I'd be good at the warning part, as a neutral observer. I could signal: green light or red, play or don't play."

Why this persistence? I said, "I don't need to add more awkwardness to what could already be the worst dinner party I ever throw."

"Me, you mean? I'm the extra dose of awkward?"

"You know why? Because no father's in a big hurry to meet his daughter's ex–fuck buddy."

There was silence at the other end. Do I wait or do I hang up? He settled that with an overly dignified response, gallant in the extreme but cold. "I'll be sure to tell him I regret nothing except this."

"Which is what?"

"The end of a friendship."

"Not my fault."

More uncharacteristic nothingness. Finally: "Well, good luck with your dinner party. I'm sure it'll be great; I'm sure your dad will really appreciate knowing about the podcast. And here's an idea: Invite Geneva. That'd make for a lively evening."

He really *had* gone to the other side. I said, "I won't dignify that with a response. For the record, I haven't seen her since our vigil — you remember that, right? How you rushed from the set to keep me company in the emergency room in another lifetime?

She must still be at her father's. Maybe she died and they buried her on Long Island."

Jeremy said, at last a note of charity detectable, "That doesn't sound like the Daphne I know."

"People change. And then they throw parties and don't invite you. And next time they run into you, they give you back your key."

"I don't need —"

"And I want the yearbook, too."

I didn't actually care where that poisonous book was being housed, but what else did I have to repossess that would sound as finito? "Have I made this very clear: The dinner party will be fine. If you were there, I'd have to explain that we're no longer seeing each other as . . . whatever we were."

"Lovers," said Jeremy before the line went dead.

Why did he have to use that word and pronounce it so solemnly?

On Saturday at exactly six, the doorman called to say that my guests had arrived and were on their way up. I opened my door to find three faces smiling at me.

"We just bumped into each other," announced Jeremy, standing between my father and Kathi.

"Like when?"

"Just now," said my dad. "He was leaving his apartment as we got off the elevator."

"I bet."

"Now, now," said Jeremy. "Don't be like that."

"Jeremy thought I'd need his help tonight, but I said it wasn't necessary," I explained.

"I hope you'll let *me* help," said Kathi.

My lovestruck father added, "Nobody clears a table like this lady!"

I said, "Thank you, but I didn't mean that kind of help."

I was effectively blocking their entry, which prompted my father to ask if they had the right night. "Of course, of course. Come in! Sorry."

"Daphne's position is that I'm crashing the party," said Jeremy.

What half-decent hostess wouldn't lie, and say, "Not true." I collected their coats and invited everyone to take a seat. They were dressed up, my dad in a suit and bow tie, Kathi in a short black dress, lacy stockings, and ropey pearls, unlike my jeans and a wrinkled shirt. "Cosmopolitans, anyone? Dad? A Manhattan?"

"Or a martini," piped up my uninvited guest.

"And, of course, I have this terrific" — I checked the label of the bottle Kathi had brought — "gewürztraminer. Which will be perfect with the chicken."

"Something does smell great," Jeremy said.

"Drunken thighs. I hope I made enough."

"Don't worry. I'm not staying," he said with a stagy pout.

When everyone had a filled glass, Kathi lifted hers. and said, "So nice to be together, and to meet you, Jeremy." Because he was checking his phone, I punished him by saying surely he had plans, this being Saturday night, with Tina the part-time professor who lived downstairs.

Kathi said, "Oh, that must be nice, having a girlfriend in the building."

This much was clear: She had no idea that Jeremy and I had been an item, which made sense. My father, ever protective, hadn't wanted to explain that I was having fun of a horizontal nature, no strings, with the nearest male.

Jeremy said, "'Girlfriend' might be an overstatement. We've hung out a couple of times, but that's really it."

I said, "I wouldn't call orchestra seats to *Hamilton* 'hanging out.'"

The *Hamilton* reference threw Kathi ecstatically off course. We then heard how she'd seen it at the Public Theater before it went to Broadway. No one could believe she'd been that lucky. Just try to get a ticket now!

"Did you love it?" Jeremy asked.

Back and forth that conversation went — about how everyone had been bummed when Lin-Manuel Miranda left and when the actors playing Aaron Burr and King George III did, too... etcetera.

Kathi asked when he and — was it Tina? — were seeing the show.

"We already did. A couple of weeks ago."

"Are we meeting her, too?" Kathi asked.

I sent my father a look that asked, *Why so clueless?* Jeremy stepped in with exactly the right subject changers. "Thanks, but Tina's away — her mother's not well, unfortunately — and I've got lines to learn."

Empathy plus an acting career. What's not to love about those two lumps of conversational sugar? Ever gracious, Kathi asked, in the correct order, "Is her mother seriously ill?" followed by "Lines? Are you in a play?"

Jeremy smiled, which I interpreted to mean *It's almost too easy.* Then, gravely, he said, "It's cancer. But the prognosis is good."

I said, "Jeremy plays a teenager in *Archie and Veronica Go to High School.*"

Jeremy said, "Aka *Riverdale.*"

How had I not noticed that his braces were gone? I tapped my own front teeth. "All done with that?"

"Yup, all done, because Timmy couldn't go off to college with braces on."

"'Off to college' as in 'off the show'?"

"No. Still on. Luckily, he got into the college right in *Riverdale*. Many of us will be enrolled there."

"Would that be Riverdale U by any chance?" I asked.

"Good guess," he said.

Next, Kathi was telling us that she once gave lessons to an actor playing a pianist — not really *playing* the piano because the music was dubbed, but she worked with him to make his hands move believably over the keyboard.

My father said, "It's another thing I love about New York! Movies, television, actors, and celebrities in your midst. Filming things right on the street!"

"Tell them about Cleopatra," said Kathi.

My dad said, "Cleopatra belongs to an opera singer, a real one. She's been an understudy at the Met."

"Cleopatra has?"

"No, Cleo's her dog, an Afghan hound."

I reminded Jeremy that my father was a professional dog walker.

Jeremy said, "I always thought a Manhattan dog walker would make a great character in a movie."

"You write movies?" Kathi asked.

"So far just screenplays that go nowhere."

How did I not know that? Months of pillow talk, yet he'd never told me he had screenwriting dreams? No wonder we were ... nothing.

"I'm going to start watching your show," said Kathi.

I stood up. "I have to check the rice," I lied.

Before I'd taken two steps toward the kitchen, Jeremy asked, "Daff — before I don't stay for dinner — did you want to tell your dad about that thing we discussed?"

No, I did *not*.

"The podcast?" he prompted.

And with only that, my father asked, "From the gal who put it together. Jennifer? I had coffee with her last month."

"Geneva," I nearly stuttered.

"Right — the woman who had us for Thanksgiving dinner."

Did I bravely explore this revelation further? Ask the when/ where/how of it? No, I excused myself, pleading rice again.

I heard Jeremy say, "I'll see if Daphne needs any help," and in seconds, he was next to me at the stove.

"You okay?" he asked.

"I'm in shock. How long has he known about the podcast! I'm afraid of what I'll find out next."

"Look, he came tonight. He seems happy. Wouldn't you have heard immediately if he never wanted to talk to you again?" Jeremy switched off the burner under the tea kettle I didn't need. "C'mon. This was why you invited him over, right? To tell all?"

"But in my own words: 'Dad, there's this podcast out there that puts your wife and your marriage in a terrible light.'"

"If you want me to, I could say there's a Nielsen rating for podcasts, and — trust me — this one's a stinker."

"I thought you had to go learn some lines."

"I do. All six of them. Leave this."

I poured another shot of vodka into the pitcher of cosmos and refilled my glass. I returned to my guests, sat down, and said, as calmly as I could, "So what was your coffee with Geneva about?"

"That thing she's doing — the radio show."

The distress must have been registering on my face and possibly excreting from my pores because Kathi asked what was wrong. I said, "He's so calm! I was scared to tell him about it. I thought he'd be furious and I'd get blamed because I let the stupid yearbook fall into her hands!"

"Furious?" my dad repeated. "Why?"

"It's about . . . people. Alleged people. From Pickering . . . friends of Mom's."

"I know all that. She told me that she had hired actors to play the roles of people a small-town teacher *might* have known. She explained that it was an adaptation. That's what Hollywood does: They take someone's life and they turn it into a musical, or put in a car chase, or set it in space."

"And didn't she tell you it was a comedy, hon?" Kathi asked him.

I could utter only a faint "Comedy?"

But the look I was getting from Jeremy was plainly *Leave it alone.*

"I listened to it for him," Kathi said.

"Apparently, it takes a special thing on a phone that I don't have," my father said. "A map."

"App," said Kathi. She shot me the same cautionary and conspiratorial look Jeremy had dispensed, adding, "As you know, you need the right phone, and it's *very* hard to install. Then the episodes get erased once you listen. Gone for good."

"So they are," said Jeremy.

It was clear: Kathi had screened the episodes and reported back something like *That podcast has nothing to do with you. You'd be bored stiff.*

Was this morally right? Did someone need to tell him the truth, and would that truth teller have to be me? Or had this been put to rest? Could I report to Holly, *Mission accomplished*? *Dad already knows about the podcast, period, case closed. By the way, never, ever discuss it with him. And if you ever write a memoir, I'll kill you.*

I told Jeremy I had enough chicken if he wanted to stay. But he was checking his phone again, which made me say, "Never mind. Obviously, you can't."

"Can I take a rain check?"

"Sure. Whenever."

He grinned, flashing a newly liberated smile. "Will there be drunken thighs again?"

Why was he acting this way? I said, "I'm not promising anything."

31

Judge and Jury

EVENTUALLY, GENEVA RETURNED to discover that *The Monadnockian* was missing. Prime and only suspect: me. She called, ranted, and threatened. I said, "I don't know what you're talking about."

"The yearbook's gone! It was in my study! I know you stole it!"

"What would I want with the yearbook at this point? The damage is done. I don't even know what *you'd* want with it at this point."

"I'm not done! I haven't even scratched the surface of the documentary. You have twenty-four hours to return it."

"How can I return something I don't have?"

"I'll get a search warrant!"

"You do that. I'm sure judges give search warrants to private citizens who think they lost someone else's high school yearbook."

"You think you're so clever? I'm calling the police as soon as I hang up."

"Good. Call 911. And you know what they'll say? 'Ma'am, really? You're missing a book? Are you sure you didn't return it to the library?'"

That took the wind out of her hysterical sails. "You still there?" I asked. "Did you take your meds today?"

"I'm fine!" she yelled. "I don't need meds!"

"Keep looking. It's probably somewhere logical in the apartment, like the clothes hamper or the refrigerator. You did have a bad knock on the head."

"I have other ways of making trouble for you," she warned.

She did, and soon I found out exactly how. As reported by my most loyal doorman, she complained about me — the professionally jealous me; the evil, criminal, and spiteful me — to everyone she encountered. The topic must have done double duty — yearbook talk was podcast talk; one missing item could be interpreted as an assault on all documentarians and artists. She worked it and worked it.

Finally, she must have found an interested party.

When the school director called, asking me to meet with her the following day before the children arrived, I had no reason to connect the summons to Geneva.

"May I ask about what?"

"A rather serious matter," she'd said.

I spent the rest of the day doing what I hadn't done since I'd started teaching: catching up on my chocolate curriculum. I covered "Bean Sources," "Time and Temperature," and "Chocolate Culture in New York City." The kitchen hiatus seemed to have done me some good because the tempering and the molding and even the flavoring was a success. I knew this because, by bedtime, I'd eaten every morsel.

We spoke privately in the director's office, which was decorated with photos of parents studying Dr. Montessori's *The Discovery of the Child* and *The Absorbent Mind*. Her hands were folded on her blotter, and her expression was bordering on the tragic. She told me that she'd received some distressing news from a parent.

My stomach and heart lurched. "Which child?" I whispered. "What happened?"

"Child? No. It's not about a child. The parent raised a rather serious concern about *you*."

"What concern? What parent?"

That earned a prim, silent rebuke, at war with her happy-lumpy papier-mâché necklace.

What she did share with me was that the unnamed parent had reported that a Daphne Maritch had stolen some valuable property from a competitor's apartment. He and his husband were not comfortable, to put it mildly, with her teaching their child. In other words, either I go or they withdraw their gifted, full-tuition son.

All I could do was sputter an inarticulate string of syllables expressing outrage and denial.

"Are you saying this is a false accusation or mistaken identity?" the director asked.

"Both! And what do they think I stole?"

"A valuable book that was — I'd have to consult my notes — one of a kind and irreplaceable. Inscribed throughout. And the source material for many media projects."

What hope did I have from a woman who'd never been a particularly sympathetic boss? I told her I wanted to talk to these accusers face to face! Like the U.S. Constitution guarantees, I improvised.

"Out of the question. I promised them my utter discretion." The director consulted a peach-colored index card. "You do live on West Fifty-fourth Street, apartment 11-D, down the hall from the apartment of the aggrieved party?"

With all the dignity I could muster, I said, "The book in question belonged to *me*; actually, it belonged to my mother who bequeathed it to me in her last will and testament."

That managed to evoke something that looked like uncertainty, so I embellished it with "In a handwritten codicil."

She checked her notes again. "What about this part, that the book is the basis of a movie script and other media?"

"First of all, there's no movie. And by the way, this source material? It's a friggin' yearbook, like fifty years old."

"Then . . . I don't understand."

"Because whoever told you this is misinformed. How can you steal what already belongs to you? *I'm* the aggrieved party."

"Daphne. I can hardly let this go. What would you do in my shoes if parents came to you with a serious charge against a teacher? They also said the police had been called—"

"I'd have heard if the police were called. More like the police were *dialed.* If anyone did the stealing, it was this crazy woman who—"

"Do you realize that if you're arrested it would make the papers, and every article would identify you as a teacher at Belvedere Montessori? I shudder to think of the consequences."

"Well, there was never anything to make the papers. And do you really think I'm capable of a felony—if you can even call the repossessing of a book that belonged to you in the first place a felony?"

"That's your story: You repossessed the book?"

"Yes, because it's not a story! The book belonged to me! And just in case you're thinking *breaking and entering,* you should know I was able to return the book to my own possession because I was inside her apartment saving the alleged owner's life!"

"Motive and opportunity," said my director, as if I'd uttered the exact inculpatory thing she was hoping to hear.

What else did I have to shake her up with but "I'm guessing these snitches were Logan's fathers?"

No affirmation or denial. What I next heard was "I'm sure you can appreciate that I have no other choice."

I never liked this woman or this job. But still I said, "What about 'innocent until proven guilty'?"

"It's all about the children. If there's even a scintilla of truth —"

"I'll sue those parents for defamation. And Belvedere Montessori for wrongful termination!"

Judge and jury was shaking her head emphatically. "You misunderstand. Danielle is coming back from maternity leave. You were hired on a temporary basis to fill in for her during her confinement. She returns on Monday."

"Since when? When you offered me the job, you hinted that Danielle might take a maternity leave that lasted until she had the next kid!"

"Then you misunderstood."

Perhaps, in the interest of keeping my job, I should've listened respectfully, maintained my innocence, and asked for another chance. I didn't. I stood up and stated with utmost dignity, "Well, fuck you, then."

Who to call for commiseration? My dad? No. He already had enough to worry about in the Daphne department. Jeremy? Another no. We maintained that we were still friends, but that was only our going through the motions of civility due to geography. Attorney Cousin Julian? No, once again. Neither unfair termination nor defamation was his kind of law. There was only one avenue, one person, one target: Geneva Wisenkorn, bane of my existence, source of all misery in my life — not counting my ex-husband, my ex-boyfriend, Tina the interloper, my sister the memoirist, Peter Armstrong the statutory seducer, Maria Montessori, and my own self.

I still had Jeremy's key. I found the yearbook nearly in plain view — if you'd call the top drawer of his bureau plain view. I took it, thoughtfully leaving a note explaining that I'd been fired and needed the yearbook for reasons I'd explain if our paths ever crossed again.

I Googled the service required and found a place right on Tenth Avenue. The pages of *The Monadnockian* were easy to rip out of their fifty-year-old binding. Without ceremony or regret, I shredded them, a handful at a time, and collected the fragments in a clear plastic bag. Even reduced to shreds, slivers of eyes, noses, ears, teeth, lips, bangs, pearls, headbands, bow ties, signatures, and ambitions made their source recognizable. My first thought was to leave the remains outside Geneva's door, silently demanding, *You wanted your precious stolen yearbook back? Well, here it is.*

But it was mine to keep, and its destruction had given me solace after the morning's indignity. Hadn't this caused me nothing but trouble for months? So, like a good kidnapper, I photographed the bulging bag propped between its two covers lest there be any doubt as to its identity. I texted the photo to Geneva, unaccompanied by words. I did, however, put some time into choosing emoji, and settled on three: a scissors, the scales of justice, and a middle finger.

32

No Turning Back

WHILE SHREDDING AND STRESSING, I'd forgotten that I'd left a note for Jeremy announcing the end of my Montessori journey. He called, and we went over the conversation I'd had with my director, culminating in her big lie that the job had never been anything but temporary.

"Is it true?" he asked.

"No! She'd said Danielle might be coming back, but it was with a verbal wink, as in 'Her maternity leave is open-ended.' The truth is that I was fired for being a burglar."

That required me to backtrack to Geneva's bigmouthing my alleged crime all over the Upper West Side until her slander reached the unforgiving ears of two Belvedere parents.

"Can you pretty much reconstruct the conversation?" Jeremy asked.

"I just did."

"No. I mean in writing."

I told him I had a whole document on my laptop titled "Yearbook Stuff." But if he was thinking it could be ammo in a lawsuit, forget it. I had no case since I happened to be guilty of that which I'd been accused.

"Are you going to be all right?" he asked.

That was delivered in a sympathetic voice that made me think he meant "all right emotionally" until he added, "Because I'm pretty sure you can collect unemployment from the state when you're fired."

"That won't be necessary. I get alimony and" — what to call my Peter Armstrong allowance? — "money from a kind of trust. I'll be fine."

I took a stab at sounding as if I could live outside my own head. "What about you? Work good? Timmy happy?"

"Very. He's writing for the *Blue and Gold*. And he kissed a girl."

I chose not to pursue that. I asked, "What about the other work, the secret screenwriting I knew nothing about until you told Kathi. Anything to report there?"

"Actually, yes, but it's still in the note-taking stage."

"Can you talk about it?"

"I'm afraid to."

I assumed that meant he was keeping the idea close to the vest, guarding his premise against copycats. I said, "I get that."

"When I have more on paper, I'd like to run it by you."

That was flattering, especially since I had no experience with scripts except for the times I'd rehearsed lines with him. I'd always been happy to be asked, especially when I got to read for Timmy's drunk mother. I asked which medium he was writing for, TV or movies?

"Neither."

"Please tell me it's not a podcast."

"It's not."

I asked what was left.

"The stage."

I'd been in New York long enough to recognize a pipedream when I heard one. "Wow. Good luck."

"Really? 'Good luck'? That sounds like 'Nice knowing you.'"

Did he need reminding about the obstacle in our path? Apparently, yes. I asked, "How is the adjunct professor? Are you having sex yet, or is that another thing you'd rather not discuss?"

"Correct."

I wanted to ask, *Is she as much fun/readily available/raring to go as I am?* Or *Are you falling for her?* Instead, I announced, "I shredded the yearbook."

He yelped. "No, you did *not!*"

"I did."

"*Literally* shredded?"

"Every page. And I kept the shreds as evidence that the yearbook's not hidden in a vault somewhere."

"What made you do it? I mean, if you had to describe your motivation . . ."

Motivation? Despite his day job, Jeremy rarely used director-speak. I said, "I couldn't stand to look at it. I didn't want it lying around. I could've hidden it —"

"Or kept it at my place. It was very happy here."

"Except it was radioactive back in my apartment."

"But you can live with the shreds?"

"It's like saving someone's ashes. Maybe I'll scatter them from the top of Mount Monadnock."

"Do that. I'll drive you up there," he said.

Why did he keep saying things like that, implying that he welcomed my company? I said, "We'll bring Geneva, too. She can make it the grand finale: I scatter the ashes and then get pushed off the mountain and die. Cue 'Are You Lonesome Tonight?'"

The old Jeremy had been a much better audience. "Does she even know the yearbook's been destroyed?" was his unsatisfying response.

"I bagged the shreds and texted her a picture of them."

"When?"

"Yesterday."

"Did you hear back?"

"No, and I don't want to."

"She must've gone ballistic. I'd lie low for a while if I were you.
And maybe not answer the door."

Doubts were creeping in. Book shredding, discussed aloud, was
sounding less and less like the act of a stable person. "Be honest.
Did I do a really stupid, impulsive thing? Maybe I should've copied the pages first, then shredded the fakes. I did think of that, but
the originals are on that nice glossy stock."

"No turning back. You have to own it. And I must say, it'll play
beautifully."

"Play where?" I asked. "Why did you say that?"

"Just a figure of speech," Jeremy said.

33
......

Two Birds with One Stone

WAS PETER ARMSTRONG really marrying his newly divorced ex–office manager and defacer of thank-you notes? Apparently so, because I was invited to their wedding via Paperless Post.

I called his cell and, without greeting or preamble, went straight to "Isn't this kind of sudden?"

"I'm sixty-eight years old. How can a wedding be sudden at sixty-eight?"

"I meant how well do you know her?"

"For starters, let's call her by her name, which is Bonnie. And I've known her since I made partner in my firm."

"Which was when?"

"A simple 'congratulations' would be nice."

"I just meant . . . she seemed cuckoo."

That was not well received if I was correctly interpreting his sharp intake of breath. "You and she had an unfortunate introduction. She'd never done anything like that before, and she's apologized."

"Not to me she hasn't!"

"We thought — we were wrong, obviously — that inviting you to the wedding *was* an apology. I'm beginning to think that this decision was misguided."

With that, he'd penetrated the fortified guilt center in my brain. I said, "I'm sorry. I got fired this week. It's made me a little crazy. I'll come and I'll behave. Okay if I bring a plus-one?"

"We figured you would. Presumably not that woman you brought to the reunion."

I told him God, no, she and I weren't speaking; in fact, it would be good to get out of town.

One doesn't invite a man to a wedding reception casually, especially if he's a frenemy. I'd start with the news that Senator Peter Armstrong was engaged, then work my way up to the ask. When to approach? ASAP, I decided, since the wedding was one month away. I waited for Jeremy's return from work, easy to calibrate since lately he'd been singing or whistling at high volume upon his arrival. Was it an attention-getting device? When I heard a spirited "Buy me some peanuts and Cracker Jacks, I don't care if I ever get back," I was ready, lipstick applied, dressed in my coat and backpack to give the impression that I was going somewhere.

I feigned surprise at finding him outside his door. He smiled, and said, "Why, it's Miss Maritch. *Qué pasa?*"

"Not much."

"Where are you off to?"

"Whole Foods. Need anything?"

"Um, probably. But I don't want to hold you up."

"Go check. I can wait."

He unlocked his door, stepped back, and gestured, *After you.* Inside, I stopped in the foyer, waiting in the manner of a delivery person who knows his place.

Without asking, he slipped my backpack off my shoulders and pointed me toward his living room. There, I planted myself picturesquely in front of his window, its river view and the lights of New Jersey beyond. Was my pose too artful? Too wistful? Would that be a bad thing?

His kitchen survey was taking more time than expected. And was that the sound of ice being harvested, then rattling in a cocktail shaker? After another few minutes, he returned with two martinis. "Gin, three olives, right?"

"It hasn't been *that* long." I took mine, leaving him free to dim the wall sconces. I'd taken off my coat, exposing the black jersey dress underneath, its deep V-neck ruling it out as daytime attire.

"Looks like there's a cocktail party at Whole Foods," he said.

"I went to one earlier and didn't bother to change," I lied. To shelve any further discussion of that nonevent, I announced, "I heard something interesting today."

He, then I, took a seat on the couch a sisterly distance away. "I'm listening," he said.

"Peter Armstrong is getting married. The senator? From the reunion?"

"Right. Your alleged father. Remind me: not already married?"

"Never! And you won't believe who he's marrying—the woman who intercepted my thank-you note—remember that?—and sent it back, defaced."

"He's marrying that crackpot?"

"Yes! And I'm invited to the wedding."

Unprompted, and to my amazement, he said, "Awesome! Think you can bring someone?"

"Meaning *you?*"

"Yes, me. I'm in!"

In? Without knowing where I stood and if he was the last man I'd ever invite? Unsure if it was a sincere *yes,* I put forward a list of out clauses: "It's not in New York. Not a taxi ride away. It's in

New Hampshire. It'll take four, five hours to get there. You haven't even asked when —"

"When is it?"

"March nineteenth, a Saturday."

"I'll make it work. In Pickering, I hope."

"No, in Exeter. At an inn." It took me a few moments and several sips of alcohol for his question to register. "Why would you be hoping for Pickering?"

"To see it. To get a feel for it."

"Except there's nothing there."

"Except the house where you grew up and Pickering High School. And there must be a main street and a diner, or a town common, maybe even with a bandstand. How far is Pickering from Exeter? Could we kill two birds with one stone and take a side trip there?"

What was this about? I confessed that I had intended to invite him as my plus-one before he beat me to it . . . which confused me . . . which would confuse any ex or relationship counselor.

"Because . . . ?" he asked.

"Because men avoid the woman they had sex with once it's over. And they certainly don't go to weddings with them!"

"And you think I'm like most men?"

"No, unfortunately you're not."

"Where does the 'unfortunately' come in?"

"I just told you: You're still around and very buddy-buddy. Whistling to announce you're home. Still trying to help. It makes no sense."

"You mean not an asshole? That's the problem?"

I was back in debate club again, having drawn the side of an argument I couldn't support. He was looking pensive and overly analytical when he said, "I think I know why I sound like such a sensitive man, always saying supportive things."

I prepared myself for a heartfelt answer that would explain his mixed messaging.

"It's occupational," he announced.

I said I didn't get that. Occupational how?

"I meant I'm exceptionally nice because women write all of my lines!" His laugh was the audible equivalent of a knee slap. *Lines? Scripts! Ha! Good one!*

"Clearly we can't have a serious discussion. You have to joke around and hide behind Timmy while I'm worrying that you want to pick up where Geneva left off with that lame documentary. Why else would you want to take a field trip to Pickering?"

"Believe me, there's no documentary in the works, which, PS, was a shit idea. Did you forget we had a long conversation about what I might be writing for the stage?"

Oh, wait. He *had* told me—which I'd quickly forgotten since it had the ring of Playwriting 101 and the work of every third Starbucks customer with an open laptop. I said, "Of course I remember. But why do you want to go to Pickering? Why my old house and PHS?"

"It's about scenery."

"Pickering for scenery? Unh-unh. You'd want Franconia Notch or Mount Washington or the Kancamagus Highway."

"Not that kind of scenery. I meant scenery as in set design. Photos to project on a screen or a white sheet."

"You're not calming my fears about this being *The Maritch Story, As Told Through a Yearbook*."

"Nothing like that. When I have something I can show you, I will."

"A play set in New Hampshire? Really?"

"Partly. I think I'll call it . . . wait; I've got it: *Our Town!* Could that work on a New York stage?"

See what I mean: Men cannot have a serious discussion. I asked what he would've done if the Armstrong nuptials hadn't come along at such a conveniently creative moment. "Jump on a bus and head north until you spotted the first bandstand on a town green?"

"Bus?" he repeated, his eyes wide. "Movie stars don't take buses. We'll rent a car. My treat."

I told him I'd have to think it over.

"Which part?"

"Everything."

Pretending there was a camera over my shoulder, he addressed it in documentary fashion: "Things are very black or white with Daphne Maritch. Because of our history, she thinks we can't take a field trip together. She questions my motives, both personal and professional. Could she just relax and stop analyzing every word I say?"

I turned around to speak to the imaginary camera. "I withdraw the question, whatever the hell it was. I accept his acceptance to the wedding. I'll also pray that a project that requires a scouting trip to Pickering won't make me sorry I ever met him."

This time he answered me directly, setting his glass on the coffee table. "You know what's progress? That you haven't asked, 'How's the professor?' six times. Or 'How can you come to the wedding if it's on a Saturday night?' Or 'Are you having sexual relations with that woman?'"

I was dying to ask *exactly* those questions. Instead, I said that there was one thing I hadn't had a chance to discuss before he signed on for the wedding.

"Which is what?"

"The party's going to be big. Lots of guests. Armstrong's a public figure and it's his first wedding."

Jeremy asked if I'd forgotten how good he was with people, how at ease. And though he hated to brag, fans of the show were everywhere.

"Yes, yes, I know you're an excellent mingler. It's not that. I meant it must be a huge party because I got the last available room, generously provided by the senator. But don't worry. It was a double, with two big beds, surely. And if not, these five-star inns always have cots for the platonic."

34

The Day Job

DAD PUT ME IN TOUCH with Sara, his relationship manager at New Leash on Life, who hired me despite my submitting fewer than the requested six letters of reference.

"Is this a joke?" I asked, upon meeting my first client, a huge slobbering English Mastiff.

"He's a cream puff," Sara said, caressing the big wrinkly forehead. "Right, boy? You two are going to fall in love. Don't wear anything too good, though."

His name was Elton John, nicknamed E. J., and his poops were the size of a hardcover book. We had bonded early—attributable to the mere sight of a human carrying a leash, the smell of fresh air clinging to her coat and treats in her pocket. His mom told me that by my third visit he'd planted himself at the front door a half hour before I was due. Was that not both brilliant and flattering, plus reassuring to an owner? I allowed a modest "My last job was as a Montessori teacher."

When my trial period ended, Sara asked if I wanted to switch to another client. I said, "Not on your life," despite the nightly ibuprofen I needed for muscles wrenched whenever a squirrel crossed our path.

My dad was, in his own words, pleased as punch.

"I told you," he said.

"Yup. The famed unconditional love."

"And the nicest possible company to work with. Did I tell you they sent me a Starbucks gift certificate at Christmas? You'll get one, too."

"Real benefits would be nice," I said.

"You'll get there."

"Where?"

"I meant a figurative 'there'—a job with health insurance and membership in something like a guild."

I laughed. "Guild! Like I'll become a mason or a candlemaker?"

He claimed not to know why he used that term, then conceded it might be Kathi's membership in a musicians' guild of some sort. She was eligible because she'd played in an orchestra pit for a whole week, subbing for the regular pianist who had bronchitis. "Isn't that New York for you? Everyone is involved with something creative—whether it's music or theater or television or publishing or art or designing skyscrapers."

"Everyone except me," I said.

Less than a week later, I received a birthday card, two and half months early, from my dad and Kathi. Folded inside was a brochure and acceptance letter announcing ten weeks of acting lessons starting almost immediately.

Acting lessons? Weren't those for actors? I checked the envelope to see if I'd opened someone else's mail. No, it was addressed to me in my dad's handwriting. I reread the enclosed letter, still puzzled. Was the Drama Factory the lowest hanging fruit on the drama-school tree since I didn't have to apply or audition? At the bottom of the card, Dad had written, "NB: The hours will not interfere with your day job." And next to that, he'd penciled a paw print and a heart.

I called him, offered thanks that must have sounded anemic

because his follow-up was "I *did* check whether I could get a re-fund if you hated the idea. But I thought it would be fun. And you'd be good at it. Jeremy thought so, too. In fact, it was his idea."

"Wait. Jeremy? When? At my dinner party?"

"No, recently. I ran into him buying bagels."

"And the topic of my *June* birthday came up?"

There was a silence I could read: *How to negotiate with Daphne when she's like this?* "Not exactly. I got the idea after Jeremy told me you enjoyed going over lines with him."

"But that was me hamming it up! What's easier than playing a drunk stepmother in the privacy of your then-boyfriend's bou-doir? And how long a conversation did you have before it got around to my alleged acting ability?"

"Not long. He was on his way to work. I said, 'Remind me what you do,' and one thing led to another."

"Does he know you signed me up?"

"I thought *you* might tell him. I guess not; I guess that would re-quire a modicum of enthusiasm."

Now I felt bad. "Let's start over," I said. "So this is me thanking you profusely for such an . . . original gift."

"You're welcome."

Elton John was taking a noisy snooze under the customers-only bench provided by a barber shop I didn't patronize. When I reached down to stroke his gigantic head, his rheumy eyes asked, *How about if I turn over and you rub my belly?*

"C'mon, you couch potato. Wanna go to school?" He loved walking by Sacred Heart of Jesus and PS 111 on West Fifty-sec-ond, or so I projected. I timed our visit to coincide with recess when his sheer immensity drew a delighted crowd behind the chain-link fence. I did some showing off: I'd throw whatever stick I'd harvested from Central Park, causing him to move not an inch or even turn his head to follow the stick's trajectory. Instead, he took it for his cue to perform his only trick, offering me his paw, which I'd shake like I was cranking the handle of a pump. That earned us the cheers and mittened applause of our pint-size onlookers.

Acting potential? I doubted it. But who didn't like an audience?

"I won't keep you," I told Kathi, who picked up after one ring. "Just calling with my thanks."

"No hurry; no student until eleven. Thanking me for . . . ?"

"The gift certificate? Great present!" That was step one of my plan: express heartfelt gratitude, then work my way toward the who/what/where/why of such a present. Since hearing how Kathi saved my father from Geneva's evil output, I'd been viewing her as the inside track. I said as casually as I could, "Dad told me he got the idea from Jeremy. You remember Jeremy — he was at my chicken dinner but left before we ate?"

"Of course. I liked him very much . . . I even entertained a secret thought that it was too bad you two can't get together."

Had Jeremy been the source of that "can't"? I didn't ask. I said, "Funny coincidence — Dad's running into him."

"Not really. It was at Pick-a-Bagel. Isn't that a block or two from your building?"

"Yes, true —"

"You know your dad. He'll strike up a conversation with any-one."

"And I guess it was natural that the conversation would get around to me, either my birthday or my hidden acting talent?"

"Your dad thought the lessons would be fun. Not like the choc-olate course where you had to buy supplies and do homework. And, most important, you might meet some new people."

That wasn't supposed to sting, but it did. Now I knew: The gift wasn't the flattering career counseling I'd taken it for; it was to get me out of the house, make friends, meet the similarly lonely and unmoored.

"You still there?" asked Kathi.

I said yes. I was on a walk with Elton John; sorry if I sounded distracted.

"I hope it's okay to say this: You have your whole life ahead of you. You can dip your toes into so many different things. You might even come full circle, discover that your true north is teaching."

E. J. was squatting and staring back at me with an apologetic look I recognized. I unrolled a plastic poop bag and a backup one. "Unlikely," I said. "Did you know I was fired from my Montessori job?"

"Your dad told me."

"For bullshit reasons!"

"I heard that, too."

"But I'm fine. I might have a case — just need a little distance on that." Thinking I'd sound motivated and mildly adventurous, I added, "Next weekend I'm getting out of the city, doing some exploring in New Hampshire. And even going to a wedding up there."

"In Exeter? That one?"

Had I already mentioned that? Or had Jeremy told my dad about our upcoming weekend? I said yes, that one.

"I wondered if you'd be going."

"Wondered *when?*"

"When I heard about it from your father."

"And how did Dad hear?"

"From the invitation."

"He got one?"

"In his email."

I was still processing this exchange as being about an ill-considered invitation that my dad had sent straight into the trash until Kathi said, "Do you know what you're wearing? The invitation said cocktail attire."

"You're *going?* Dad actually accepted?"

"He felt he should. The groom isn't only a Pickering High grad, but he's also now a state senator *representing* Pickering."

I stumbled through a litany of questions: Did they really want to go, considering the complications? The podcast? The drama that could unfold after a few drinks?

"Your father feels it's a way to right a wrong."

"Which wrong?"

"The one he refers to as storming the State House."

"And going to this party erases that? Retracts what the *Concord Monitor* wrote about the two of them going at it?"

"He feels — and maybe you should talk to him directly — that the invitation was a sincere apology from an ex-student to his old principal. And your father is big enough to let it be water under the bridge."

"What a hypocrite!"

"Your father?"

"No, Armstrong. He had Dad dragged from his office and arrested!"

"But the trespassing charge was dismissed, correct?"

"I still don't consider it water under the bridge."

"Did I misunderstand? I thought you said you were going to the wedding, that it was just the getaway you needed."

I said yes, true, I was. I didn't tell her what my own reasons were — that Peter Armstrong was keeping me afloat. And thanks to a white lie about a fully booked inn, Jeremy would be sleeping one bed away.

35

Take Your Seat, Daphne

E BEGAN BY LYING FLAT on the dirty rehearsal-room floor, doing stretching exercises, then breathing from the abdominals, then moving and swaying around the room in a fashion I found not only awkward but embarrassing. Was I really about to impersonate colors?

"Orange!" our gray-haired, ponytailed teacher called out. "Blue!" And inevitably the downer, "Black!" Bodies sagged. Fingertips brushed the floor. Why was everyone else so into it, so earnest and eager to please?

Next the lecture: Acting is reacting. Good acting is listening. Feel it from the inside out. Mining what you are. He himself, in the late 1990s, had read the stage directions while rehearsing Sanford Meisner. In a single evening with that brilliant practitioner of the Method, he'd gleaned infinite wisdom about the "reality of doing."

Next: Each would get a folding chair from a stack against the wall, then reach into the paper bag containing our clues. This, we were told, was the Who's Knocking? exercise. One by one we'd leave the room, close the door, then knock in the manner of the character named on our folded piece of paper, returning only when someone guessed the correct identity.

Any volunteers? Of course the handsomest guy — I guessed Italian mother, Irish father, or vice versa — stood up, but then had to sit down because he announced proudly that his knocker was a census taker.

"The point is to have your fellow classmates *guess* who is knocking," said the instructor.

The next volunteer, a short, pretty blonde woman with straight hair to her chin, walked out the door, closed it, and delivered a pounding that sounded frantic.

I volunteered, "Someone who hears her neighbor calling for help, and even though they're not on friendly terms, her Good Samaritan instincts kick in —"

Incorrect.

"An angry wife who's showing up at her husband's secret love nest!" someone else yelled.

That wasn't it, but at least I was enjoying the audience-participation part of acting.

A woman with very long, very black hair yelled out, "There's a fire in the building!"

The instructor said, "So who's knocking? Remember, it's the person's identity we need."

"A fireman!" she called.

The door opened and the blonde woman returned, smiling and waving the unfolded piece of paper. "Firefighter arriving at a burning building," she read.

Which would've been fine, but the handsome guy announced he was a real-life firefighter. "Who knocks? Maybe if you're going house to house raising money for the families of the fallen."

My slip of paper said, "Doctor approaching an examining room." With such a booby-prize situation, I didn't volunteer. Neither did anyone else. Probably because I had my head down in an effort to disappear, the instructor said, "You. At the end of the row in the yellow T-shirt. You're up."

I said, "I have a real stinker. I'll pass."

"You can't," he said.

Once outside, I knocked tentatively, earning no guesses. I tried a louder knock, which must've sounded more authoritative than I intended because I heard someone say, "A parent who thinks his kid is smoking dope in his room?"

I tried to act from the inside out, making myself the patient, sitting on the examining table, under paper, naked from the waist down, waiting for the gynecologist. This time I went for the quick rap from the impatient doctor who'd already kept me waiting an hour.

"A twelve-year-old kid," yelled our twelve-year-old classmate, whose mother had been taking notes from her own row. "Maybe he hit a home run that broke a window and his father made him come over and apologize."

Oh, brother. This could go on all night. I knocked again, willy-nilly. Who cared? What a stupid exercise.

"A teacher on her first day of school," someone tried.

Really? Why would a teacher be knocking on her own classroom door?

"A casualty-notification officer?" said a sad male voice.

No and no. Was I getting everyone's life story? Was this the point? Against the rules, I called out, "How about one more guess?"

"No words," warned the instructor.

One final, uninspired knock by me.

I heard "UPS guy" followed by "Bill collector?"

Bill collector? What century was this? I opened the door. "Give up?"

The various classmates said yes, no, get back out there.

I didn't. I held up my piece of paper. "Didn't my knock sound exactly like ... wait for it ... a doctor approaching the examination room?"

Our instructor asked my name. I told him.

"This isn't improv, Daphne. Please take your seat."

There was no mistaking from his tone that he considered improv a lesser form of the dramatic arts. This was serious scholarship, he was trained in the Stanislavski method, and I'd effectively flunked the first exam.

36

What's So Secret?

I TOOK OVER AS SOON AS we crossed into New England, mainly to show off one of my few proficiencies: driving a manual transmission. Our plan was to check into the inn, unpack, walk around the Exeter campus, slip into the five o'clock wedding, eat, drink, dance if there was a band—all the while keeping my ear out for insensitive remarks directed at my father on topics such as his wasting no time finding an attractive, younger girlfriend.

The hometown-scouting part of the trip would be on Sunday morning. From the passenger seat, Jeremy asked whether I could introduce him to Pickering natives who might have tips on what to see and where to go.

"*I'm* your Pickering native," I said.

"But what about places off the beaten path? Maybe hangouts for the class of '68. I'm going to need a lot of slides for the PowerPoint presentation."

Ha, ha, good one: PowerPoint presentation! That snooze—except that Jeremy was saying, "No. I'm serious. I'm planning slides in the background, big ones."

"Background of what?"

"The thing I'm working on."

"The 'thing'! The Manhattan Project of top-secret theatrical works in progress!"

"How is it a secret? You know it's a piece for the stage. And you know, for starters, that I need to see Pickering—"

"That doesn't help! It makes me think you're pulling a Geneva."

"Which you define as . . . ?"

"An unhealthy yearbook obsession channeled into some kind of show! Why else would you need a guided tour of hangouts frequented by the class of 1968?"

"What yearbook? The one that's history? You saw to that."

Ouch. That was new, that edge. If we hadn't been on the turnpike, I'd have pulled sharply over to the side of the road and braked with a decisive jerk. Instead, I remained silent, knowing there was a service plaza coming up that would serve my purposes.

He must've been aware that I was stewing because he tried to make conversation, starting with the unwise question of when I'd last seen Geneva.

"Not since the emergency room. The last conversation we had was after the yearbook went missing."

"Went missing? Or met a shredder at FedEx?"

I was no longer proud of that. I admitted: bad that I'd destroyed my mother's prized possession; good riddance when I thought of it as Geneva's so-called intellectual property.

I could hear the *click-click* of his typing. "Are you writing down what I said?"

"Just making a note."

"Be sure *not* to tell me why," I huffed. A sign announced that the Charlton Service Plaza was upcoming, a mile ahead. At the half-mile point, I put my blinker on.

"Bathroom?" he asked.

"No. We're pulling over, and I'm not moving until you tell me what this secret project is."

He pointed to the glove compartment. "I don't think you can hold me hostage if the rental car's in my name."

"Try me," I said.

I pulled into a spot inconvenient to bathrooms, drive-through refreshment, and fuel. Jeremy busied himself, leaning over the front seat, patting his garment bag flat on the back seat, turning it over, patting it some more. "Just making sure my charger and camera are in there."

"Are they? Is that settled? Anything else? Or can you now tell me what the fuck you're writing?"

"C'mon, Daff. What more do you need to know? I've told you it's for the stage—"

"And set in New Hampshire, which I find more than annoying."

"Listen . . . New Hampshire, okay . . . the place is sort of a character in the story. I need to evoke it without actually setting it there." He tapped the stick shift as if to say, *Now we can go.*

"There's still something missing, something you're not saying."

"Trust me, you'll be the first person to read it. I want to get it into really good shape. Then we'll discuss—"

"Why do you care what I think of it? You're the pro. I'm no script doctor. I don't know what makes a play work."

He slid downward until his head was resting on the back of the seat. "Believe me, I need you on board."

"Because . . . ?"

"Because . . . it's a one-woman show."

That explained his stalling, his nerves: He knew I'd never go along with a play about my mortal enemy. I said, "I could never give my permission for that."

"Without even reading it?"

I shrugged. I supposed it wouldn't kill me to read a project that would never see the light of day. I'd probably find it satisfying to see Geneva portrayed as a bigger-than-life thief and villain. "Maybe it has potential," I said to be charitable, "but I don't think you'll ever get her permission. She's probably writing her own one-woman show as we speak."

"Her own show?" he repeated. "Whose did you think I was talking about?"

"Geneva's!"

"Not Geneva's," he said. "Yours."

37

Be Nice

WE DISCUSSED HIS PIPE DREAM of a project for the rest of the ride. "Let's just say you got this off the ground. Who'd play me?" I asked.

"You'd play you."

That introduced a new level of shell shock. I, who knew nothing about the world of theater, expounded anyway. "A producer would want a name actress. Not a nobody, especially a nobody whose only experience was a month of acting classes and understudy to the female lead in a fully clothed high school production of *Hair*."

"But the charm would be that it's your story. And don't think of a one-woman show as acting. It's essentially stand-up, and I've seen you do stand-up."

"No, you haven't!"

"Not in a club," he said. "In life."

"Ridiculous. Forget it." But after another few miles, I asked, "Not that I'm warming to the idea, but how long would I have to stand up there talking about myself?"

"I won't know until it's finished, but I'd say ninety minutes max."

"Could I sit on a stool or would I have to move around the stage?"

"You could sit on a stool part of the time, and when you were talking about something that riled you up, you could pace."

I thought about the exercises from acting lessons, supposedly using our bodies as . . . I forgot. Conveying emotion? Acting from the inside out, the Stella Adler method. Or was that outside in? I might have a well of hatred for Geneva that I could tap from either side.

Still protesting, I said, "Who in the world would put money into a show about a nobody *starring* the nobody?"

"We'd start small, at festivals."

"Would it be my life to date or just since I've known you?"

"It would begin with Geneva's taking possession of the yearbook. I've been in on that pretty much from the beginning."

"But *she* wouldn't be in it, right?"

"Correct. Just you. Hence the 'one-woman.'"

I pondered this some more. Airing grievances in public could be therapeutic if I didn't have stage fright. "Could it include some things about my horrible ex and his horrible mother?"

"Maybe. I couldn't stop you from improvising."

"Would I have to use my real name?"

"Hard to avoid in a one-woman show."

I continued to play the skeptic through Worcester and up I-495. Approaching Lowell, I asked why he wouldn't use one of his fellow actresses from his show. Or an old girlfriend from Tisch.

"Just a hunch about what would work. And we'd start small. We'd do a staged reading."

"In front of an audience?"

"Depending on who was interested, but that's when the potential agents and backers scope it out."

"You'd better not give up your day job. This sounds like it has the same chances as Geneva's documentary, i.e., stillborn."

"Have a little faith. At least wait to read it."

"How long till you finish?"

"Weeks? Months? Depends on my schedule. But I don't want you to see it until it's as polished as I can make it."

Though pretending I was adjusting the rearview mirror for better visibility, I was stealing a glance at my face. Would these laugh lines be visible from the orchestra seats? Was this head-shot material? I'd never thought of myself as a one-woman anything, but I guess Jeremy the professional knew best.

Our room was small. The registration desk told me it was a "traditional queen," which sounded grand enough to accommodate nonpartners. It wasn't. There was a double bed, just one, and a squeeze of a bathroom with a loopy scatter rug that kept the door from closing.

Jeremy said, checking out the nonview from the one window and squeezing past me to appraise the tubless shower, "Fine with me."

I didn't admit that it was fine with me, too. But because I'd be sharing this space with someone I was no longer having sex with, I felt it was my duty to ask, "Should we try to get a cot or a separate room?"

"We're adults," he said.

"I consider that answer nonresponsive."

"I was going for that. Can we just play it by ear?"

"Did you bring pajamas?"

"Darn it. I forgot."

I made myself busy unpacking my toothbrush and toothpaste. We hung up our wedding finery; in gentlemanly fashion, he insisted I get the one padded hanger.

There was a light rain falling, so we did an abbreviated circuit around campus, peeked into the library and church, saw catalogue-worthy students of all descriptions. We had coffee in town, both agreeing to change the subject away from the work in progress to the topic of the upcoming wedding and its potentially awkward moments.

I said, "I'm going to try to be as pleasant as possible to the bride. Clean slate. If she apologizes for making a horrible first impression—"

"She won't."

"But if she does, I'm going to be so gracious that you won't believe it's me."

"See. There's your method acting."

I noticed that two girls, teenagers easily identified as Exonians by their maroon and white scarves, were gaping at Jeremy. "Even here in the boonies," I said.

Jeremy gave a nod that said, *Yes, I'm him; I'm who you think I am.*

One of the two called over, "I love the show. And I voted for it in the Teen Choice Awards."

"Thank you so much."

"There's going to be a third season, right?" asked the other one, who suddenly had no need for her glasses.

"Can we get your autograph?" the first one asked.

Jeremy said, "Sure." When they were standing next to us, he said, "Let me introduce Daphne Maritch. We're collaborators."

Their interest in me, if any, was as my role of photographer with each of their smartphones.

"Wanna go?" Jeremy asked after the fans had returned to their table, autographs signed.

"I'm used to it. It's fine." I did wonder how I looked to these girls, hoping the rain hadn't had a deleterious effect on my hair or the cappuccino on my lip gloss.

. . .

Like two professional actors sharing a trailer, we were unself-conscious about getting undressed and dressed. My interpretation of "cocktail attire" had led me to the pale gray chiffon thing, tastefully ruffled, expensive simplicity personified, that I'd worn only once — to my own rehearsal dinner. I'd shopped with my sister, who'd flown in from LA for the wedding and insisted we go to Bergdorf's, her treat.

I needed help with the tiny cloth-covered buttons up the back. Jeremy said, "Good thing I'm here. What would you have done otherwise?"

"I'd have flagged down a housekeeper."

"I was going after something more like 'Yes, I thank my lucky stars that you and your nimble fingers are here.'"

"That, too." I turned around, fully buttoned, for inspection.

"Quite spectacular," he said.

I took a step back, and said, *"Vous, aussi."* I also noted that his silver tie made us look coordinated.

"I brought three ties up with me, so not so much of a coincidence."

"Very thoughtful," I said. It was ten to five. "We should go now."

He offered me his arm even though it was just a walk out of our room to the elevator. Two couples, the men in tuxes, older, joined us when it stopped at a lower floor.

"Are we all going to the Armstrong wedding?" I asked.

They answered with smiles and nods.

One woman, who was wearing a purple-feathered fascinator, asked, "Are you the couple from New York?"

Jeremy, grinning, asked, "What gave us away?"

"Bonnie said that Peter had a daughter she hadn't met yet who lived in New York."

Just like that.

I said, "The daughter part of that hasn't quite been established."

"Oh! I'm sorry! Bonnie gave me the distinct impression . . ."

The bigmouth's husband said, "Sheila and Bonnie are very close."

As the doors opened, I made myself say, "Enjoy the evening," in dignified fashion rather than the scolding she deserved. Life had taught me that the Sheila you have words with on your way to an event is the Sheila who inevitably ends up at your table.

I'd met Peter Armstrong exactly once, at the reunion, newly elected to state office and having fulfilled his most-likely-to-succeed early promise. He was a very good-looking sixty-eight-year-old groom, dressed in black, the kind of sharp suit actors wear to the Academy Awards instead of a tux. Bonnie came down the aisle on the arm of what must've been her father, who was wearing a kilt, which explained the bagpipe soloist. In its understated elegance, her dress, with its deep ivory silk, its sleeves to the elbow, the pearls of a political wife, seemed to say, *Yes, this is my second marriage; I know that, so I'm not going over-the-top bridal.*

Her two daughters were also manifestations of good taste: empire-waisted matching black velvet dresses with lace collars, skewing younger than their preteen ages.

Had I been expecting cheesy? I must've. I hadn't been to a wedding since my own, which had been a bare-bones ceremony without—I could see in retrospect—any feeling. This one was unexpectedly touching, performed by a judge who seemed to know—in fact, love—them both. Maybe Bonnie wasn't the adulteress I'd pegged her for, or Peter the sexual harasser of his office manager. I checked the seats around me—the underpopulated groom's side, where the oldest celebrants were sitting—in case Peter's parents were there. Dead or alive? I'd never asked. His best man, next to him at the makeshift altar, looked enough like Peter to be a brother. Had he gone to Pickering High, too? My dad would know.

And then there were the vows delivered by the bride and groom facing each other, voices choked. Maybe I shouldn't have let one crazy act of mail vandalism color my opinion. Bonnie seemed so committed, so adoring. And today she was beautiful. The very act of hiring her must've sealed this lifelong bachelor's fate.

I found myself getting teary-eyed. I looked over to my father and Kathi, in our row, and caught the moment that my father reached for Kathi's hand. Weddings did that to people. Just as I was thinking it was too bad I wasn't here with a boyfriend who'd be similarly moved by the juxtaposition of wedding vows and me, Jeremy took my hand.

It was the familiar service, very *Book of Common Prayer*–ish, plus customized vows about their domestic life, pets, the State House, their always-and-foreverness, the two girls he was getting in the bargain. And then they were pronounced husband and wife to a round of applause, a bagpipe recessional, and, though I could've been mistaken, a smile from Peter that landed directly on me.

Our table: my dad and Kathi, plus the mayor of Pickering, who was a son of the groom's high school classmate who'd died tragically and heroically trying to rescue the driver of an overturned car on I-93. How had I not known that Pickering had elected a gay mayor? Or did Pickering not realize they had?

I told him I'd moved away two-plus years ago but surely would've voted for him.

"Did you change your voter registration?" he asked.

"He's thinking absentee ballot," my father explained.

Also seated with us: the mayor's mother. And, oddly not at some secondary head table, were Bonnie's mother and stepfather. Was this because I was considered a branch of the family? They'd driven up from Danbury, Connecticut, and would be taking the granddaughters back with them when Bonnie and Peter headed to Santa Barbara for their honeymoon.

To me, they looked a little tight-lipped about the marriage we'd just witnessed. I didn't have to imagine the whys and wherefores of that because, upon hearing that my father had been Peter's high school principal, Bonnie's mom asked what kind of youngster Peter had been. "As the twig is bent, so grows the tree," the stepfather added.

My father said, "Top student. Went on to Dartmouth."

"And was voted most likely to succeed," I added.

"Did he date in high school?" she asked.

My father said, "That sort of thing doesn't make its way into the principal's office unless there's some kind of trouble. Why do you ask?"

The bride's mom said, "I guess . . . a lifelong bachelor."

"Some of us are late bloomers," said Jeremy, knocking his shoulder into mine.

I checked the mayor's expression. He was looking a little tight-lipped himself. His mother said, "I went to high school with Pete, and I can tell you this: He was *not* a late bloomer."

Kathi must've been avoiding the same thing I was, which was the topic of the groom's past love life, because she said to the bride's mother, "Your granddaughters are adorable."

Their dual ungenerous, churchy responses were looks that conveyed, *Handsome is as handsome does.*

I thought all of this prickliness deserved a quasi-rude question: "They won't be staying with their father while their mother's away?"

"Their father . . . hasn't quite made peace with the divorce yet," said the stepdad. And even though most of us had started in on our salads, he changed the subject by asking if we could say grace. One by one we joined hands. Jeremy and I kept our eyes open while Pastor Stepdad—as it turned out—intoned, "Dear Lord, thank you for the blessing of bringing Bonnie and Peter together in marriage today. We ask you to bless their marriage and their family. Help them stay strong in any adversity and treasure and protect the joy of marriage. Please bless this food we are about to receive, and let this reception be an honor to You. In Jesus' name. Amen."

"Amen," we echoed. Jeremy gave me an ironic New York City smile. Kathi said, "That was lovely. Thank you."

I said, "Very positive."

"You're a man of the cloth?" asked the mayor's mother.

"I am. Retired."

I asked why he hadn't performed the ceremony.

There was a brief silence. His wife said, "The reverend doesn't perform ceremonies for divorced people."

It begged the question, *But aren't you Bonnie's stepfather? Doesn't that mean, by definition, that you married a divorcée?*

The mayor asked, "Do you perform same-sex ceremonies?"

That earned only a frown from the stepdad and a shake of his wife's head.

"Not because you're homophobic, though, right?" I asked.

My father was giving me a look. *Don't spoil the party. Be nice.*

I said, "I withdraw the question."

Kathi, skilled changer of subjects, asked Jeremy if he'd started shooting a third season, then offered, "Jeremy stars in a television series called *Riverdale.*"

"Not stars in," he corrected. "Just a minor character."

The mayor said, "*Riverdale!* No kidding! I love that show."

His mother asked, "Do I watch that with you?"

"Not so far. I watch it over at Greg's."

Jeremy asked, as if it were his own fondest wish, "You get to live with your mom? How great is that?"

His mom said, "Just since I lost my husband."

The mayor said, "It doesn't hurt me at the ballot box. I make jokes about it — not about my dad, about my mom being my campaign manager —"

"Though I'm not. He likes to say that."

"And I'm known at city hall for the lunches she packs me."

"I don't know why," said his mom. "Tuna fish five days a week. Even though I warn him about the mercury."

Kathi said, "Maybe just the novelty of a mayor brown-bagging it."

I said, "I don't live with my dad, but we're neighbors. He moved to New York after my mom died" — my messaging to the wet blankets: not divorced but widowed.

"We both walk dogs for the same outfit," my dad said.

"Which is how we met," said Kathi. "He walked my Westie."

"Still do," said my dad.

A waiter was circling, asking, "Salmon or filet mignon?" and pouring either red or white accordingly.

And then the bride and groom were standing behind Bonnie's mom and stepdad, and asking if everyone was having a good time.

I said, "So far so good."

"This must be Jeremy," Peter said.

"Thank you for having me. The ceremony was beautiful. As is the bride."

Bonnie said, "I like him!"

My dad said, "And I'm Daphne's father."

"A lot more than that," said Peter. "Everyone here know that he was the principal of PHS? And a great one? Though young, right? You were just out of grad school back in the day?"

My dad said, "Well, three years out. I always hoped you wise-acres thought I was older than I was."

"Wiseacres?" repeated Bonnie's mother.

"Not I," said Peter. "Right, Mr. Maritch?" He smiled. "Still can't call him Tom."

The bride smiled, but I sensed she was hearing Pickering lore at every table and had had enough. She said to her mother, "Dad did a great job, didn't he?"

"Walking you down the aisle? Not much he could've gotten wrong." Then to the table: "He was the one in the kilt. Which he didn't even wear at his own wedding."

"Did he remarry, too?" I asked.

"I meant to me. He wasn't so taken with his roots then."

Bonnie explained: "I gave him a gift certificate to an Ancestry dot com DNA test where you send in your sputum. He came back more than half-Scottish, so he's all in."

"How did he know which tartan if he wasn't sure about his roots?" asked my father.

"Some names he pulled up — maiden names of grandmothers. He just picked the tartan he liked best."

Peter said to his new mother-in-law and step-father-in-law, "And you've had the pleasure of meeting Hizzoner and Mrs. Wojcik?"

"Yes. We've all been chatting," said Bonnie's mom.

"And you've met Daphne?"

"We've met everybody," she said.

Bride Bonnie was staring at me, not so much in a hostile manner but in a diagnostic one. I knew she was conducting a mental DNA test. Was there anything about me that suggested I'd been sired by her new husband?

During the ongoing awkwardness of this table-hop, no one had introduced Kathi, which we discovered when she volunteered, "I'm Kathi Krauss, Tom's plus-one"—prompting an apology from my father for not introducing her in proper sequence.

"Plus-one hardly says it all," I added, smiling at Kathi.

"Same over there," said my dad.

Whoops. He meant Jeremy and me. I said, "Um, Jeremy lives across the hall from me in New York."

"Directly across," Jeremy said.

"He's an actor," said the mayor's mother. "I'm going to start watching his show. Remind me what it's called."

"*Riverdale*," said at least three of us in unison.

"It's based on the Archie comic books," said Kathi. "But it's not a cartoon."

Was Bonnie still staring at me? I was capable—too capable—of matching her tactless gaze, but I pretended not to notice, pretended the small talk around me was fascinating.

"What a group of luminaries! If I didn't have to circulate, this is the table I'd want to be at," boomed Peter.

"Why?" asked Bonnie's mother.

"You! The reverend and the mayor and his mother and my friend Tom and his lovely partner." He then walked around the table and put his hands on my shoulders. "And a young woman I've known for only a few months, but whose presence here today means a great deal to me."

Oh, God. Was he going to say more?

Seated on my left, my father, the nicest guy in America, looked up at the man treating us to filet mignon, potatoes dauphinoise, a fine burgundy, and said, "That's enough, Pete."

Senator Armstrong snapped out of whatever wistful paternal state he'd fallen into, and said, "You're right. I'm sorry. Too much champagne already."

Bonnie said, "Darling, we'd better keep moving. Our first dance was supposed to be between the salad and entrée."

He said, with one last squeeze of my shoulders, "And I hope to dance with every one of you ladies. The night is young."

I didn't answer. Jeremy was passing the basket of rolls. I took one and busied myself shredding it.

38

Just That Simple

I HADN'T ACCEPTED THE WEDDING INVITATION to do what I was about to do: say a final good-bye to Peter Armstrong, careless broadcaster of genetic truths. Following a fox-trot with the real father of my heart and a Kahlúa espresso, I'd come up with what I considered pretty good grounds for a permanent parting—a new DNA test vastly improved over the primitive, unreliable one available at the time of my birth.

I confided this while the band was playing "My Funny Valentine" and I was dancing with the groom. I thought, after hearing my father's warning—"Enough!"—and because he'd given every other female guest a whirl, alternating songs with the new Mrs. Armstrong, that he'd bypass me as a partner. But when Jeremy and I were dancing to yet another Beach Boys' hit circa 1965, Peter cut in.

There was no need for conversation while he smiled and nodded, presumably at constituents. "Having a good time?" he finally asked me. I said yes, lovely wedding. Delicious food. Good band. Bonnie very nice. And when the song wasn't going to last much longer, I announced that I'd gotten a state-of-the-art DNA test and it had told the tale: Tom Maritch was my real father.

He didn't miss a step or a beat at the same time he said, "You're lying."

I didn't cave. Just the opposite. I said, "Tom Maritch is unquestionably a match. I have the letter from the lab to prove it."

We did a few more whirls before he said, "You did this through a reputable lab, not some mail-in, fly-by-night outfit?"

"I went to Mount Sinai."

"And Tom participated?"

Oh, a minor point I'd forgotten to weave into my fabrication — what piece of male DNA was I matching against mine?

"I didn't have to involve him. We see each other all the time. I just had to fish a dirty Kleenex of his out of my wastebasket."

"Very resourceful," said Peter, grimly.

"I'm sorry if it got your hopes up that you had a biological child—"

"Just that simple," he said.

"You can't go around telling people that I'm your daughter. That was reckless, and that's over. You had a fling with my mother. Okay. Everyone has flings. It was huge to you because she was your teacher—"

"Ex-teacher."

"Fine, ex-teacher. But you have to drop it."

"We shouldn't be having this conversation at my wedding. Can I call you?"

"No, bad idea. And, of course, I'll return the money you've been sending me."

He whispered, right above my ear, "Don't. She told me you were mine. She used to send me baby pictures."

Maybe this would be the last time I'd have to endure accounts of my mother's disloyalty. I said, "Well, she was wrong."

The song was ending and Jeremy was back at my side.

"Everything okay?" he asked.

I said, "I told him about the new test," hoping my accompanying look signaled *Just play along.*

"Yes, it had to be said," Jeremy granted ever so solemnly. "Sometimes ripping the Band-Aid off is the only way."

We two improvisational talents nodded, *Yes, so very true.* I asked Jeremy if he wanted to call it a night.

"We haven't cut the cake yet," said Peter.

"It's been a very long day," I said.

"Too long. I wish it had ended before we had this conversation."

"I hope you have a long and happy marriage. I really do."

"I didn't handle this very well, did I? I plowed right in the first time we met. You're wiser than I ever was at your age," said Peter.

"Hey, c'mon. It's not good-bye," said Jeremy. "It's just good night."

"I'm afraid you're wrong," said Peter.

We wound our way over to Kathi and my dad, who hadn't left the dance floor since the deejay had declared the newlyweds' first dance, "Can't Take My Eyes Off of You," now open to all.

"Your father never told me he was a dancer!" said Kathi.

"I chaperoned more than my share of hops. You pick up the moves," said my dad.

"I heard that people can go dancing in the borough of Manhattan," said Jeremy. "Maybe you two can look into that."

I could tell that Kathi was thinking, *Sad. We like Jeremy so much. Is there any hope?*

In the elevator, just the two of us plus the half-empty bottle of burgundy he'd taken from an abandoned table, Jeremy asked what bomb I'd dropped on Armstrong.

"I told him I'd had a fancy new DNA test that showed that my dad was my dad—"

"Tom?"

"Of course Tom!"

"Did you, in fact, have a test?"

It occurred to me that I could lie to Jeremy, too. But I didn't. I said, "No test. Just me wanting to put an end to the whole damn thing. I wanted to clear him out of my head. I wanted to go back to the first three decades of my dad being my real dad. He deserves that."

"Pete did look a little shell-shocked. I think he was planning on this event doing double duty—as in 'A big round of applause for my illegitimate daughter at table one!'"

"You and me both. When my dad told him to scram, we were about thirty seconds away from being the subject of a boozy toast. That did it." Our floor number pinged. I said, "He'll get over it. He's known me for about a minute in the great scheme of things. And now he's got two stepdaughters he can daddy."

I took my shoes off as soon as we stepped out of the elevator onto the carpeted hallway. "You know what I think?" Jeremy asked.

I said no, tell me.

"I think he's in love with you."

I emitted an automatic *yuck* and *eeew*, but what I was really focusing on was *Does Jeremy think of me as a woman whom a handsome state senator would be in love with?*

"Aren't you supposed to look a lot like your mother, the alleged love of his life?"

Oh, that. "Some people think so."

I took the plastic key card from my tiny satin purse, opened the door, closed the curtains, and turned on the overhead light. Jeremy turned it off.

I said, "You're not going to be able to find the buttons that need unbuttoning."

That seemed to be his cue to pat me here and there, pretending it was too dark to know breast from clavicle.

"They're on the upper back, remember?"

"Got 'em. But I'm noting that they don't serve any real purpose. And there's a zipper. Do you want me to unzip you, too?"

"As long as you're there, sure."

I could feel my dress opening wider. Then noticeably closer to my ear: "Your bra seems to have an excessive number of hooks. Should I help with that, or do you want to take care of it yourself?"

"That depends . . ."

He dropped his hands. "I sense you have a speech you'd like to make."

I did, one I'd been preparing since seeing the size of the room we'd been assigned. I held on to the slipping bodice of my dress for dignity's sake, then began. "I know when we first met, and I had a martini, I was ultracool, very cavalier, about jumping into bed with you. It was like I was experimenting, trying to be the kind of woman who could have casual sex with someone she'd just met. No emotional investment."

"But . . . ?"

"But now, if I'm being very honest, which I probably shouldn't be, I have an emotional investment. And if this thing now went from unbuttoning and unzipping to sleeping together, and if we had sex, would it be accidental because we were side by side and naked? I also have to ask if you have a girlfriend. And would you wake up all sorry because you were cheating on she who must not be named?"

Now, having turned me around, and counting on three fingers, he said, "No. No. And no."

I shimmied, dress halfway down, over to the bureau and took a sip of our stolen wine straight from the bottle. "Okay, but what about this? Would it be sex for old times' sake . . . or would we be back together?"

"You're such an idiot," he said.

"In a good way?"

"In a way good enough that made me miss it."

I offered him the bottle. Before taking a swig, he said, "And for the record, Tina and I never had sex."

"But . . ." I had to search for whatever was left that I hadn't exhausted. "Even so, she's around. Your bikes are stored side by side. And isn't it true that a woman could get the idea that casual dates might qualify someone as her boyfriend?"

"If you'd ever had to talk about sustainability over dinner, you wouldn't have to ask."

Because those words had been spoken with his lips on my neck, I didn't pursue the Tina topic any further. I didn't need to. I'd stepped out of the gauzy puddle that was my dress. And somehow, without my help, Jeremy's trousers and boxers were no longer confining his responsive lower body.

I said, "I have to get something in my cosmetics bag. I brought them just in case."

When I came out of the bathroom, he was in bed. I joined him. He wasn't a handsome specimen, but he was beautiful.

39

Mind If I Take a Few Pictures?

NOT THAT I'D SLEPT WELL, having fallen, postcoitally, into a pinch-me state of best-case insomnia. Jeremy, though, was dozing between my conversational pinball. I had to ask, didn't I, about the hiatus he'd initiated — the why of it, and whether the breakup helped us get to where we were now?

He murmured, facing the viny wallpaper, "Izznit obvious we broke up 'cuz I was falling in love with you?"

That made me hitch myself up on my elbows to ask, "How does that make sense? Continue, please."

"Tomorrow..."

"Now, please."

He turned back in my direction. "Okay. I was twenty-five. I thought: *Twenty. Fucking. Five. She's been married and divorced. I never even came close. Maybe I need to get out there.*"

"Out there? You work on a TV show surrounded by beautiful actresses" — but that's where I stopped, reminding myself that he was testifying as to why he was lying next to me, not why he was plotting his escape. Of course, I couldn't leave it there. "Can I play devil's advocate, against my own self-interest?"

"Sure —" he said, followed by a fake snore.

"It was a pretty short break. You didn't go off for a year like a Mormon missionary to a foreign land."

"Very true but not what I'd call an apt analogy."

"I just meant you had a little PG fling, then you came back. After only—what was it, two months?"

"It looked like two months. I was back before that. In spirit. Mentally."

I did know that. Who wouldn't have noticed his non-disappearance, his checking in? I thought it only right to say, "The falling in love part? I had that, too."

No answer, just some murmured syllables. Was he back asleep? I asked if we were going public.

"I think we have."

"I don't mean at the wedding. I mean if the play got produced, can we put an extra little spin on 'collaborators' so people get that we're together?"

"Sure."

I moved my pillow closer so we'd be falling asleep ear to ear. I said, "Have I told you yet that I find you delightful?"

"Thank you. I try."

"And one more thing: When I said I'd also fallen in love—did that sound like I was speaking in the past tense?"

"I can't say I noticed the tense—"

"I may not have said it aloud lately. Like tonight. By which I mean the love part. Because it's *extremely* present tense."

"Thank you. Now go to sleep." He reached over and found a thigh to pat.

A few minutes later, I heard a faint "You looked beautiful tonight." Was he in REM sleep already, delivering a line of dialogue meant for Veronica or Betty or even the hateful Cheryl Blossom, *Riverdale*'s villain? I didn't nudge him to ask, *Were you speaking to me?* I accepted the compliment, silently for once, smiling in the dark.

· · ·

On the ride to Pickering, borrowing from a *Riverdale* voice-over, Jeremy intoned, "This story is about a town, once fulsome and in-nocent, now forever changed by the disappearance and eventual murder of a cherished yearbook." Earlier, I'd woken up thinking that our one-woman show was doable, or at least no longer the worst idea I'd ever heard. I could imagine myself reciting lines on stage in front of pixelated images of the town. Life had sorted it-self out, and I was turning into an excellent tour guide.

First stop on this unseasonably warm March day was a no-brainer: the high school, built in 1920, with its flag pole, its bronze memorial plaque to fallen graduates, its double-wide doors painted so many times that their high-gloss black finish was crackled. Now that PHS was a regional high school, the word PICKERING had disappeared from above the door. I reminded Jeremy that he could blow up the yearbook's black-and-white photo, which would look appropriately antiquey and — whoops. Maybe not.

"As if I didn't ask the mayor's mother and that guy who told us a dozen times that he'd driven all the way from Buffalo to attend the wedding — which he wouldn't have missed for the world be-cause he'd played water polo with Pete — if I could borrow their yearbook for a project I was working on."

"And when they heard you were an actor, they said, 'Oh, boy. You bet.'"

"Just about."

"Clever."

"And if they don't come through, I'll put an ad in the Pickering *Sentinel* offering to buy a 1968 yearbook."

Once again, I expressed regret over my impulsive shredding.

"Don't worry. That bag of shreds could open the show, as a prop, I mean. Where to now?"

I drove to the first house I lived in, 198 Front Street, and the second house, from age six to eighteen, at 55 Olde Coach Road. I said, "We should ask permission first. A neighbor is probably taking down our license plate and calling the police as we speak."

"So we do what?"

I got out of the car and, at both locations, rang the doorbell, introduced myself, and said, "I used to live here. Do you mind if I take a few pictures — just the outside?"

Both owners said, "Fine, take what you need," without even the slightest curiosity about why. Jeremy noted, "It's like 'Maritch' is the golden ticket. Is there anyone here who *didn't* go to the high school?"

The owner at Olde Coach Road had bought the house from my dad only a year before. She felt compelled to question whether the master bathroom's tub had drained as slowly during our tenure as it was draining now. I told her to use a plunger, like she would for a toilet. Worked like a charm for us. Photo okay? I asked again. "I'm documenting my life."

"Oh, sure. Good luck with that."

Next, the public library and the Knights of Columbus Hall where the eventful reunion took place, then moody shots of goalposts and empty bleachers, then the bandstand on the town green and the former Nagle's department store, now a branch of New Hampshire Technical Institute.

"Any other place that still speaks to you? A high school hangout?"

That led us to the Rialto, no longer a movie theater but an indoor flea market on weekends, marquee intact and proclaiming OVER 50 BOOTHS! Then, a few miles out of town, to the Ice Cream Barn, closed for the season, but not an inch of it changed, its perennial flavors posted on wooden slats. I said, "I used to get either rum raisin or burnt sugar. The scoops were huge," which led Jeremy to make a note.

At the town's only red light, he asked, "How far a drive to the motel where your mother hooked up with Armstrong?"

"Forget that! My father's coming to this show, and I'd prefer if he didn't leave in the middle. Promise me you're not writing a slutty-mom part."

"I'm not. Besides, you're the boss. You're the one delivering the lines, which should take your slutty mother and the question of your paternity off the table."

"My paternity is no longer a question, remember? I fixed that. Done. Over."

"Got it. Your dad is your dad."

"Exactly."

"Except . . . he knows he's not."

"Immaterial! My birth certificate says 'Thomas Maritch' next to 'father,' and you can take that to the bank."

"Along with the fantasy DNA test."

"No comment," I said.

Our last stop was the extant Pretty Good Diner, where we had weak coffee in thick mugs and shared a grilled cheese-and-tomato sandwich. Jeremy was charmed by the multipage laminated menu with "International Specialties" (lasagna, moussaka, French onion soup, chili con carne) and "All desserts homemade except the chocolate pudding." We ordered frappes, one vanilla, one chocolate, aka "milkshakes," an homage to everyone's favorite beverage at Pop's Chock'lit Shoppe on *Riverdale*.

I took at least a half-dozen selfies with the two of us practically cheek to cheek, achievable because we were occupying the same side of the booth. As soon as we'd placed our order, Jeremy walked to the juke box and spent a long time there. When he returned, it was with a sly grin, attributable, he said, to the bargain rate of four songs for a dollar. But then he sat opposite me, looking unusually solemn, taking my hands across the table, clinically, in the manner of a bearer of bad news.

"Are you —?"

"*Shhh*, listen," he said.

What then filled the Pretty Good were love songs of the seriously earnest kind — classics — by the Righteous Brothers, then Paul McCartney, then Roberta Flack.

And finally — oh, God — the late, great Whitney Houston belting out what I now call our anthem. Was Jeremy even *born* when she recorded "I Will Always Love You"?

40

Pie in the Sky?

LL WAS GOOD — so good that we were soon referring to my apartment as the guest room/ Airbnb/storage facility across the hall.

After much beseeching, Jeremy gave me a sneak preview of the as-yet-untitled draft. Very wisely, he'd repurposed Geneva as a man, moved her/him from Manhattan to Pickering, where he drove around town on garbage day, salvaging things like used furniture and tin cans, except one lucky day — or so he thought — when he came upon a dog-eared, overly notated high school yearbook.

And that so-called Eugene Palumbo had a son who was graduating from Emerson College and needed a topic for his senior thesis in documentary filmmaking. Could anyone guess the real-life identity of the villain from this setup? Surely only Geneva.

I still had to worry about the rest of it, which was the Daphne story nibbling around the edges of my mother's infidelity. Jeremy had done a good job covering my marriage and divorce: how I met Holden (now Chauncey) at the Registry of Motor Vehicles instead of CVS; how he courted and married me under false pretenses, driven by trust-fund greed.

I didn't mind that I came across as lovable-wacky, knocking on the playwright's door the first minute I'd moved in, juggling

plants, complaining about a yappy dog he didn't own. Had he
made notes of our early conversations, or did he have a recording
device for an ear? He'd remembered the inedible wasabi truffles,
the dialogue over the making and drinking of our first martini,
then my free fall into easy virtue.

Jeremy had me going to the reunion reluctantly, sitting with
Peter—now named Dr. Brendan Carswell—along with fellow
graduates, including Eugene Palumbo. The doctor asked me
to dance, then told me he'd been in love with his teacher, my
mother, since the first yearbook staff meeting.

"Nope, we're dropping that," I told him.

Jeremy explained that the Peter-Brendan digression was necessary. All drama needs tension, a will-she-or-won't-she thread;
in this case, will Daphne have to spend the rest of her life wondering if Dr. Carswell was telling the truth?

"Since when is this a drama? What do I need tension for?"

He shuffled some pages. "Give me a few days," he said.

I did. Before I read the new draft, he prefaced it with "I went a
little meta."

The fix: He borrowed from his own show, echoing the *Riverdale*
subplot in which Archie the high schooler has an affair with Miss
Grundy, the music teacher. Jeremy made it sound as if he'd taken
a flight of narrative fancy—that he, the love interest/actor across
the hall, had conflated real life with television.

"Wow. Not only does it work, but I think my dad could see this
version of it."

"Yes, he will, and he'll take a bow. First, we'll enlist Kathi."

"For what?"

"She'll work the poetic-license angle—that what did or didn't
go on between your mother and Brendon Carswell is left to the
audience's imagination."

I said, "I don't know . . ."

"She's been great. I can't imagine her turning down that request."

"I'm just wondering if Kathi is a little sick of helping me lie to
my dad."

We were side by side in his kitchen, him chopping vegetables,
me sautéing. There was a pause, his knife no longer hitting the
cutting board, which is when he asked, "Did you ever wonder why
your dad has to protect your mother? She cheated on him for who
knows how long, and he took it. Maybe he's been holding it in all
these years. Maybe it would be therapeutic to come clean. Maybe
he'd like the world to know the real June Maritch—"

"No! What happened is so embarrassing—she was the teacher,
he was the principal, she ends up having an affair right under his
nose, and he takes her back! If you think he'd like to air our dirty
laundry, then you don't know my dad."

"Sorry. Just had to ask." He nudged me. "For art's sake. And remember what we discussed in the car: This isn't ventriloquism.
You're in charge. You'll deliver only what you want the audience
to hear."

What audience? I thought. *Was this just pie in the sky?* I did
a little whining about how bad I was in acting class and how I
dreaded the remaining lessons. Couldn't I drop out now that I
sort of had an acting job?

"No, you're sticking it out, and you'll tell your thankless
teacher that you've been cast as the lead in a show that's in previews."

Sort of true. I was the one woman in a one-woman show. And
who's not to say that our repeated readings within these four walls
weren't previews? How's this for the "reality of doing"? What had
my instructor ever done anyway? *Law & Order: SVU*? What New

York actor hadn't? And the disrespectful way he talked over and around me when it came to lectures on the craft, he'd be lucky if we comped him a ticket.

Geneva was still down the hall, surely seething over my act of treachery, but there was an unaccustomed lack of harassment. No emails, no pounding on my door, no summons from some administrative agency that handled alleged stolen property of questionable ownership. Yet we wondered: Could Jeremy and I produce a show on the down low? Could we write about my trials and tribulations *without* naming the cause of them?

Unlike me, Jeremy didn't feel the need to steer clear of her. He emailed, hinting he had something of a professional nature to discuss. She wrote back, "How's tonight?"

I stayed behind. I baked cheesecake brownies. I rewatched the episode of *Riverdale* where Archie and Miss Grundy are busted for falling in love. After a longer-than-expected absence, Jeremy was back, announcing, "We're all set. You hungry? How about pizza?"

"All set with, like, everything? Did she mention the shredding?"

"Only a dozen times. I told her a replacement was on its way."

"Not that she's getting it!"

"I don't think she has any use for it. She's not feeling too ambitious these days."

It was hard for me to feign concern about Geneva's well-being, but I did force myself to ask, "Is it her health?"

"Nope. It's professional. The money's dried up."

"I thought her father funded everything."

"Not anymore."

"Yikes. Did she say why?"

"She tried to change the subject, but I kept at it. Eventually, she admitted that he'd listened to the podcast — she blames us, by the way; he hadn't known about it till we tipped him off in the emergency room. It sounds like he went slightly ballistic."

"Because he hated it that much?"

"More like he figured out that the actors were impersonating real people, reading bullshit scripts, which apparently can land a producer in court."

Suddenly, this was turning into a very enjoyable conversation. I led him to the gray tufted couch in the living room and put my feet up on the coffee table. "I'm surprised she told you that much."

"She didn't. She was testing the waters. She asked if anyone I knew, maybe people from New Hampshire, had listened to it. And if so, did they have . . . issues? So, of course, I had to run with it."

"How?"

"I told her your family was considering a giant lawsuit."

How nice to have a boyfriend so skilled at improvising. I offered my hand for a high five. "And our show? You got to that?"

That earned me one of his signature when-did-I-ever-let-you-down looks. "I told her that I'm writing a one-woman show for you, the premise being what you've endured since the family heirloom fell into her hands, including getting fired thanks to her bad-mouthing you all over town. I threw in slander, defamation, character assassination. Oh, and on the spot I named the show *The Yearbook Thief*, which caused a little conniption. So I reassured her that I'd given her a new identity, that the title character who helped herself to the yearbook was not Geneva Wisenkorn but a man who drove around Pickering on garbage day searching for collectibles."

"And the reason for your reassurances to the enemy?" I asked.

He paused. "I know you won't love this. I know you'll think it's like asking your major asshole rival in a campaign to join your ticket, to which your loyal family members say, 'No way; how could you ask him to be your vice president after all those awful things he said about you?'"

"Okay, now I'm nervous."

"Don't be. It's so nothing. I told her, since she did make the story possible — and, believe me, she knew that 'making the story possible' meant the grief she caused you. So, here's the deal: In lieu of suing her for X, Y, and Z, or her suing us for dramatizing her bad deeds . . . she'd give her blessing to the project."

"That's it? We want her blessing?"

"She's running it by Daddy or, as she put it, 'consulting with my attorney.'"

"And we're not worried that when Daddy hears his daughter's the villain of a one-woman show —"

"She's not. Eugene Palumbo is. And you can put money on the fact that Lawyer Dad is saying, 'That's it? They're not gonna sue you if you let them put on a play about a yearbook stolen by a guy named Palumbo in Bumblefuck, New Hampshire?'"

I said, "You're good."

"Thank you."

"When do we hear?"

"I told her we'd have to know by the end of the week, or else we'd name someone else as an executive producer."

Did he just say "executive producer"?

"Actually, coexecutive producer, i.e., nothing. She just gets her name in the playbill and she tries to raise some money."

I asked if I'd have to meet with her and/or be nice to her.

That was Jeremy's cue to slip into a new favorite role, impresario reassuring the ingénue. "You're the star, darling. Always better to be a gracious leading lady than a diva."

Diva . . . some days I pictured the press release chronicling my rise from high school *Hair* to Montessori failure to Drama Factory dud to leading lady—plucked from obscurity like a twenty-first-century Lana Turner.

Was that even true, that she was discovered in Schwab's drug-store or was that just Hollywood legend? I'd be embarrassed to ask Jeremy. Next time I was back in my own apartment, I'd Google it.

41

Just Like That

WE INVITED MY FATHER and Kathi to Jeremy's apartment, where we'd begin the reading as soon as the sun had set over the Hudson. First, we lubricated them with drinks made from Jeremy's well-stocked bar. My father's Manhattan got a perfect stemmed cherry, and Kathi's mojito looked like our host had just returned from the farmers' market.

I stood in front of the picture window and began with "You know how shocked I was when you gave me acting lessons? Remember? I thought you were just feeling sorry for me — no job, no social life" — I smiled at Jeremy — "at that *particular* time? Getting back to school would give me a purpose in life or at least a reason to leave the apartment."

"Guilty," said my father. "But are you going to tell us that it paid off in some way?"

"Shush," said Kathi. "I think she's leading up to something."

As choreographed, Jeremy joined me from the doorway between living room and hallway. "When I suggested acting lessons for Daff? That wasn't random. I had an ulterior motive."

The matching looks on both my father's and Kathi's faces was guessing-game earnest — eager to hear what might be next. "Did you get an acting job?" my father asked.

I checked with Jeremy. He said, "If all goes well, yes. We have something in the works. There's a long road ahead. We're going to start small — a reading and then, if we're lucky, a festival and even a backer."

I could see my father was trying not to look deflated. "Were you hoping I was getting a job on Jeremy's show?" I asked him.

"Not really," he fibbed.

Kathi said, "So it's a play?"

I said, "Sort of. It's a one-woman show partly about my experience with Geneva, the wannabe documentarian."

"And producer of unnecessary podcasts," Kathi finished.

"Unnecessary and a lawsuit waiting to happen," I said. "Which is why we were able to gag her."

Jeremy said, "I wouldn't put it exactly that way —"

"I meant, I was petrified of Geneva. She's just down the hall, and the day she fainted and I called 911, I was able to repossess it and eventually . . . I destroyed the evidence."

"Evidence? What evidence?" my father asked.

"The yearbook. I destroyed it."

"This is what your play's about?" my father asked.

"Well, the plot isn't 'I shredded a yearbook.' It's more like . . ."

"Daphne's journey," said Jeremy.

"Not literally," I said. "Not from Olde Coach Road to West Fifty-fourth Street, but starting with my bogus marriage, the divorce, the ups and downs with jobs, then to Geneva finding the yearbook and those complications."

"It sounds to me as if the play is about bullying," Kathi said.

"Very timely," said my father. "In fact, it sounds like something that you could perform at high schools."

I said, "We're getting ahead of ourselves. We just need to find a venue or an open mic."

Kathi asked if Jeremy's connections — his being a real actor — would be of any help.

"Hope so," he said. "I'm networking."

"When do we get to see it?" asked my father.

Jeremy said, "That's exactly why we're here tonight."

Preplanned was this semidelicate question: "Dad? Kathi knows about your marriage to Mom? How she might've been —?"

"Less than faithful?" Kathi filled in, with an edge in her voice — anger toward the woman who'd hurt her impeccably loyal boyfriend.

"I guess we know the answer to *that*," said Jeremy.

"Does your play get into my journey, too?" my dad asked.

"Had to," I said. "It's all interwoven with the yearbook and Mom's obsession with it."

Jeremy said, "Mr. Maritch — please keep in mind that we put a spin on the events to make them pop from the stage. I was going for . . . well . . . entertainment."

I said, "Believe me — I started out a nonbeliever. I mean *me?* A one-woman show? Airing the family's dirty laundry? How could he? How could *I?* But that was only till I read it."

"Anyone need a refill before Daphne begins?" Jeremy asked.

A yes, a no, a thanks, top it off . . . finally, we were ready. I hadn't memorized much, so I read with an open laptop in the crook of my elbow. Every few lines, I'd look up to check my dad's face. Was that worry? Disapproval? Queasiness?

He raised his hand when I got to Eugene Palumbo, second-string garbage man. "May I make a suggestion?" he asked.

I said, "Of course."

"Here's what I'm thinking: that it's more believable if this Palumbo guy hung around the dump rather than drove around checking out what people left on the curb. The Pickering landfill has almost a party atmosphere on weekends."

That's how I knew he was on board. Jeremy got it, too. And Kathi was smiling. Yes, there was a grimace, but a resigned one, when I introduced Brendan Carswell, now demoted to mere crush.

After about a half hour, I said, "I could go on, but it's about getting fired from Montessori and my chocolate career, and then the New Leash job. Do you want me to keep reading, or should we run out for dinner?"

My dad said, "If the rest is this enjoyable, I vote to save it for Broadway." He turned to Kathi. "Do you agree—save some for opening night so it'll be fresh and new to us?"

I could tell that Jeremy, like me, was pondering whether to disabuse him of all thoughts of Broadway, but we didn't.

Kathi stood up. "Agree. *Totally.* Save the rest for opening night, wherever that may be."

"Did I hear a vote for grabbing dinner?" I asked.

"Starved," said my dad. "But first, I'd like a private word with Daphne."

Both Jeremy and Kathi said sure, of course; they'd discuss where to eat and make a reservation.

Once we were alone, my father said, "Somewhere in the story, do you ever speak kindly of your mother?"

I couldn't tell from his expression whether that would be a good thing or an unwelcome one.

"She wasn't perfect," he said. "But she had many wonderful qualities. Her students testified to that. I mean, seniors don't dedicate a yearbook to a teacher unless she was everyone's favorite. And, honey, you were so broken up when she died. Maybe you could think about that, the terrible loss, what you felt like when the call from the hospital came, when I told you she didn't make it. And not that it's my bailiwick, but wouldn't it be a very dramatic moment on the stage, re-creating that phone call?"

I said, "It would be, for sure."

"She loved her girls," he said. "And I know you loved her back."

What harm in saying that his fond wish had already come true, that there were beautiful lines toward the end about how we all loved one another despite bumps in the road? "Done," I said.

"I didn't want to meddle, but what a relief."

Also ahead, still unaired, was a question it took a playwright in search of motivation to answer: Why did my mother want me to have the yearbook?

To Jeremy, her thinking was clear: She'd been younger than my dad and healthy. Surely she'd outlive him. He would die, then she would die, and I'd be an orphan, unlike Holly who had a husband and children. My mother would have wanted me to know that I wasn't alone, that there was a spare parent on the bench. The yearbook was never meant to be a puzzle; she'd merely died before she'd had the chance to turn down the corner of Peter Armstrong's page.

As soon as we were alone after dinner, Jeremy asked me what the powwow had been about.

"My mother. He was reminding me that I loved her."

"I knew that."

"I'd forgotten," I said.

42

Sisters

THE SHOW WAS AS FINE-TUNED as we could make it. We'd applied to every festival that had a reasonable submission deadline; we'd sent out what we thought was a charming and wry fund-raising appeal, and mounted a Crowd-Rise campaign that brought in $525.

Who did we know who had money to spare? "Any chance your sister would want to have her name on this as producer?" Jeremy asked me one morning.

I called Holly as soon as it was a decent hour in Los Angeles. First, I raved about the recent photo of her boys at their jujitsu-belt promotion ceremony. Then I asked if she missed work, not that I was discounting, no, not at all, full-time motherhood; but would she welcome an opportunity to flex her organizational and entrepreneurial muscles?

"I'm listening," she said.

I explained that Jeremy had written a show starring me, and we needed a producer. And who better than a young, ambitious go-getter who lived in LA, had a year of law school, a nanny, and might welcome a new professional identity?

"Is this about money?" she asked.

"Somewhat. Plus the title, the prestige, and a very nice thing to have on your CV."

"Let me talk to Doug," she said.

We sent her Jeremy's impressive credentials and the script, which she pronounced "cute," an adjective we found slightly patronizing but not enough to turn down her first check. With it, she'd sent a contract stating that if her investment (postcards, my head shot, a portable projector, a case of wine for the reading) was a box-office hit, it would return to her 90 percent of the profits.

"It's fine, since it won't make a penny," Jeremy said, handing me the pen. The assistant bank manager, acting as notary, asked if that was true.

I said, "We're putting on a play."

"Got it," he said.

Dad, Kathi, Holly, Jeremy, and I dined together the night before the staged reading. I tried to talk Holly out of a get-together due to my superstition and nerves. But Holly was host and concierge, even in a city she didn't know. She'd dropped her own name as producer of *Dirty Laundry*, scoring a table at Orso, chosen for its theatergoing cred.

We'd just been handed menus. Which daughter noticed first? Me. "Is that what I think it is?" I yelped.

Kathi looked down at her hand at the oval sapphire with its halo of tiny diamonds, then said apologetically, "It is."

I jumped up, kissed her first, then my red-eyed dad. "It's fine," I whispered. "All good."

"When were you going to tell us?" Holly asked.

"Day after tomorrow," my dad said. "You'd come for brunch before you'd leave. We didn't want to steal your sister's thunder."

"I considered leaving it at home tonight," said Kathi. "I was picturing Holly meeting her father's girlfriend for the first time, and boom, she's his fiancée." Her hand was splayed and she was gazing fondly at it. "But I can't bring myself to take it off."

Holly said, "Dad — nice job. It's a beauty."

"I think so, too."

"The ring!"

Thankfully, she didn't ask where he'd bought it, its weight in carats, or the retailer's country of origin.

"We picked it out together," said Kathi.

"Good move," said Jeremy. "I'm making a note of that."

I rose, tapped my water glass with my knife, inadvertently catching the attention of strangers at surrounding tables. "Sorry, please carry on," I told my expanded audience. "But you're welcome to listen because we just got some thrilling news."

Glass raised, I said, "Our father and this lovely woman are newly engaged!"

Applause at our table and beyond.

"My sister and I" — Holly identified herself with a wiggle of fingers — "were gathering for another reason, to celebrate what might be a one-woman show —"

Jeremy twirled his finger: *Wind it up.*

I said, "Okay, just this: Despite the waterworks, I've never seen my father happier. And for that, we thank this woman, Kathleen Krauss, who, I should add, specializes in piano lessons for adults —"

"Who gave up the piano as a child but regret that decision," said my dad.

I heard Jeremy say to Kathi, "Maritch and Maritch Public Relations."

"Did acting lessons do this to her?" asked Holly.

I said, "I yield my remaining time to the gentleman from New Hampshire."

My dad didn't stand up. He took a sip of water. "Daphne . . . Holly. I know this is sudden, but I hope my girls will understand and forgive me when I say I've been waiting for something like this my whole life." He smiled a wobbly smile at Kathi. "We didn't want to use this dinner as an engagement party. But here we all are—well, not Doug and the boys—but something tells me they're going to get a text before dessert comes."

"When's the wedding?" Holly asked.

"We haven't gotten that far," said Kathi.

Holly asked her if she'd ever been married before.

"Holly!" said my dad.

"It's fine," said Kathi. "I'd want to know that, too. Nope. He's the first."

Jeremy said, "And *I* want to toast producer Holly Maritch-McMaster, without whom we'd be applying for grants we'd never get."

Holly said, "I'm getting you two out to LA when this run ends."

Well, that was nice, but what run—tomorrow's reading in a windowless fifth-floor room reached by a creaky elevator?

Jeremy added, "Wait'll you see Daphne in action. She's gonna kill. Give her a villain, and she lights up the stage."

Epilogue

I know now: It's harder than it looks. We didn't make it to Broadway, or off-Broadway, or extremely-far-off-Broadway, unless you count one night at the Long Beach Playhouse's New Works Festival, thanks to Holly making herself useful back home.

Kathi and my father traveled to California for the opening. I was lucky that, either with footlights or spotlights — who knows? — blinding me, and the audience in the dark, I couldn't see my dad's reaction. Backstage after the show, he told me it had been a very interesting experience and that I'd done a nifty job learning all those lines.

"And the audience loved it," said Kathi. "People all around us were laughing, and when it was over, I heard nothing but praise." Unsaid: the fifty friends of Holly and Doug's who had a free night and a babysitter.

"You okay with it?" I asked my dad.

"Pretty good," he said. "Maybe next time you won't ask me to stand up and take a bow."

"I did that on impulse," I said. "It's not in the script."

"She's become quite the ad-libber," said Jeremy.

We never told Geneva about the out-of-town debut. Except for polite exchanges in the hallway and mailroom about nothing, Jeremy and I didn't engage her, figuring she'd let us know if she ever raised a dollar. I Google her every few weeks to see if she's producing, directing, or humiliating anyone new, but all there is in her IMDb profile is *The Last Matzo Man* and her wedding-video website.

My dad and Kathi were married at New York City Hall on the first of September and honeymooned in Paris, a first visit for both. Holly had flown in for the ceremony, insisting that even the simplest civil wedding needed flowers, a trip to Bergdorf's, and two maids of honor. What a brick my annoying little sister has turned out to be.

To the bottomless delight of Sammi the dog, her beloved handler and new dad moved into Kathi's loft upon their return.

I hear from Peter Armstrong regularly only because I'm on his constituent mailing list. There's no need to respond to or even read these emails with subject lines such as "Stand with Me Against Hate" and "I Need Your Help in My Final Push." I'd never told him about *Dirty Laundry* or asked for a contribution. If it ever gets to White Mountains Regional High School, I'll send him a ticket.

My father above anyone else holds the highest, unrealistic hopes for the eventual success of *Dirty Laundry.* Or maybe it's his faith in me and wishful thinking about his acting lessons bearing fruit. He's careful not to ask if there are any bites, any more festivals soliciting new work, churches or synagogues in search of an excellent night's entertainment. I usually explain that success comes in many forms; that this one-woman flop, ironically, had brought me back to life.

"I know what you mean, but isn't that a little melodramatic?" he asked.

I said yes, he was right: an overstatement, me being hyperbolic.

When Jeremy characterizes our show as dead on arrival, I correct that, too. I tell him, only half teasing, that if we ever make it to another stage, I'll end by asking the audience to hold their applause; no curtain calls and no bouquets, either. It will look like I'm making one of those cast appeals for a favorite charity, but it'll be me assuring the audience that despite its uphill battle, its rough patches, its flubbed lines, the so-called journey of Daphne has delivered its own form of success. So thank you for coming. Drive safely. Oh, and I probably should add: When your friends ask what you did this evening, it's okay to tell them you were misled; that you thought you'd bought tickets for a one-woman show but what you heard, in lines spoken and unspoken, was a love story.

Acknowledgments

There would be no *Good Riddance* if Jonathan Greenberg hadn't found an orphaned high school yearbook at the Stormville, New York, Airport Antique Show and Flea Market. Once home, he discovered that his new piece of Americana ("Ha," said I) had belonged to the yearbook advisor to whom it had been dedicated. As the otherwise entirely fictional June Winter Maritch did, its owner faithfully attended reunions and made notes.

For every one of my books and beyond, I've had the wise and doting early editing of Mameve Medwed and Stacy Schiff.

I am beyond grateful to have Lauren Wein once again as my editor. Her sense and sensibility make every page more of what I want in the first place. Extremely helpful as the extra set of eyes is Houghton's Pilar Garcia-Brown, who spotted and fixed what I had not.

I love being asked "Who's your agent?" so I can say, "Suzanne Gluck," my steadfast and quick-witted ally.

In the advice and verisimilitude department, I thank Sharissa Jones for her insider Montessori tips; Jake Lipman, actor, producer, and founder of Tongue in Cheek Theatre, for guiding Daphne's stumble into acting; Frances Broudie of Chocarella for chocolatiering lessons; Rebecca Bogart for insights about teaching piano to adult students; and once again, Chief (ret.) James E.

Mulligan of the Georgetown, Massachusetts, Police Department for advice on all matters police-related.

I do know that the TV series *Riverdale* is not filmed in New York. I took liberties with the cast, plot, and location for narrative convenience.

I thank my readers, new and old, met and unmet. Truly, I write these novels for you.

Q&A with Elinor Lipman

What, if anything, prompted a yearbook obsession as a plot line?

It began with a chance purchase at a flea market in Stormville, New York. My significant other, who'd grown up in England without yearbooks (at least not at the Quarry Bank School in Liverpool) bought it proudly for $12 when I wasn't looking. "Why would you want this?" I asked. "Americana," he said. When he got it home and studied it, he realized that the book had belonged to the teacher and yearbook advisor to whom it was dedicated. As he examined it, he saw that she had attended reunions faithfully and had made notes. Eventually I went through every page. But the story and the hanky-panky are entirely my invention.

How soon after reading the yearbook did you know this would become the basis of your next novel?

I didn't know until a sentence popped into my head, months later, something close to "I am in possession of a yearbook that was dedicated to my mother."

Can you say what the real-life high school was?

No! Oh, okay: Keene, New Hampshire. But let me repeat: I made it all up! No persons were hurt in the production of this novel!

When you began with the premise of a teacher overinvolved with her students, did you know where it would lead you?

Hardly at all, and I hope that doesn't show. I knew that the year-book would be bequeathed to a daughter, who'd throw it out, and it would be found by someone who'd put it to some embarrassing use. Enter Geneva.

Is it okay to call her the novel's villain?

Oh, be my guest! I didn't give her a break. She's my runner-up villain to the anti-Semitic innkeeper from *The Inn at Lake Devine*, whom I never redeemed. Geneva is clueless about her talents and prospects, just lucky enough to have a father with deep pockets. I'm hoping that her unearned self-esteem rings a bell with readers who've known overly ambitious, underachieving busybodies like her.

Does Daphne have more of an edge than many of your other narrators?

Definitely. I welcomed that departure, and sometimes wonder whether she was Elinor unleashed. It's a challenge to make a not-always-polite character sympathetic. Of course, much of her bite is bluster, especially her embrace of loose-womanhood. Not much has gone right for her when the novel opens — profession-ally or romantically — so her sharp tongue is earned.

Then, happily, enter Jeremy.

Thank you, yes. He appeared across the hall the day I became worried that the story was underpopulated. Daphne needed a friend. At first (just as Daphne thought) he was going to be something of a boy toy. But then they surprised me.

Is Tom Maritch, her father, so supportive and loving that he's too good to be true?

Take that back! No. He is a sweet man and something of a country mouse. It was fun to create a fish out of water who was utterly comfortable and enthusiastic about the big city. I didn't expect that *Good Riddance* would be a father-daughter buddy story, but that happened almost with their first conversation. If it's okay to love a character of one's own creation, it would be true that I love Daphne's dad.

He surprises Daphne throughout, though. And the reader, too.

He does. She never knew he had a lifelong New York dream, nor had she known the secrets in her parents' marriage. She sees a new side of him, quite charming and a little flirtatious. Suddenly he's a dog walker, which leads him to Kathi, making Sammi, effectively, the matchmaker. I love dogs and find them innately comical. One in Tom's pack, Gizmo, is named after a rescue dog in my building.

The phrase "good riddance" refers to what aspect of the story?

I saw it as applying to the twin nuisances of the boomeranging yearbook and the unrelenting Geneva.

Any acting or acting lessons in your past?

Just in high school plays (*Arsenic and Old Lace* and *The Petrified Forest*). No lessons though and didn't love it. I have a recurring dream where I'm on stage and haven't quite learned all my lines. For The Drama Factory, I researched acting school curricula online, wrote the chapter covering Daphne's first acting lesson, and ran it by Jake Lipman (no relation), who adapted and produced *The Inn at Lake Devine* for the stage in 2015.

Did you consider making Daphne's one-woman show a hit?

Never. Not that I'm happy-ending averse, but that would've been pure Cinderella. I was so happy to have my decision reinforced by Anita Shreve, who read it in manuscript. She wrote me: "I'm so glad you didn't make the play a huge success. While it might have pleased your fans, it would have disappointed me on the grounds of highly improbable. But your ending was so right." That meant so much. *She* meant so much. I was able to tell her a week before she died that *Good Riddance* would be dedicated to her.

Recommended Reading from
Elinor Lipman

None of these novels are new or on my nightstand at this moment, but they are among my favorites and always will be.

The Republic of Love by Carol Shields   A 35-year-old high-achieving folklorist who studies mermaid legends meets a thrice-divorced 40-year-old radio deejay, provoking an instant, intense devotion that neither — as romance-starved as they are — can fully metabolize. A touching, elegantly funny, luscious work of fiction.

The New Yorkers by Cathleen Schine   I even love its flap copy ("Dogs bring people together unexpectedly, acting as cupids for the quiet, the struggling, sometimes lonely, eccentric people...") and its dedication: "To the memory of Buster, who in eighteen months taught me more about the city than I had discovered in thirty years."

How Elizabeth Barrett Browning Saved My Life by Mameve Medwed   Another smart, even laugh-out-loud gem of a novel, this one set in Cambridge, Massachusetts, behind the downmarket stall in an antiques emporium. Everything changes for the depressed Abby Randolph when she goes on *Antiques Roadshow* ...

Happy All the Time by Laurie Colwin   When Guido Morris spots

Holly Sturgis for the first time he immediately senses that she will be difficult, quirky, and hard to live with. His cousin and best friend, Vincent Cardworthy, meets Misty Berkowitz — who from the get-go is cranky, bored, misanthropic. The story gives us four memorable characters who find love in spite of themselves.

Selling the Lite of Heaven by Suzanne Strempek Shea   The premise alone tickles me: Not only left at the altar but *for* it when fiancé Eddie Balicki chooses the priesthood over marriage, the 32-year-old narrator is trying to sell her 2.75-karat engagement ring in the local *Pennysaver.*

Fill your shelves
with Elinor Lipman!

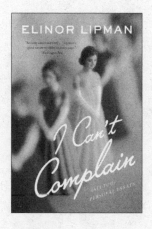

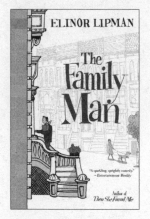